THE METER'S ALWAYS RUNNING

A HAUNTED CITY MYSTERY

C.A. ROWLAND

SHADOW DANCE PUBLISHING LTD

The Meter's Always Running

Cover art copyright © 2020 by Shadow Dance Publishing Ltd.

Cover art design by Liana Moisescu 2020

ISBN: 978-1-946279-01-9

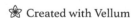 Created with Vellum

To Kari, Linda S., Lane, Linda E., Lourdes
and Emily for all your thoughtful comments on this manuscript. You helped
me grow as a writer and a person through this process.

1

A woman inviting a total stranger into her car might not be the smartest idea, but that was my job as a taxi driver. It sounded a bit crazy, I know.

I knew something about crazy. My aunt Harriett always said she could hear the whispers in the live oaks gracing the twenty-two squares within the Savannah downtown historic district. Sometimes the murmurs of the trees raised goose bumps on my arms, and I wondered what they were saying that my body understood but my mind couldn't yet comprehend.

Honk.

I inched forward, now first in the taxi cab line at the Savannah/Hilton Head International Airport, glad to not be sitting in a desk in an office somewhere, even in the heat of early fall. And glad this was my final fare of the day. I could almost taste the wine spritzer I'd pour myself at home later tonight, sliding over my tongue and down my dry throat.

I preferred driving in the historic district across cobblestone streets filled with tourists enjoying the history of my city, both real and imagined. I could tell the fares great ghost and otherworldly stories involving the older homes, including my family's home.

Today, I found myself outside this massive concrete island from which metal and glass grew, surrounded by asphalt roads and runways, waiting for tired travelers to emerge. I sat, wrapped within the idling purr of the SUV engine, cool air flowing out and around me, a contrast to the humidity outside, where jet fuel fumes mixed with vehicle exhaust.

Waiting.

Watching the doors for the crew.

The terminal door opened, and the flight crew from the DC shuttle to Savannah exited. Traveler's Taxi was their preferred taxi service, and two of the five company cabs always picked up each flight crew. Secure, reliable fares.

I shut off the engine, climbed out to meet them, and immediately noted the new guy. A wiry pencil-thin guy whose strut screamed for someone to notice him. The uniformed women in the flight crew were pointing toward my SUV and sending him my way.

As he swaggered over, he stared intently at what I guessed was my figure, almost to the point of being offensive. I'd dealt with lots of different people, and I'd found the best way to deal with this was to ignore what was happening and just be nice. Sounded a bit cliché, but I didn't know what they'd had to deal with, so I did my best to make their day a bit easier.

"Can I help you with something?" I asked.

The man didn't even blink as his gaze rose to meet mine. "Not really." He moved toward the other cab again. Kinda rude, but whatever. Maybe the other driver would squeeze him in.

I got all kinds of looks from people, surprised I was a woman driver—from those who stared at the pink hair extensions for breast cancer month to mouth-dropping stares. This guy's look made my skin crawl, and I was glad he wouldn't be in my cab.

I turned to pick up the luggage for the other two men. "Hi, Josh. Ryan."

The pilot and copilot were both about six feet tall—Josh with wavy chocolate brown hair thinning on top, and Ryan with straight sandy brown hair.

"Hi, Patricia," Josh said. "I thought Savannah cooled down in October."

I laughed and took both men's bags.

"Not yet. Who's the new guy?" I loaded the two men's bags in the back of the tan SUV.

"You mean the leering flight attendant? That's Brandon. Been flying with us for several months—usually on the earlier routes," Josh said. "Heather's out on sick leave for at least a few days. He's her replacement for now."

A genuine smile lit up my face as I moved to open the side door for them. The other taxi with the three women flight attendants drove around us and headed out.

"Hey, what about my luggage, Pink Patty?" Brandon had joined the two men.

I grimaced at the use of the nickname I hated, swallowed the retort, and decided I'd take that as a statement he was just trying to be cute.

"Actually, it's Patricia. I'm getting your luggage now. Why don't you grab a seat, and we'll head out as soon as I finish loading these."

"Got it. Bad day?"

"Not really. Just a long one. I'm sure you know how that is."

Brandon gave me a half-smile as he muttered under his breath.

"Tough day for you? Our jobs aren't so different, what with dealing with passengers all day." I gave him my friendliest smile as I stepped around him to shut the tailgate door.

"Huh? I have a lot more responsibility than just driving people around," Brandon said.

I swallowed at the insult. "Looks like Josh and Ryan are already in the SUV. Why don't you join them, and I'll get you all to where you need to go," I said with as much of a smile as I could muster.

Brandon continued grumbling as he walked to the open side of the vehicle and took a seat. He launched into a stream of complaints about the recent flight. I could understand venting after a long day, but he appeared to be looking for a fight.

I closed the door and hurried around to the driver's side in my

Converse denim sneakers. Why me? I'd hoped for a stress-free quick ride and drop-off. I wasn't so sure now.

I took a deep breath and forced my shoulders to relax.

Settling into my seat, I adjusted my secondhand designer denim skirt and peeled my damp blue cotton shirt off my back. I placed my cell phone underneath my leg. While flight crews were mostly safe for a woman taxi driver, you couldn't be too careful. My cell phone was set on vibrate, since all my calls were through my radio. I kept it safely close by in case I needed to hit the speed dial.

"Where to? Pondside Inn? Everybody?" I looked over my shoulder.

Josh nodded.

"Me too, but only to pick up my car. I'm headed home from there," Brandon said.

"I'm with you on that. I head home after this too." I turned the key to start the engine. I maneuvered into traffic.

"Hey, Pink Patty. Anything special going on in town tonight? I've been gone most of the week," Brandon said.

I could swear I almost heard him winking at me. I frowned. Eleven p.m., eighty-plus degrees, ninety percent humidity. I was grateful for air-conditioning and last fares.

"Don't know. I work most nights and spend the others with my boyfriend. Please don't call me Patty."

I drew another long breath, trying to calm the acid rolling around in my stomach, and decided to ignore Brandon for the trip, no matter what he said.

"No offense intended. I knew a Patricia once. She went by Patty. She was lots of fun. Liked to change up her hair too."

My stomach eased a bit. Quiet reigned in the SUV for a minute or so before Brandon launched into a rant. I tuned him out for the first two blocks, and then he let out a string of curse words.

A quick look in the rearview mirror confirmed Josh's frown was deepening by the minute.

I started to respond, but Josh beat me to it. "Can you tone it down some? We've all had a long day."

"What's the big deal? It's important to my story."

"None of us want to hear your story. We just want quiet time to end the day," Josh said.

"Right, I'm in a trash heap and supposed to shut up?" Brandon asked.

I almost busted a gut. I worked hard to keep the interior as clean as possible and deserved a little respect. Then I took a couple of breaths, determined to ignore the slights and just finish the drive.

But the comment nagged at me and I started to protest. Josh beat me to it. "Come on, Brandon. Drop it, okay? We'll be at the hotel shortly."

"It's a dump. I'm only saying what's here," Brandon said.

I sniffed. Under the vanilla candle smell I'd used to mask the dregs from an early-morning sick kid, a slight hint remained. I'd cleaned up as best I could without doing a wet vacuum, which I'd do tomorrow before work. Any other bits on the floor were from the last fare. A dump? Not by any stretch.

"You're in this cab because the flight attendants didn't want you in theirs. Lighten up or get out and call your own," Josh said.

"There wasn't room in the other one. We're off work. I don't have to listen to you."

"Look, we've all had a long day," Ryan said. "Let's just relax and get to the hotel."

"Josh started this. I can talk if I want to. A little venting won't hurt you," Brandon said.

"No, it doesn't, but you're inching close to crossing a line here," Josh said.

"Don't tell me what to do. You're not the boss of me when I'm off the job," Brandon said.

"We have to work together, so I'm going to let that pass. Just tone it down some," Josh said.

"Aren't you doing *me* a favor? I'll do what I please and say what I want on my own time."

"Have it your way. Patricia, pull over. Brandon's getting out," Josh said.

"Are you sure?" I'd never put anyone out of my cab, so this was gonna be a first. I pulled over to the curb. "We're not far from the hotel."

"No. We're on our own time, and I'm paying for this cab. He can walk," Josh said.

Brandon's face went from shock to a frown in my rearview mirror as he crossed his arms and stared at the back of the front seat. "You mean the airline is paying."

I gave them a couple of seconds, but when no one said anything, I walked to the back and yanked Brandon's suitcase out. As I set it on the sidewalk, Brandon got out and glared at me. I was glad I wasn't going to have to try to muscle his wannabe rock star self to the curb. He'd lost some of the swagger, and his large mouth was in a deep frown. Yes, I loved the old rockers and their music.

"Sorry. The pilot trumps, as far as I'm concerned. You'll have to call somebody else to get you where you're going."

"But there's nothing here," Brandon said. "I'm going to call your supervisor. Tell him about how you treat people, dumping them to the curb."

I'd felt somewhat bad about putting him out, but I was tired of his attitude. This strip of road was mainly warehouses, quiet at night, except for the occasional homeless person or night janitor. There'd been a number of robberies in the past weeks, but the police had a suspect in custody. My gaze searched the area. Nothing stirred, although the streetlights created shadows beside the buildings.

Still, I didn't want trouble, so I tried again, "Want me to call a different cab company? Not sure how long it will take."

"No, I'll do it."

"Okay. You live in Savannah, right? And you've been on this route for a while. The hotel is a quarter-mile or so away." I pointed down the street in the general direction he'd need to go.

"I know. Mostly I work on earlier flights. Looks a bit different in the dark. I can find my way."

I nodded and climbed back into the SUV.

I drove the next two blocks in silence, not daring to peek at my other passengers. At the corner, I turned right and pulled over to the curb.

"I can go back and get him, if you want." I turned around. "He might be okay for the rest of the ride."

"Are you kidding? He's got a cell phone. Another cab might come by, right?" Josh asked.

"Not really, but he can call one. Or he might try Uber. Might take a while, but there might be one returning from the hotel as well."

Josh and Ryan's smiles grew.

"Serves him right," Ryan said. "I've wanted someone to teach that asshole a lesson. I've been listening to his complaints for weeks. Let him find his own way."

I nodded and shifted back into the right lane. Five blocks later, we entered the long asphalt drive to the Pondside Inn, around the quiet pond framed by live oaks and under the covered entrance. After I unloaded Josh's suitcase from the back, he paid the fare and tipped me twenty dollars.

I must have gasped.

"It was well worth it."

Ryan's tip was twenty dollars too. He was laughing as he choked out the words to thank me.

I started to close the side door and caught a flash of something on the floor. Reaching down, I picked up a cell phone.

"Hey, guys," I called.

They were already entering the hotel.

I ran inside, dodging a group of costumed people, a woman wearing square black glittery sunglasses and a man in a three-piece baby blue suit and matching flat golf cap. Only in Savannah. There was always a themed party or movie being filmed or convention going on—more than I could ever keep up with.

The pilot and copilot stood at the front desk.

"Guys? Did either of you leave your cell phone in the SUV?"

Both men turned and checked their pockets. Both pulled out cell phones.

"Not ours," Josh said. "Must be Brandon's."

They laughed, but my stomach turned over.

"I guess he couldn't call a different company after all," Josh said.

"It's a fairly short walk. I'm sure Brandon'll be here any minute. Can I leave the phone with one of you?" I asked.

"I doubt he'll check in with me. I think you should leave it with the desk clerk," Josh said.

Leaving the phone behind, I headed back outside and climbed into the SUV. What Brandon didn't know was that my boss was a woman. Sylvie didn't take trash talk from anyone, workers or clients. She might not like what had just happened, but she was reasonable and backed up her drivers. The look on Brandon's face had been priceless. He might complain, even though it was Josh's decision. If he did, I'd deal with it. In Sylvie's book, the customer wasn't always right.

I let go of the nagging thought I should have called him a replacement cab. At this point, there were several streets he could have turned down, and I wasn't sure where to even direct a taxi to pick him up. It was a short distance, and any cab would take longer to reach him than if he walked.

Right then, I wanted to put my feet up, relax my shoulder muscles, and forget about the day. I headed out of the covered area at Pondside. In an hour or two, Bill would arrive and I'd settle into his strong arms, safe and sound. I was glad nothing worse had happened.

2

Tires crunched on the crushed gravel driveway as I pulled in beside the Victorian in the downtown historic district. I'd inherited the house when Aunt Harriett died. I tried to shake my unease. Putting a client out of my cab midtrip was within my rights. Sure, I put Brandon out at the request of the pilot, but I decided this was the first and only time I would ever do such a thing.

I bounded up the three broad wooden steps and almost tripped over a pot of marigolds—Aunt Harriett's favorite. What were they doing there? Hadn't I shifted them to the other side of the porch for the sun this morning? This was the second time I'd moved them to a new spot only to find them moved when I got home. I carried the container back to the other side and placed them in the spot where Aunt Harriett always kept them. She'd said the sun was the best for them there.

I paused, listening for the wind as Aunt Harriett used to do. Nothing. Big surprise. Only a few leaves swirled around the yard with what looked like a bit of stirred-up dust devil of black dirt.

I walked through the front door, tossing my keys into the ceramic shell I'd picked up in Cozumel three years ago. The shell pitched on the glass-and-metal accent table and straightened. It would be an hour or two before Bill arrived for our date. He had a smile that made me weak in the knees, dreamy brown eyes, and a gentleness that hid the strength I knew he used in his work as a paramedic. I'd met him through my fireman brother, Jackson. Not on purpose, of course. Jackson was horrified I was dating one of his coworkers.

Home. A whiff of Aunt Harriett's favorite perfume, Chantilly, grazed my nose. She'd been gone for nine months, but I could almost feel her presence here at times. I swore I'd heard her favorite song, "Moon River," playing in her old room at times during the last three months, but each time I'd gone looking for the source of the music it stopped as I reached the top of the stairs. The women in my family had a history of unique "talents." I wondered if someone was trying to tell me something.

The inheritance of her house came with all the Queen Anne furniture she'd collected over the years. Creamy brown armchairs complemented the beige-flowered couch reigning in the living room off the front door. I'd spent hours reading on the baby blue cushions in the window seat at the front. I could have used a hug from Aunt Harriett about now. She had the best hugs—ones that swept you up in a way where the world and any problems melted away. I'd left her upstairs bedroom intact, and sometimes when I heard a strange sound, I'd turn around to talk to her—realizing as I did that it was merely the creaking of an old house.

I started up the stairs, the oak handrail slick from years of use and numerous slides down by daring kids. I turned right, away from Aunt Harriett's room, and past the spare room set up for Stephanie, if she ever decided to come home.

I'd picked the one with three large windows letting in lots of light, with a view of the backyard and its garden. Spring brought the aroma of gardenias and crepe myrtles amid the lemony-sweet smell of the magnolias. I surveyed my tiny closet, so common in Victorians, before I slipped into my favorite lounging outfit, a cropped formfitting T-shirt and skimpy shorts, both of which Bill would appreciate.

Back downstairs, Possum, my rescue tabby, slinked in, meowing for food. A bowl of cat food on the floor, and I could turn back to what I wanted—wine with ginger ale. I settled on the couch. I flipped on the TV and watched for a couple of hours, trying to distract my mind while I waited. The white noise of a talk show, the warmth of the house, and the wine worked their magic.

Sunlight streamed through a window as I struggled to open my eyes. I must have fallen asleep. I clicked the TV off. What time was it? The clock read nine, which was extra early for me on a Saturday.

Where was Bill? Was that my doorbell? Maybe he had to work late last night. In my sleepy haze, I stumbled to the door. I unlocked it and drew it wide open. "Hi there, hand..."

I stared into the face of Officer John Davidson.

"You're not who I expected." I stumbled over the words.

"I can see that, Trisha." He grinned.

"I'll be right back." My face began to burn in a way that told me I was turning the same shade of red as the T-shirt. I slammed the door and raced down the hall and up the stairs. After pulling my denim jeans back on and a blouse covering a bit more of my chest, I headed back down, trying to compose myself, all the while wondering what was going on.

John Davidson and I had been in kindergarten through high school together. Like my other longtime friends, he always called me Trisha. I couldn't imagine my life without him, and we'd even met regularly for just friends' dinners when I was divorced. I wasn't his type. Showing up unannounced at my house? Even as good friends, he'd never do that. It wasn't his style. What on earth was he doing here?

John wore the same smile as I reopened the door.

"Nice outfit."

"Funny. I haven't seen you in months. What's up?"

John's smile evaporated. "Can we come in?"

For the first time, I realized John was in uniform, and his partner was standing in the shadows. Male. Young with peach fuzz for facial hair. Shorter than John's six-foot solid frame. Dark brown hair and almost solid black eyes. Silent. I guessed John was paired with a rookie.

"Of course. Come on in." I opened the door wider. I led them into the living room and settled into the brown armchair, the farthest from the door.

"Have a seat."

John settled on the couch, while his partner took the other brown armchair.

John asked, "Do you know a Brandon Jennings?"

"No. Should I?"

He ignored my question. "Where were you last night?"

"I was working. I had fares up until about eleven thirty."

"Tell me about your last fare."

"Flight crew off the Golden Wings Airways shuttle from DC. Routine run."

"Anything different about this fare?"

"One of the crew was rude, but nothing I couldn't handle. Why all the questions?"

"What happened?"

"Nothing much. Bad language, obnoxious personality, and then it got worse. I finally put him out of my cab at the request of the pilot. Is that what this is about? Was a complaint made?"

"Not exactly," John said. "What was the man's name?"

"Brandon. He didn't give me his last name."

"Where did you leave him?"

"Down on Dean Forest Road. About six blocks from the Pondside Inn. It's less than a half mile away from the hotel."

John took notes. "Who else was in the cab?"

"The pilots—Josh and Ryan. I don't know their last names."

"Were there other flight attendants?" John asked.

"They were in the other cab." I hesitated. "Am I in trouble? Did he file a complaint or what? The pilot can confirm this."

"We've already talked to the pilot," John said. "Brandon Jennings is dead. You wouldn't know anything about that, would you?"

3

After what seemed like hours, John and his partner left, leaving behind coffee and mugs in my sink. How many different ways could I say I'd put the guy out of my cab? At least five. I'd repeated it over and over. And all the questions on how long I'd been driving and who else I picked up during the day. I had respect for the police, but this was a bit much.

John knew I couldn't kill a fare. This was all crazy. I mulled over what he had told me, which wasn't much. Someone had seen Brandon's body and called the police. John and his partner had talked to the pilot and copilot. Then the clerk at Pondside. The pilot had been the one to tell them about the cab ride and the argument leading to Brandon being ejected from the taxi. Next was the dispatcher for Traveler's Taxi. The police were moving fast on this case.

John had a job to do. I didn't know anything about the man's murder. Or maybe I was assuming it was murder. John hadn't exactly said. With Brandon's attitude and mouth, I wasn't surprised he'd been attacked and killed, but it wasn't me.

Before leaving, John gave me a firm reminder they might have more questions. I looked at the clock. Great. It was already eleven. Where was Bill?

My cell phone vibrated on the mahogany side table.

What the...?

I yawned and rubbed my eyes. First, the cops were here early, and now someone was calling me at this hour. Everyone who knew me knew I slept in until early afternoon on Saturdays. It was my boss, so I let it roll to voice mail. I'd see what she wanted after I made another pot of coffee.

John and his partner had accepted my offer for the brew after the first round of questions, and two rounds later, all the coffee I'd made was gone. The pot sat on the white marble granite countertop and soon filled the room with a deep aroma. I was fixing to pour a cup when I heard music floating down from above. It stopped when the doorbell rang. What next?

As I swung the door open, Bill stepped forward.

"Are you okay? I've been trying to reach you for hours."

I almost laughed. I'd have to tell the story again.

"Come on in. I'm fine. I forgot to take the phone off vibrate and fell asleep. I didn't hear it. Then the police showed up this morning. Want breakfast? It's a bit of a tale. Where were you, anyway?"

His blue eyes widened as he stared at me for a moment and then followed me into the kitchen.

Coffee in hand, we walked to the dining room on the other side of the kitchen wall. He sank into the mahogany chair with a navy-and-white cushion at the head of the matching table. I joined him in the chair to his right.

"I had to work a bad wreck. None of what you've said makes sense. Can you start over from the beginning?" Bill's eyes were smiling.

He already knew me well enough to know sometimes the words and story came out all jumbled up in a mishmash. As I brought him up to date, I realized I was starving after having had a liquid supper. We moved back into the kitchen, and I started blueberry pancakes and bacon. There was nothing like the smell of bacon frying to relieve a bit of tension, but it wasn't working today.

Bill's face had gone from concern to irritation to curious and was now stony. I could see he was wondering what to think about all this. I was glad to have food to concentrate on.

"Why didn't you take him to the hotel if it was so close?"

"I don't know. I probably should have known better, but the guy's language and attitude sucked to the point I couldn't stand it. When the pilot said to stop, I didn't argue as hard as I might have."

My brain started to wander. Why had Brandon been killed? Was it a robbery? A random act? An act of revenge? The cops sure asked me enough questions about what happened. Was I responsible? It was way too early to go down that road.

"You might want to turn those, or is it your goal to have blackened pancakes this morning?"

My eyes refocused on the pan, and I quickly turned them. "They're a little browner than I normally cook them." I gave a small laugh.

"Do you think your boss will back you up for putting out a fare?"

"I think so, but I won't know until I have a chance to talk to her. I haven't been arrested, and I didn't kill anyone. If I'm a suspect, then the flight crew are likely ones as well. Sylvie might already know, and she might have to suspend me—if my actions were against company policy." Which would be disastrous for me, since I had little savings for emergencies.

Bill moved behind me and wrapped his arms around my waist. "I know you didn't. And if the worst happens, we'll figure things out. Okay?"

I about melted to the floor. I ignored the pancakes and, turning, planted a big kiss on Bill's mouth. A broad smile was my reward before he moved back so I could finish up breakfast. I hit the switch to start the coffeepot. The dark liquid began to dribble in. I wondered if Brandon's blood had trickled out. How morbid. I wasn't even sure how Brandon had died. The cops hadn't answered any of my questions. As I thought back, neither John nor his partner had told me much of anything.

Soothing wafts of the brewing mixture filled my nose. I looked around for something else to focus on. No more coffee, or I'd be a jittery mess all day.

Bill and I ate breakfast as he told me about the accident on the interstate. He usually didn't like to talk about what happened at work, so I wasn't sure if he was telling me to distract me or if it was so bad he needed to vent.

We rescheduled for later in the week. I had the monthly Saturday work meeting, then maybe a nap before I had to work my shift.

After he left, I checked for my voice messages, but there weren't any. Strange. My boss never called this early on Saturday, plus I would have expected her to leave a message. What was up? She liked quick responses, or she'd stew about whatever she was calling for.

The phone vibrated again. The caller ID read "Sylvie." I braced myself.

4

"Triiishaaaa?" Sylvie drawled.

A true Southern belle, right down to her perfectly manicured French-tipped toenails and coiffed silvery gray hair, she could drag out her vowels like nobody's business. But she was also tough as nails, even though she was only a few inches taller than me and had a slender frame. She was always expertly made up, but in a way that didn't try to hide the wrinkles she'd earned. Running a taxi business wasn't for the fainthearted. I was glad she had her husband, Derek, as a partner.

"Yeah. Just fixin' to call you back. What's up?"

"Can you come in thirty minutes early for the staff meeting today? I need to talk to you."

Oh great. First the cops, now my boss. The idea of a nap was fading fast. Would I have a job later? Or maybe I should quit now, before she had a chance to fire me. I wanted to cry.

A pity party wasn't going to help me. I sucked in a breath and steeled myself to be upbeat. "Sure. I'll be there. Everything okay?"

"Derek had a bad night, so I'm trying to let him sleep. It's why I didn't wait for you to call me back. And I'd like to hear about last night from you," Sylvie said.

At sixty-five, Derek was two years older than Sylvie, with far more health problems. He'd relocated to Savannah thirty years ago to help with his chronic congestion and allergies. While the humidity might not have been the best remedy for his lungs, he'd met Sylvie and married her. A couple of inches taller than Sylvie, Derek was stocky and the exact opposite of Sylvie—more fragile than he looked.

"Is he alright?" He'd been released two days ago after a two-week hospital visit for pneumonia. The doctors fixed one thing only to have another go wrong.

"He's just tired. Did too much yesterday. Thinks he's got his old strength back, but he's still weak."

"Okay. I'll see you at the office."

We hung up.

Time to face the world. Or, at least, the shower.

Steamy hot water pelted my face. The last of the tension melted as my shoulders relaxed. If I could stay in the shower all day, all would be right with the world. The water began to cool as my skin puckered. I'd wear my lucky black underwear today. Not sure it was really lucky, but things went better when I wore it. After yesterday, I wasn't willing to chance it.

I dressed in my usual uniform—a clean pair of blue jeans and a work shirt. My Velcroed sneakers were at the front door. I was ready.

Shoot. I hadn't called my daughter, Steph, for our Saturday morning call. I dialed, and it went to voice mail.

My stomach tightened at the thought of having to call my ex, but there was no other way around it. I hated making these calls when Steph didn't answer. I dreaded whatever was the drama for the week at Mike's house. Steph had a cell phone, but it was a crapshoot as to whether she would pick up. Mike's phone was always on if he was home, and I could count on him asking Steph to talk to me.

I dialed. My second ex-husband answered.

"Hey, Mike. It's me. How are things? Anything I should know about?"

The first bad part. I hated not knowing what was going on with my daughter. She was fifteen when I got the second divorce two years ago. Earlier this year, after Aunt Harriett died, she'd said she wanted to live with Mike, who she knew best and who'd been around for most of her life, not her birth father. That would have been my first ex-husband, who had remarried and moved away.

I'll never forget her words: "I can't stand it here anymore."

I'm not sure what was worse: going through a divorce, again; being broke and not sure where we were going to live; Aunt Harriett's recent death and my brother contesting the will for her house; or my daughter being obsessed with all things Goth and moving out to live with one of my exes.

After pleasantries, Mike called Steph to the phone.

"Hello." Boredom and lack of interest dripped from her voice. I pictured her black fingernails drumming the kitchen counter before she ran her fingers through her spiky black hair. She must have shifted the phone as I heard her metal-pierced earrings connect to the plastic phone. Unless it was her nose ring. I shivered at the thought and wondered if I'd get used to it before she grew out of what I hoped was a passing phase.

"Hi, Steph. How's school?" I wanted to bite my tongue as soon as I'd said it, knowing what was coming.

"Mom. It's Stephanie. I'm grown up now. Use my real name." The disdain rolled off her tongue like boulders rolled down hills. I felt like one had landed on my back.

"Sorry. Old habits, you know. I'll work harder to remember. How was your week?"

"The same. Classes. Hung out with friends."

I choked back all my questions. I wanted things to go back to what they had been like before she moved. When we talked, giggled, and did things together. She was growing up, but I wanted details. It was maddening, and I missed our closeness.

"I'm off tomorrow. Would you like to have lunch at the house or out somewhere? Maybe an hour or so?" I hated to sound like I was begging, but it had been several weeks since I'd seen her. I wanted to know about her classes and teachers. Our telephone calls were short.

She barely said anything. I'd really get to know things if I could sit with her in person. Or at least that was the idea.

"I've got plans."

"What about next Sunday night? I could pick you up for dinner. A quick bite, and then I'll have you back."

"Dad says I have to go to a church function with them. Sorry."

I let the silence hang for a while. "I miss you, Stephanie. I just want to see you, know you're okay."

"I'm fine, Mom. Really. I need to be here for a while. Can you understand?"

I swallowed my frustration. "I can. It's hard not to have you at home with me. I have the house all fixed up now. My job is going pretty well." Well, except for the little problem of my customer getting murdered, but she didn't need to know that. "If you decide you want to come home, you have your room and space."

"I know, Mom. I need some time. Gotta go."

"Okay. Put your dad back on."

Mike picked up the phone.

"How is she really?"

"She's doing great. Her routine is better. Attending classes regularly. She likes her teachers. Give her time."

I wanted to strangle him. He was almost as bad as Steph. If I knew his wife better, I would've asked her. Women always got the details, but his wife had no time for me. I wasn't sure what it was, but she didn't talk to me unless absolutely necessary. Filling me in on my daughter's life wasn't on her list of essential things.

"How's Jennifer feeling?" His new wife, Jennifer, was pregnant with their first child. I wasn't sure how Steph would cope with a baby, but I expected the change could cause another crisis for her.

"She's fine. Thanks for asking. She's over morning sickness, so we're hoping it will be an uneventful rest of the term."

"How's Steph taking all this?"

"She seems excited there will be a new baby in the house."

I could imagine. It might seem fun, but I wondered how the reality of not being the main focus was going to bear on her. The good news was it might send her back to me, but I hated the thought of one more disappointment in her life. My last divorce had hurt her, but at least Mike cared about her and had stayed in her life. My first husband was out of our lives and had settled into a relationship with kids of his own. Steph had been a toddler when we divorced, so they never talked. I couldn't understand how my ex, who'd been in her life for three years, could walk away so easily. I'd talked to him a few times, and he'd agreed to stay in contact with her. Then he'd met his new wife, and those intentions went out the window. I ached to the deepest marrow of my bones for her.

"I've got to run. Jennifer wants me to get her onion rings." He laughed. "You know how pregnant women are."

"Got it. One more thing. I'd love to have lunch or dinner with Steph. Sundays seem to be best. Can you help me out on this?"

"I'll try. You know how teenagers are."

"Okay. I'll call you next Saturday."

I frowned, glad Steph couldn't see my face. Being interested in a particular kind of music your parents didn't get, I got. My generation had gone through the same things. But all the fascination with black and death I didn't understand. At least she was talking to me. I wished there were a topic we could talk about that would fascinate her. Maybe inspiration would strike me on my drive to work.

5
_____

My brain was working through ideas as I made the ten-minute ride to the office on Oglethorpe Road in what I called my street car, a silver Honda Accord. Several years old and purchased when I was married, it was reliable and didn't require a lot of maintenance.

Green lights all the way. I passed a red on-off tour bus partly filled with tourists. I was right. My lucky underwear had been a good choice.

I pulled into the office parking lot, bumping over the passenger side curb. Good grief. My good luck was working only on the road, not parking. I didn't know if I had woken up spatially messed up or what. But I'd been here before. Probably because I had been awakened way too early on a Saturday and slept on the couch. The shower had relaxed me, and now, I forced myself to pay a bit more attention to driving.

I checked to make sure no one was around and breathed in deeply, clearing my head before I slid into a parking space in front of the office.

As I opened the door, it dawned on me there had been a second driver last night. I'd seen the cab but not the driver. Who had that been, and had the police talked to him too? John hadn't mentioned checking out anyone else. His expression said he believed me, but if there were more questions, I wanted to be prepared. I'd check with the dispatcher after the meeting. At least my brain was working okay.

My tennis shoes scuffed along the concrete parking lot as I moved to the building. I took a deep breath, clearing my head. The concrete industrial park where the office was located felt dead to me. I much preferred being among trees and nature. All more alive.

I sucked in more air. I wasn't sure it would do any good, but hey, it was worth a shot, and Aunt Harriett always said clearing the air helped.

I stared at the small rectangular white with navy lettering sign over the metal door of the drab building. Traveler's Taxi. Boring. And the grayish-brown building, well, was just butt ugly. As my grandma used to say, "You can dress up a porcupine, but it doesn't get rid of the bristles." That was the point. I laughed. Where was Angie? I had to remember to tell her about this. She loved old sayings that applied today almost as much as a good pun.

Angie and I had been best friends from the first day we met in kindergarten. Where we also met John. She'd gotten the best of him with a knock-knock joke. I'd followed up with, "Why did the pony go to the doctor?"

She'd started to laugh even before she answered. "Cuz, it was a little horse." It had sealed our friendship.

I'd learned a lot about reading people being around her. We'd eventually graduated from jokes to puns and old sayings, trying to outdo each other when we got together.

The office door opened into a large stuffy room. Rectangular desks were lined up in two rows from wall to wall with a wide aisle in the center of the beige linoleum floor. A window air-conditioning unit blocked the light from one of the small windows near the top of the front wall. Long, white fluorescent fixtures hung from the ceiling.

Geoff and Mark, two other drivers, manned two of the desks. Geoff was a burly barrel type of guy who played defense in high school football, complete with a thick neck and broad shoulders.

Mark, who also worked dispatch many nights, was a young guy, lean, almost frail-looking, but all muscle, like every other driver except me.

Sylvie ran a tight, no-nonsense ship. Only the dispatcher's area in the far corner had a cubical wall to shield for noise. Behind it, the phones that controlled our business covered a lonely wooden desk.

In the other corner was a small office with opaque glass half-walls on the inside and a door to close for privacy. From any vantage point, Sylvie, or Derek, if he was working, could see everything—which we all knew. For a five-car taxi company, we stayed busy.

"Sylvie in her office?" I walked in, not immediately seeing her in the office.

"Yep," Mark said. "Came in about ten minutes ago. She looks tired. Must have been a rough night."

I frowned. Sylvie had started Traveler's Taxi twenty-five years ago, and when she married Derek, he became her partner. What would happen when they retired? Geoff was their most senior driver, and he hated me. Not me exactly, but women taxi drivers. Thought it was a man's job. I couldn't see myself working for him. Or for anyone other than Sylvie, for that matter. Geoff was quick on his feet and held strong Southern values, a lot like my uncle, when it came to a woman's place in the world. But he respected Sylvie, mostly. Having Derek back her up helped with guys like Geoff.

"I thought I heard you." Sylvie came out of her office. "Come on in. Let's chat."

I took a seat in front of her desk and took a close look at her. She had bags under her eyes. Dressed in navy khakis and a button-down shirt, her hair gave away the fact she wasn't much younger. She had on full makeup, like my mother had always worn and which I hated, but somehow it worked on her. She was about three inches taller than me, but her slender frame and straight-up posture made it seem more.

Sylvie closed the door and moved to the back corner, closing a box she must have been sorting through when I arrived. Her actions were both calming and nerve-wracking. Pictures of Rome, Egypt, and

Moscow plastered the white walls. All places she and Derek had toured. Places I would love to visit someday.

Sylvie sat in the dirt-brown office chair and wheeled up to the small cherry desk.

I tensed. Maybe my underwear was only good for traffic.

"Trisha, remind me how long you've been working for us?" Sylvie asked.

"Almost two years. It was when I divorced my last husband. You hired me when most wouldn't have. I know I haven't told you lately, but I won't ever forget you doing that, no matter what happens."

Her forehead wrinkled as if she were going to ask me what I meant and then changed her mind. "That's right. You've been a great driver. I wonder if you wouldn't like a different challenge."

"I like driving. I always have."

Sylvie remained silent.

"Look, about last night. I could have handled the situation better. Not put the guy out. It won't happen again. I've learned my lesson."

Sylvie laughed. "From what I hear, he deserved it. And yes, the police called me, but it sounded like routine questions. Besides, you know I don't interfere with my drivers' decisions unless I have to. Although I don't encourage it, I want to be sure you, the other drivers, and the police know I take it seriously. We have a reputation to maintain. But I stand by you." She paused. "No, I have a different idea."

"I don't understand. If this isn't about last night, why am I here?"

"You know Derek's been sick."

"Yes. But he's getting better, right?"

"He is, but we're not as young as we used to be. And frankly, we think it's time for a change. Or at least starting to consider our options." She paused. "We may sell the company or at least engage a person to run it, with a sale in the future. I've been talking to Derek, and he's coming around to the idea."

My mouth dropped open. Sylvie loved working with the drivers and hearing the stories. Sure, she was in her sixties, but she was mostly in the office part-time, and the company almost ran itself. Sylvie *was* Traveler's Taxi.

"I don't understand." I felt like an idiot repeating it, but I really didn't get it. What was she trying to tell me?

"I thought you might be interested in buying it."

"I...I don't know the first thing about running a company."

"Sure you do. You filled in for me when Derek and I went to Scotland this past year. You drive a cab. There's not much more. Working with the accountant, but I could help you with everything at the start. Didn't you help one of your husbands with a business?"

My face heated. I doubted this was all that simple, and I laughed softly.

"I don't think you give yourself enough credit for what you've built here."

Maybe she was trying to ease me into thinking about it. It was working. But the idea of my owning and running my own company was a lot to take in.

"What about Geoff? He's the most senior. And I would bet money he wants this."

"But I really want you. And I think you're the best person for this. You've got the right temperament, at least most of the time. And you know most of the business. You're smart. You've worked hard this past year, and I've noticed." She paused and stared at papers on her desk before she looked up again. "You'll learn what you need to know. If you're interested and would prefer it, we could handle this in stages—a progression as you get more managerial experience."

"I did help my second husband with the business. He was in charge of managing everything, so I'd be starting over on the learning curve. But even if I could master what it takes to run this company, I don't have any money to buy this."

"If you're interested, we can work out the terms. You inherited Harriett's house, didn't you? Maybe a loan using your home as collateral?" Sylvie asked. "Of course, you'll need to be eligible to transfer all the licenses if you buy the business. They don't look kindly on any type of illegal activity by the owners, or even any suspicion for crimes. Let's hope the police can solve this unfortunate incident quickly. I don't see how this could affect anything, but the licensing board can be tricky. That shouldn't be a problem, should it? And I'd be around for a while to help with the transition. So would Derek. What do you say?"

"Can I think about it?" I wasn't sure I wanted to be in debt again and trying to make a loan payment. It felt like I was only now getting firmly back on my feet.

"Sure. Don't take too long. If you aren't interested, then I need to decide on an alternative. And if you have any questions or want to look at the financial information, let me know. We'll work on an agreement. Also, you need to set an example for the others, so no more stunts like the one last night. I support my drivers, but I don't want everyone thinking they can do that without considering there may be consequences. To make a point, I am moving you to dispatch for one day. I want to be sure anyone inquiring of the incident— police or otherwise—knows I took this seriously. However, this is more to protect you and this business, as well as to keep the other drivers in line."

"Okay. I understand, and thanks. At this point, I'm not sure what to ask. I'll think about it. I'm sure I'll have questions. And I'll let you know quickly." I paused. "You know, I do have a question I've been meaning to ask. More about the business in general. How are Uber and Lyft affecting us?"

Sylvie smiled. I guessed it was at the "us" I'd used.

"It is an issue—part of why the airport permit is so important. We can talk more about strategy if you decide to pursue this. For now, I'll have Sam in a cab and you on dispatch for the late shift. They'll know you've been pulled off the driving roster, but don't let them get to you. Plan on working tomorrow instead. And if you're interested in this, let's talk about how you can help me while Derek is on the mend. Kind of a test period for both of us."

I know I nodded before I walked out, but my head was spinning. I bumped into a desk.

"Hey, watch it," Geoff snapped.

"Sorry."

The clock read 2:45. Fifteen minutes to kill.

6

Hmm, I told myself to focus. A business opportunity was the last thing I thought Sylvie would talk to me about. I had a lot of thinking to do. For now, what to do with the time before the meeting?

All drivers were required to attend these weekly meetings, even if you were working at the dispatch desk. I traded barbs with the other drivers, two milling around in search of coffee, and one on a computer. Geoff was eyeing me, so I took a seat at one of the tables with a computer as far from him as possible. Relief had flooded me when Sylvie had confirmed my job was safe, but her news and the one-day work on dispatch made me wonder if I shouldn't see what I could find out about Brandon and the murder. I wouldn't have much time once I started staffing the dispatch desk.

I clicked the computer on. What to search? First, news. I read the local articles. Nothing there I didn't already know, except the body had been found at the hotel, not the area where I dropped him off. That changed everything. I'd need to retrace the route and see what might have happened.

Since I didn't know Brandon, maybe it was time to figure out who he was. Googling Brandon Jennings, I found a couple of doctors,

Facebook profiles, and a reference to a character on a popular emergency room TV drama. No chance Brandon was a doctor.

Facebook might be a better choice. I signed in and typed his name. Three guys stared out. One too old. Two more in the wrong states. A tap on "See More" brought me a long list. I scrolled down. Good grief. There were a lot of them. I had no idea how popular and common the name was. A change in tactics was needed.

"Brandon Jennings, Savannah" gave me two, and there he was, smiling. His profile showed he was a football fan and posted lots of pictures of himself. There were photos of him, blond hair and tan, in his car, playing volleyball, having a cold one outside, with a blonde or two on his arm—the poster boy for Southern beach life.

The movie list was interesting—*The Usual Suspects*, *The Breakfast Club*, *War Horse*, *The African Queen,* and *Taking Chance.* He liked a lot of the same ones I did. Maybe I had gotten the wrong impression, and there had been more to this guy than I realized. He was clearly a movie buff and outdoor kinda guy, with a lot of friends commenting on his posts. Could it have been we both had a bad day? No time for more scrolling through his posts. The meeting would start soon. I'd have to check more later. I powered down the computer.

Promptly at three, the room quieted as Sylvie emerged from her office to stand in front of the desks. Talking to her hadn't been what I expected. Could I do this? Did I want to? I'd have to deal with Geoff. I wasn't sure he'd work for me. And what about the other drivers? I had mostly good relationships with them. But as a boss? Who knew? Wow, my own company. The cars could be painted to look like denim. That would be unique.

Or not. I hadn't managed to keep a marriage together for more than a couple of years. I was better at being a worker bee than a queen, so how would I manage a company? And all the paperwork to transfer the licenses. Ugh.

Sylvie was right, I'd need those, especially the airport license, which was the key to this business. Otherwise, I'd have to depend on hotels and random calls. Taxi drivers could starve waiting on those.

But I could do this, couldn't I? I rearranged myself in my chair as I listened to Sylvie start her regular pep talk.

My mind drifted, and I stared at the walls. Several maps and posters for the company littered one side of the room. Otherwise, drab walls stared back at me. It was functional and, with the beating the desks took from the drivers, I understood the rationale for the cheap furniture. Funny how your perspective changed in a snap.

As I looked around, I wondered if Sylvie owned the warehouse complex. Or maybe she owned the one-story building strip at the back of this warehouse business center we officed in. Or did she rent the office? My shoulders slumped. I didn't even know what this business included. How could I ever hope to buy it, much less run it? I didn't completely understand what Sylvie wanted to do. If she owned the building, she and Derek might want to keep it and rent it, or they might want to sell over time. I should stop obsessing and talk to her about what this opportunity might mean. Or at least start making a list of questions.

I refocused on what Sylvie was saying. It was more of the usual—keeping good receipts, being on time, etc. I tried to listen more closely today to make sure I didn't miss anything important, although it sounded like most of the reminders she gave.

"Remember, a lot of our business is from flight crews. They remember good service and ask for us by name. I hope all of you will help protect this business."

"Yeah, well, it helps if they don't get killed on our watch," Geoff said as the other drivers laughed.

Heat surged up my neck.

"Okay," Sylvie said. "That's enough. We all know a flight crew member was killed. But let me remind you. This can be a dangerous business. Everyone has the right to refuse a client if they're concerned about their safety. And by everyone, and I do mean everybody"—Sylvie stared at Geoff— "has the right to put any fare out of their cab who is misbehaving or acting up."

"That leaves out working late Friday and Saturday nights," Geoff said.

Again, soft laughter floated across the room.

"If we leave out all the drunks and party boys and girls, we won't have any fares, now will we?"

"I think you know what I mean. And, so it's clear, I don't condone that sort of conduct. However, as this matter is still under investigation by the police, I'm taking Trisha off the rotation for today. Sam will be handling her shift."

Geoff smirked. "Maybe she should be on dispatch permanently. Safer for a girl. Where's Derek? This is the third meeting he's missed. I don't remember him ever missing many before."

Sylvie grimaced. "Derek's still recovering from his bout of pneumonia. He probably won't be at a meeting for several weeks while he regains his strength. But it shouldn't affect operations. And Trisha is on dispatch for today. Then back in her cab."

Geoff persisted. "But Derek's always been here to back you up. Isn't that going to create problems? Sometimes it takes a man to deal with things. And if he can't return, what does that mean?"

Sylvie's mouth turned into a thin, drawn line. "First of all, this is my business. I started it long before any of you were my drivers. And long before I met and married Derek. Derek's been an enormous help over the years, but it's *my* business. And if he can't return, then I'll run it, as I always have. And I'll make any decisions needed. Speaking of which, I received two applications from drivers who'd like to join the company. I don't think we need additional drivers at this time, but I'll keep them on file in case we have any openings."

I almost giggled out loud as Geoff folded his arms across his chest. This was a small taste of what I could expect as the owner. Sylvie had turned things on their head, and I wasn't sure I could have done it quite as well. I'd give a week's pay to know what was going on in Geoff's head at that moment. Serious cussing, I decided. Not worth a nickel.

"Don't need more drivers. It's hard enough now with Uber and Lyft out there, plus new cab companies opening. If it weren't for the fact the airport isn't issuing any new permits for those new companies, there'd be more even competition for passengers," Geoff said.

The words hung in the air for a minute. Sylvie appeared to be assessing the room. "You're right. Our airport permit is important, to me and each of you, since you operate under the company's permit. And Derek and I are working on strategies to deal with Uber as we plan the future. I appreciate everything each of you does as part of this company. If you have any other suggestions, my office door is always open. Anything else?"

Silence met her. "That's it then. Back to the pavement."

I stared at the desk for a moment and, as I rose, I turned, right into Geoff's chest.

"Killed anyone else?" He wore the proverbial Joker's smile.

"Hardly. But then again, I haven't picked you up as a passenger. Care to take a ride?"

Unlike the Joker, Geoff's smile transformed into a frown almost as obscene as the smile had been. He whispered, "Don't threaten me, little girl. Bad things happen to little girls who don't behave."

Chills ran down my back, and it wasn't from the air-conditioning unit that had kicked in. I'd never liked Geoff, but he'd always kept his distance. I sensed he was the kind of guy who acted on any weakness, and I couldn't let it pass.

"Perhaps. But bad things happen to men who don't behave themselves as well. You know what happened to the flight attendant." It was probably not the smartest thing I could have said, but if I wanted to work here, whether I bought this business or not, which I couldn't even comprehend fully yet, then I was going to have to stand up to this guy. Or, if for no other reason than general principles.

"Maybe. But I heard you left him alive and kicking. Kinda makes you wonder what goes on around you when you're not looking, doesn't it?" Geoff threw his head back, laughed, and walked away.

Now, what the hell did that mean? I stared at his back. Did he know something? How could he? Great. If he was this way now, what would it be like to deal with him if he knew Sylvie had talked to me about the business?

I sucked in a breath and switched gears. Geoff was either guessing, or the police had questioned him. Sounded like he might have been the other driver. He did seem to know details about Friday night. Easy enough to find out. The trouble was, I wasn't on dispatch until later, and I wanted to know now. I looked back at the dispatch desk. Mark had moved from the chair he'd sat in for the meeting to the dispatcher area. I wanted to dance or jump up and down. Mark was susceptible to flirting and being friendly. He could also be counted on not to ask too many questions. I straightened my shoulders and sashayed my way back to the corner to check the logs.

"Hi, Mark."

"Hey, Trisha, what's up?"

"You were working last night, weren't you?"

Mark's eyebrow rose. "Yeah, why?"

"Just wondering. I appreciate you giving me the airport run."

"Yeah."

I could see the questions on his face. Better to just ask. "Was wondering who was in the other cab. Mind if I look at the log?"

"Sure, but I can tell you. Geoff was next on the list, so he got it."

Well, wasn't that interesting? Did Geoff have any skeletons in his closet? Was I right he might have been questioned already too?

7

Back in the Accord, I turned over the key and headed out of the parking lot. My thoughts were bouncing around like a tennis match —first, the idea of owning a business and then back to the murder.

My own company. No college education and running a business. That would show all the smart kids in my high school, wouldn't it? But was that what I wanted? Right now, sleep was next on my list. I'd need to be as awake on dispatch as driving, so a nap was necessary.

My standard route back through Savannah from the office to my house was almost its own cruise control. I realized I hadn't been paying attention to what was around me as I neared the house. A police cruiser was parked in front. Oh great, was this going to be round two? That was what always happened on television right before things got a lot worse.

John stepped out. I ran my hand through my hair, calming any stray strands. It felt like it was going in all directions, just like my mind. How on earth did that man always manage to look so hot and all together? And in the humidity, as well. Must've been the navy-blue uniform.

"Hey, Trisha. Seems like we just left you. Where've you been?"

I bristled. "Had a meeting at the office. What are you doing here?"

"I need to ask you to come down to the station. We've got a few follow-up questions for you."

"I already answered everything I know. Why do I have to go through that again?"

"We need to confirm several details. I need you to come in and talk to us about those."

I couldn't imagine what they could have missed. "Seems to me y'all asked the same questions over and over this morning. And I'm tired. I need a nap. Can't this wait?"

"'Fraid not. I'm gonna have to insist."

Visions of John insisting in other situations caused a tingle to run up my spine. Maybe spending the afternoon with John wasn't so bad. I must have grinned.

"This isn't a laughing matter, Trisha. I need you to come in now."

"Got it." I was glad I'd put on fresh clothes. My best armor was called for in what I suspected was going to be a very long day.

I followed John in my Accord down Oglethorpe Street. The historic three-story red brick Habersham Street station sat on the corner. Moss-draped magnolia trees extended down the center of Oglethorpe Street for as far as the eye could see. Period homes lined this street, and there were usually tourists and residents alike walking the area.

The station was near Colonial Park Cemetery, and I trod lightly on the sidewalks. When the streets were widened, a number of the graves were covered in concrete to create the new walkways beside the central part of the cemetery. A terrific story for visitors, but I was a bit squeamish about walking over the remains of the dead.

Inside the Habersham station, I was shown into a small, grayish-white room with a rectangular metal table and two chairs. John indicated I should sit in the chair facing the mirrored wall. The air-conditioning was on and blowing ice cold. Everything about the room said they wanted me as uncomfortable as possible. Great. Just like on TV, although I didn't think a handsome detective would be coming through the doorway. At least I hoped not. I would have a hard time concentrating if he were a cute hunk.

Ten minutes later, I was fidgeting, despite my best efforts. I picked at a fingernail before I tried to bite it and wondered how long I would have to be here.

The door opened and I turned toward it, like I suspected everyone else in this situation did. No handsome detective. No John, either. Instead, a new face.

"Ms. Reede. I'm Officer Stanley."

Hmmm. Was that his first or last name? He had a serious face that looked like there'd been a long drought between smiles. The frown lines arched back to his receding salt-and-pepper hair. A joke was probably out of order right now. Biting my tongue, I reflected on the restraint I had today. Must have been lack of sleep. My half-bit finger-nails dug into my hands, and I unclenched my fists. I reached up to rub my arm instead of crossing my arms. The last thing I wanted was to be seen as defensive.

"Cold?"

"Not really. Just had to scratch." I'll say, I had a major itch to get out of here.

"Well, I won't take up much of your time. Only a few follow-up questions."

"Okay. John told me that."

"John?"

Oh great. I shouldn't have used his first name. "Yeah, Officer Davidson. We've known each other since grade school."

He appeared to accept this, but who knew? I searched for any clue of what he was thinking. Nada. Zip. I settled back into the cold metal chair. I hadn't done anything wrong. Putting a rude passenger out wasn't against the law. My shoulders relaxed a bit. Officer Stanley continued to watch me as he set his clipboard on the table and took a seat. I felt a little like a mouse in a cage with a cat, waiting for it to strike.

"Let's run through this one more time."

I groaned inside. Great. I was tired of repeating this story.

"You picked up the flight crew at the airport?"

I relayed the same story I had told John that morning. I figured I might get out of there quicker if I volunteered the information I had already given them.

"Anything out of the ordinary?"

"You already know all this. I've already told you guys several times what happened."

"They asked you to take them to their hotel? Where they were staying?"

"Yes, well, no. The pilot and copilot were going to the Pondside Inn. The deceased, Brandon, was picking up his car."

Officer Stanley's eyebrow rose. "The victim wasn't staying there?"

"No. From what he said, he lives in town."

"Did he tell you where?"

"No, but he wasn't staying at the hotel."

"They were all going to the hotel? Did you go straight there? Direct route?"

I nodded.

Officer Stanley wrote notes. I crossed my arms. Questioning me about what happened was one thing, but how I did my job was a whole different matter. I was a good driver. I never "gave 'em the tour," so to speak, by taking long detours so I could increase the fare. Priming the pump was simply wrong. I cared about how I treated my customers. Who was he to question my motives? What was going on?

"Okay, let's move on."

We covered the conversation in the cab and why I asked Brandon to get out of the cab.

"Okay. Then you drove straight to the hotel?"

"Yes."

"Didn't do anything else until you let the other passengers off?"

"No."

"No other stop?"

Oh crap. I'd forgotten. And someone had told him. Geez. Would this never end? Time to fess up.

"After I put Brandon out of the cab, I stopped to ask the other passengers if they were okay with my actions or if I should go back."

"Where?"

"At the intersection of Highway 1 and Burton Street. Right after I turned the corner."

Officer Stanley made more notes. "You asked them if you should return to pick up the victim?"

"Yeah."

"If you didn't want to lose a client, why put him out? Wouldn't that be a problem for you?"

"Maybe, but he was insulting, and it was the pilot who made the decision, not me. Our business depends on the flight crews, but I was also trying to do right by all my customers. I stopped to let the pilot think about whether Brandon had learned his lesson and if I should go back. If he'd said yes, I would have."

"Why didn't you tell Officer Davidson about this?"

"I forgot."

My stomach started to roll. I fought the acidic feeling in my throat. Who was it that said you should never let them see you sweat? It was a cliché, but I wished I had worn my short-sleeve top. Droplets had developed under my arms. It was threatening to be a downpour rather than a sprinkle. I hadn't even done anything wrong. How did real criminals sit in here for hours and remain cool? I almost wished I had done more wrong stuff as a kid. At least it would've prepared me for this. Almost, but not entirely. I wouldn't have wanted to experience this as a teenager, either.

"Ms. Reede. Did you hear what I said? You know withholding information is a crime."

It was a statement, not a question. I stared back at him. I could almost feel the adrenaline charging through my veins. I grabbed my right hand to keep it from shaking. What could I say? Last night wasn't my finest moment. I'd already told him I forgot. What more did he want?

"I'm sorry. I didn't remember it or think it was important. It wasn't intentional."

He stared at me for a minute. I wondered if he thought the silence would prompt me to talk. If I knew what to say to fix this, I would. But I didn't. We could sit here all day in the quiet and nothing would change. I'd love to say I was waiting him out, power trip to power trip, but no, I was at a complete loss for words. And that didn't happen often.

His shoulders relaxed. "Then what happened?"

"I dropped them off at the hotel."

Officer Stanley continued the same questions for what seemed like hours. He wrote a few more notes and looked up. "Didn't it strike you as strange Mr. Jennings wasn't parked at the airport?"

I stared at him. "I didn't think about it. I know the rules for taxis but not for employees. Since he was with the flight crew, I didn't give it a second thought." I was rambling, but I didn't know what to say— food for later thought.

"Okay. So, what did you do after you dropped off the pilot and copilot?"

"I headed home. My boyfriend, Bill, was coming over."

"Your boyfriend's last name?"

"Traynor. William Traynor."

Officer Stanley nodded. "And what time was that?"

"I don't know. Eleven thirty or so."

"And when did your boyfriend show up?"

"Not until this morning. Bill's a paramedic, and there was a bad accident on the interstate, so he ended up working late into the night. I fell asleep waiting for him. Officer Davidson rang the doorbell waking me."

"And about what time?"

"Maybe nine. You'd have to ask him. I didn't look at the clock."

"Was anyone with you between the time of the last fare and when Officer Davidson arrived?"

"No."

"Can anyone verify any of this?"

"Other than Officer Davidson confirming the time?"

Officer Stanley nodded.

"No."

"You could have gone back to where you put the victim out, couldn't you?"

"I guess, but I didn't. I went directly home to wait for my boyfriend. We had plans."

"We'll want to talk to him."

We sat in silence.

Officer Stanley made more notes and then put down his pen. "Okay, Ms. Reede. A couple more questions and you can go. There's an old complaint here by one of your husbands. It seems you and men don't last long together. Care to tell me about it?"

The hair on the back of my neck stood up. "That was years ago. And my first ex-husband made the accusation in connection with a nasty divorce. As you already know, it was withdrawn."

Officer Stanley stared at me. "But you do seem to have a problem with men and relationships."

"No. I have made mistakes in my marriages, but so did the men. We divorced. That's not a crime."

"Anyone else accuse you of threatening them? Being violent toward them?"

"You've already looked me up, so you know there's not."

"Maybe something no one filed a report on." He let the words hang in the air.

"No."

"Well, we'll be asking around. Don't leave town. We may have additional questions for you. And if you think of anything else you've forgotten, please give me a call."

What could I have forgotten? What was he implying? And what did that mean? I hadn't had many run-ins with the police in my lifetime. Just to make sure, I asked, "Am I a suspect?"

"Not at this time. But we haven't ruled anyone out. Especially not with your record. Plus, you're a potential witness."

I stared at the card Officer Stanley handed me as we stood. Detective S. Stanley.

No first name, only an initial. Maybe a family name he didn't want printed like Stonewall or Snowball or even, Samwise. Although he didn't look like a hobbit. Or worse, maybe they named him Stanley. The nervous giggle started low, and all I could think about was a kid named Stanley Stanley. His name would've made for a tough childhood. I could barely hold the laugh in and realized the stress was making me silly. My face must have been turning green from the effort.

Officer Stanley opened the door. "Are you alright? Let me show you the way out."

I followed him down the hall and almost ran out of the station before I lost it.

Bubbling up came giggles, anxious laughter, hot tears, and the anxiety of the last twenty-four hours. I couldn't wait to get home, crawl in bed, and pull the sheets over my head. Staying there for the near future was appealing, but I also knew I'd see Bill after my shift on the desk tonight. Bill might not be a detective, but he was a good-looking man and so much more. Maybe I'd greet him with a special drink or other surprise. If I could get my brain to slow down long enough for a nap, I'd be set. What were the odds?

8

Lifting my head, I sucked in two deep breaths. Ahh, that helped. I looked around and saw John walking out the doors of the police station. I reconsidered heading home immediately and, instead, started toward him. If nothing else, maybe he could tell me what was going on.

"Hey. Wait up."

John turned to face me. "I thought you'd already left."

"I'm on my way now. And I need explanations."

"What do you mean? I don't know anything."

"Don't start that dumb Southern redneck act with me. I know you know what's going on. Why was I dragged back here? And what's all this about me not being ruled out as a suspect?"

John frowned, and his neck reddened. "You know I can't talk about an ongoing investigation."

I stepped forward, hands on my hips, stretching my neck to get my face somewhere close to being in front of his. It was the most intimidating stance I could muster, given he was at least seven inches taller than me. "Oh, please. When did you ever keep all the rules?"

John tried not to grin. He knew that look. "Look, there's the incident with your ex-husband."

"My first ex? You mean the complaint where he said I attacked him?"

John nodded.

"That was dismissed. It was all part of the divorce tactics. He didn't want to pay child support. We resolved things, and he didn't pursue it. Besides, that was years ago. You know that."

"I know. But now we have a dead man, and you were the last to see him. Plus, add in the old complaint. The investigator had questions." He held up his hands.

My face heated with anger. "I wasn't the only one. The pilot and copilot were there. They were the last ones to see him too."

"Don't shoot the messenger. I know it has no merit, but the others don't know you as I do. Now you're stopping me in front of the station. I can't be seen talking to a material witness here."

"John. Are you comin' or not?" a tall thin male cop with sandy brown hair asked.

"That's my partner. I've gotta go. I can't talk here."

"How about later?"

"Gotta run." John turned and headed to a squad car.

I stomped my foot against the pavement and turned in the direction of my car. We'd been friends for ages. I deserved better than a quick brushoff. We might have been in front of the station, but he could've given me a better answer or suggested a different time when he could talk.

What now? John had an eight-hour shift. I hated waiting. Even if I found him afterward, I wasn't sure he'd tell me anything. Then there was my shift. I'd have to wait until tomorrow to talk to him. What could I do in the meantime?

I walked in silence, head down. I started to cross the street and jumped at the horn. I'd almost walked in front of a moving car. Near the station, drivers slowed down; otherwise, I could have been toast laying on the asphalt.

I focused and paid more attention to what I was doing. Going home and catching a quick nap as I'd planned was no longer an option. With all this going on, I probably wouldn't sleep. And it was a couple of hours before I headed back to work dispatch. Until then, I'd be pacing and antsy. I wanted some answers before I went back. But what?

A drive. It always calmed me down. I headed to my car.

As I walked, I reconsidered what I knew—not much. A guy I had picked up at the airport was dead. And the pilot had said he was a substitute. He left his car at the hotel because he lived in Savannah. I'd never picked him up before, but that didn't mean much. Maybe he'd lived here a while, and I didn't know him. Or he usually parked at the airport. Savannah, after all, while a small city in many ways, was a big city in others. And why hadn't he parked in the airport lot? I suspected he either couldn't or it was cheaper, meaning free, to park at Pondside Inn and piggyback on the cab rides of the other crew members staying there.

Brandon had displayed the attitude of a player, so he might be known in certain social circles. I'd do more research later—at the office if it were quiet. Or at home, if not.

I'd been dating Bill the last six months, so unfortunately I was out of any single circles for the most part. But Angie might know, and I could set up a hair appointment.

9

Angie and I had bonded in kindergarten. She was blond and lithe, almost waiflike, and a full four inches taller than me. It wasn't apparent to most people we would be friends. She had grace where I was clumsy, and she was good with her hands and people savvy. Me, not so much, although I was getting better with every cab fare.

She'd picked up lots of jokes and funny material from her older brother that she shared with me. We'd laughed for hours. Then we'd tell them to John. We'd been friends after that, but once we helped him with vocabulary tests in first grade, we'd become an inseparable trio.

I started the car and drove through the historic district to East Congress Lane near Johnson Square. Driving in the historic district meant dodging the local buses ferrying tourists between the fifteen stops. It was better than more cars being on the road, but the frequent stops with off-loading and people getting on backed up traffic. So I took as many streets that weren't on the route as possible. The streets ended at squares and you had to go around them to get back on track. Knowing the district was crucial for a driver, so sometimes I'd simply drive around to find easier or faster routes.

Evenings were even worse, as the ghost and gravestones trolleys and walking tours with large groups crossing the streets made navigating a nightmare of a different kind. Still, tourists were my lifeblood.

Angie would be at her hair salon, Shear Designs. Hers was the trendiest salon in Savannah, an experience in itself, with a glass of champagne or wine while you had your hair styled. It was located in a historic building she had renovated, with a cream finish, baby blue shutters, and a bright grass-green front door with an oval etched-glass insert.

She also had a room for luxury pedicures or manicures in a separate spa area. It helped that Angie's brother, Stuart, was a famous director—lending a certain cachet to her salon. She'd left her previous well-paying hair salon job to work on one of his films.

Then she came back and started her salon. Too much stress and sitting around, she'd said. I think she missed being in the midst of things in Savannah. Here she was a minor celebrity, a sought-after stylist who could keep a secret—well, mostly. Plus, Savannah was in her blood just as much as mine. That was hard to escape.

She was a much bigger fish in our smaller pond of a world. On a film, she was just one of the crew. She didn't share much gossip from her clients, but she might know who Brandon was or at least his reputation. And if she didn't know, she'd know who to ask.

Dodging a black ghost tour trolley, I found a parking space on Drayton Street, around the corner from her salon. Saturday was her busiest day, but I hoped to catch her in between clients for a quick chat.

"Hi," I said to her petite receptionist with purple-streaked hair. "Is Angie around or with a client?"

"She's in the back."

I walked back to the hair products room, which doubled as a break room. Angie was seated at a bistro-style café table with a steaming cup of herbal tea. Like the rest of the salon, the walls were tan with white accent molding. Instead of the plasma TV on the wall playing loops of fashion and hair shows all day long, accompanied by jazz music, here the walls held Paris street scenes, with faint strains of popular dance tunes seeping inside. Three new life-sized headshots leaning against the wall held Angie's attention.

"Hey, girlfriend," she said. "Your tips are fading. I can't fit you in today, but sometime next week would work. We could have lunch and catch up."

"Yes, to all, but also wondering if you've got a minute."

"Barely. I have a weave and a single-process color back to back in about five minutes."

"What are the new pictures for?" Now that I was here, and although we were friends, I wasn't sure how to approach this.

"I styled hair for the upcoming Jeremy Adames competition. The photographer dropped off the pictures. What's up?"

"They're great. Did you do the styling on them all? Have you already entered?"

"Yeah. I'm hoping to make it to the semifinals this year or better. And you're stalling."

"Yeah, I know. I didn't want you to get the wrong idea. I'm looking for information on a guy and thought you might have heard of him."

"A guy? You and Bill having problems? Or are you just looking around?"

My face heated, despite my best efforts and the fact I had nothing to be embarrassed about. Angie laughed, which didn't help.

"It's not what you think. Bill and I are just fine, thank you very much. I need some info."

"Sure. Sure. Got a name?"

"Brandon or Brandon Jennings."

"Nope, never heard of him. But then again, most of my clients normally use first names or a nickname when they're in the chair. I wouldn't know if it were him unless he has a weird tattoo I've seen or a strange detail the ladies might have mentioned."

"He's nice-looking, slender, and not too tall. Blond and I think he could be a real charmer when he wanted to. I found him obnoxious, but I can see where certain women might like his kind of come-on."

"Well, that doesn't narrow it down much. Sorry I can't help you without more."

"Okay. Thanks. Guess my wannabe rock star will remain a mystery."

"Rock star...wait a minute. You know, there were two of my clients, Judy and Cindi, talking about a guy they called the Stone. What do you think?"

"Dunno. What did they say?"

"Just bits and pieces. I didn't pay much attention, since I didn't know who it was. But...hmmm. Have to check the schedule, but I think Cindi might be in next week for a cut."

"Can you check? Could you ask her a few questions?"

"You know that's not how it works. I listen while I work."

"But if she knows him, you could ask a leading question to get her started. And I could come in to have my pink tips updated at the same time. Then I could listen in as well."

Angie frowned. "Who is this guy, really? And what's he done?"

"Well...I picked him up in a cab Friday night."

"Yeah, and..."

"And he was rude and obnoxious, so when the pilot said to put him out on Dean Forest Road, I did."

"I bet there's a lot more to this since you're here."

Angie's assistant poked her head in the room. "Your three o'clock is here."

"I'm on my way. Now, spill it quick. What's the whole truth? Or I won't do a thing."

"The guy was killed, and now the police are questioning me."

"What??? That doesn't make any sense with what you just told me. Why didn't you tell me all this first? Darn. I have a client. You stay right here. I want the whole story."

"I can't. I am on dispatch later, and then Bill is coming over. Plus, I need a nap. John got me up early this morning knocking on my door about what happened last night. Then Sylvie called, and I had to go in to talk to her before our weekly meeting. But let's talk tomorrow. How about a late breakfast? You can check your schedule, and we can make a plan. And it's not as bad as it sounds. I'm not a suspect or anything, at least I don't think so. I'm a material witness. John says so. And I want to hear about the competition."

"Oh, great. John is involved. This can't be good," she said. "I have to take care of my client. But you owe me the whole story tomorrow. I'll tell you about the competition then too. And I'll see when Cindi is coming in. Got it?"

I nodded. I got it. Loud and clear. If I knew Angie, she'd dig all the details out of me and have insights on how I might find out more on Brandon.

10

After a quick goodbye, I left and walked back to my car. What to do now? John wouldn't be off duty for hours, but I knew there was some truth to cops and coffee. Except for John, who along the way had found a taste for herbal tea. Go figure. Normally the cab drivers and cops frequented many of the same spots.

It was past lunchtime, but I knew John would stop for his break when he didn't have any calls. He preferred his herbal tea with a healthy wrap to fuel the rest of his shift. They'd swing by the Krispy Kreamery for his partner's coffee, but they were never there long enough for a conversation. Right about now, he could be at The Tea Shoppe on West Harris Street, unless he had a call. The shop was known for tasty food. It was a bit out of the way, but I would only stew if I went home, so I decided to swing by.

I spotted the squad car a block away. John wouldn't be by himself, but I thought I could get him alone. At least then I'd have a chance of learning why I'd been called in for the second round of questions.

After parking, I walked to the front door, peering through the glass to make sure he was there. The Tea Shoppe was like many of Savannah's restaurants. Small and intimate, with tables for two and four. This one had a country retro feel, with metal tables and chairs and pastoral pictures on the wall. Flowers in tiny vases held court in the center of each table.

Ordering was at one end of the counter, where a blackboard menu hung and a cold storage unit containing all the fixings for wraps and salads ran along the length. The other end of the worktop had a single organic coffee machine and the hot water for the extensive choice of teas.

Sunlight streamed in, and any shadows were sent packing with Tiffany pendant stained-glass lighting. Sure enough, against the side-wall, John was having what was likely mango tea with a veggie wrap —no mayo or other dressing. Predictable. He liked eating healthy. His partner sat across the table, finishing the last bite of a sandwich, his foot tapping. I guessed he was headed for coffee or wanted to get back on the road.

Before opening the door, I took a deep breath. As I pushed it open, bells tinkled. John lifted his gaze to the door as he was taking a bite. The owner of The Tea Shoppe loved the idea of having an old-fashioned store where you heard each customer enter. He'd installed the bells that jingled all day long. The employees ignored the sound. But every single customer turned to stare at each newcomer. Walking in was a strange experience, one in which you were put in the spotlight for a brief moment for a nutritious snack or meal.

John's eyes rolled even as he sank his teeth into the wheat wrap. Contentment mixed with irritation. He wasn't pleased to see me.

I crossed to his table. John looked at his partner, a lean but muscular guy with a crew cut, the same guy who'd been at my house. "Give us a minute."

The other cop pushed back his chair and rose, all six feet of him. "See you in the car in five." He didn't smile or give any indication he'd taken any notice of me, although I knew he had, just like any cop would. Stranger even as he'd had coffee at my house and been friendly enough then.

As the cop walked away, I pulled out the metal chair matching the retro chrome table and sat down.

John said, "You now have four and a half minutes. What are you doing here? Do you want to get me in trouble?"

The shock must have shown on my face. The bells jingled and I looked up, but no one walked through the door. Must have been a final ring as John's partner left. I turned in time to see John's frown soften a bit.

"Look, I can't be seen talking to you. And I can't discuss an open case with you."

"I know," I said before he could tell me to leave. "I don't want to know anything confidential. Why was I called in a second time? I told you everything I know. Can you at least tell me that?"

John stared at me, and, for a moment, I thought he was going to get up and leave without answering. We both looked up as the bells on the door jingled again. Weird. The door hadn't closed or opened.

John drew my attention back. "Like I already said, you didn't tell us everything in the first interview. We have to check into all inconsistencies or any missing information. Then there's the prior complaint. You were the last one to see him alive. That makes you a material witness, at the very least. There's no more."

"Why does everyone keep saying that? The pilot and copilot were in the cab too when I dropped off Brandon. You know the complaint was a tactic used by the lawyer in my divorce. Plus, I wasn't the last one to see Brandon. Whoever killed him was." My heart started to pound again.

"Exactly. And until we know who that is, you're the last one we know of. I can't talk to you about this. Let us do our job."

I frowned, pursing my lips. I deserved to be treated better than this by him. "Have you talked to Geoff?"

"Who?" John asked.

"Don't play dumb—the other cab driver who picked up the rest of the flight crew. He would have taken the same route I took to the same hotel. I know it was Geoff. I checked the log."

"We talk to a lot of people," John said.

"What's the big secret? You talked to Sylvie too. She told me."

"Stay out of this. It's a murder investigation, remember, and dangerous. It's police business. That's what we do."

My mouth dropped open.

"Look, we've been friends for a long time. I'd tell you if I could. It's early in the investigation. We're talking to people. I mean it. Let us handle this."

His jaw was locked. He wasn't gonna tell me anything further, and I couldn't figure out a good response. I wanted to strangle him, but then there'd be a second body. That wouldn't be good. I calmed down, and started working through all this. John gulped his tea, grabbed what remained of his lunch, and stood, leaving me at the empty table. The bells rang out again as John opened the door.

Stunned, I sat there, breathing deeply to slow my beating heart. After a few minutes, I left and walked back to the car. What on earth was I going to do until tomorrow? Now that I was on dispatch, I'd be home earlier. I wanted to bring Bill up to date and make sure he was going to be there.

I rooted around in my denim purse for my cell phone. I texted Bill. **On dispatch tonight. We still on? Will explain later.**

I yawned. Driving always cleared my head, so I thought I'd take the long way back. I turned the car and crossed over to Abercorn Street.

A block later, a driver cut in front of me. I slammed on the brakes, knowing no one was behind me. What the...? I wanted to scream at the driver. Out-of-state license plates. A tourist without any idea where they were going. Usually I watched for them. I took a couple of breaths to calm down.

The light at the intersection turned red, and I stopped. My phone dinged. I reached over and grabbed it while I waited.

Bill had texted me. **Hey, hon. See you at 11:30 or so.**

I smiled. I hated to lose a day's fares, but spending more time with Bill was worth it.

11

I pulled into the driveway. The pots on the front porch looked wrong, again. I could have sworn I'd switched the pots of marigolds with the Bachelor Buttons pot yesterday so the marigolds could take in the sun. But they were now where Aunt Harriett always had them. With all the activity, I must have forgotten to do that. I'd take care of Possum and then come out and move them.

Inside, Possum meowed. I refilled her water bowl and watched her slurp. She was quite a pill. I smiled as I thought back to the pet store. The whole reason I'd gotten her was her personality. I hadn't been disappointed. She sure kept me entertained. Bill, on the other hand, was more of a dog person. He had a Dalmatian, Eripio. When I'd looked quizzical as he said the name, Bill had explained that Eripio was Latin for rescue. I had to admit I hadn't been quite that clever with Possum's name. But a Dalmatian was so appropriate for a firefighter, or rather an emergency medical technician now. Some would say it was stereotypical, but Bill didn't care. I wasn't sure which of the two loved their runs together more.

What would happen if we ever moved in together? Having met Eripio, I already knew he was smarter than the mixed breed next door. The mutt fell for Possum's quivering paw act before falling to the ground in a dead faint act every time. She was always a bit removed, outside the wire fence. Possum bored quickly of the barking and banging against the fence. At that point, she regally rose and wandered off. But no matter how many times she did it, the dog never remembered anything from the time before. Maybe the dog was an eternal optimist that this time the cat might actually be within his reach. I thought Eripio would catch on after the first instance and might keep Possum on her toes. Hmm, it might be fun to watch—a bit like Bill and me. I kept hoping I could catch Possum on film and send it to *America's Funniest Pets* or *Home Videos*. But she was too quick and unpredictable in her torment. It sure would be fun to win based on her performance. Maybe I'd win enough for a beach vacation.

I poured myself a glass of sweet tea from the pitcher I kept in the fridge and plopped down on the couch. I set the alarm on my cell phone in case I dozed off. I told myself I'd rest my eyes before I headed back outside.

"Trisha?"

I recognized the voice, but it was hazy.

"Trisha, girl. Open your eyes. It's important."

I managed to squeeze one eyelid up. Aunt Harriett. But that couldn't be right. She was dead. It mostly looked like her. Same short curly white hair. Petite in a short-sleeved cotton candy pink dress with white pearls and matching clip-on earrings. Fuzzy, like I wasn't seeing right or she was transparent. A gray mist hovered all around her and stretched out behind her—sort of like being in a dream sequence in a movie.

"I know you think I'm dead, dear, and well, I am, but I'm also really here. You need to pay more attention. Who do you think has been moving the marigold pots on the front porch? And tinkling bells at the tea shop? Really? I can't believe you didn't notice. Do you know how hard it is for the dead to move objects? Now get your head together before I have to knock some sense into you." Aunt Harriett's soft laughter brought me out of my slump and upright.

I wasn't sure what a dead person could do, so I tried to focus. I hadn't been imagining those things. Aunt Harriett had been trying to get my attention?

"Much better, dear. I haven't much time. Eddie's due to take me out, so I'll make it quick."

What? Stepping out as a ghost? Things hadn't changed much. I hesitated to think about where they might go. Old comments about a club being dead on a particular night suddenly had new meaning. I smiled. Angie would love that one.

"Listen. I know this is a lot for you to handle, but you must be careful," Aunt Harriett said. "There's a dark spirit searching for you. I don't like the rumblings I'm hearing."

Okay, now she had my interest. "What are you talking about?"

"Something's happened, and there's an angry presence approaching you. Take a look at anything you might have done that would cause this. You must resolve it, or you'll have that black cloud affecting everything you do."

Her head turned to look out into the cloudy gray mist. "Oops. Must go. Eddie's here, and he doesn't believe we should commune with the living. He's so straightlaced. Not at all as progressive as I am. I so hate to offend. I'll be back. I'll see what I can learn, but I wanted to warn you. And I may need your help with another task. Remember to rely on Bill. He's a good man. And, dear, the marigolds are fine where they are. No need to move them. They get plenty of sun where they are. Toodles, T."

I felt like someone had reached in and squeezed my insides. No one else ever called me T. And toodles? I hadn't heard that in years.

"Wait..."

She was already gone. What on earth did all this mean? And what was happening to me? Maybe I hadn't forgotten to move the marigolds. Could Aunt Harriett have pushed them back? And she wanted my help? How did you help a ghost?

Great. I could have used a hug from my aunt right now. The kind where Chantilly clung to me all day. I was so tired. Maybe this was all a dream. I had anxiety dreams sometimes that felt like they were real. Mostly those involved my being at a party with my PJs on while everyone else was dressed up.

Focus. But the air around me swam in darkness, and then everything faded into nothingness.

12

It seemed like only a minute later when I awoke to the sounds of my cell phone alarm. A big fur ball had balanced on my chest and now stretched, her paws flexing as she dug her claws into me. Her odd eyes—one blue, one green—stared at me.

"Okay. Stop. I know you want your dinner." I struggled with what I remembered.

I wasn't sure if Aunt Harriett was a ghost appearing to me in dreams or if my subconscious used her to get messages across. Or maybe my cat was a medium that channeled Aunt Harriett. The last would be exciting but a bit too woo-woo even for my family.

Visions of a club for the dead and the thought of my...what? Departed, she certainly hadn't. Lifeless? It would seem not. Deceased? That was it—my deceased eighty-year-old aunt being the progressive one. Both sent shivers down my spine. And who the heck was Eddie?

The dark presence worried me. Even as a kid, Aunt Harriett had been in my dreams, but this was somewhat different. In one dream, when she was once alive, she had warned about a darkness around Bill. She'd also said there was a brightness hidden in a haze. I hadn't taken it too seriously, especially as there was light near him too. Plus, it was a dream, right?

A week later, Bill and I had been outside, drinking wine coolers and watching a gorgeous sunset. He'd been the first to smell smoke. Walking out front, we'd surveyed the street. Two doors down, Bill had spotted smoke coming from an upstairs window. As I dashed inside to call the fire department, Bill had run to alert the family.

Later I would find out that, getting no response, Bill had broken a window and climbed inside. The mom was at work. The dad was trying to help the kids get out, but the youngest son was missing. Bill took the stairs two at a time. By the time he'd reached the boy's room, Bill was crouched low and covering his mouth and nose with his shirt against the smoke. He'd gotten the boy out, but both had spent the night in the hospital for smoke inhalation.

The brightness had been the fire, and I'd wrongly thought it would protect him. Instead, it was his training that saved them both. Now I wondered if Aunt Harriett was real and not a dream. But a ghost talking to me? That didn't seem real, even with my family's history. A darkness around me was disturbing, and I couldn't help but think that it was related to Brandon. I shivered.

I was going to have to come to terms with the fact Aunt Harriett might be around. And if the dream was her first warning, then this appearance was the second one. I wondered if it might not be better not to know.

"Meow." Possum's answer interrupted my thoughts. She relaxed her paws and jumped down.

I tried to shake off the dread. I crossed to the kitchen and dumped more tuna and cheese into her bowl, as well as crunchies.

I decided I'd prep for our dinner of steak and baked potatoes later tonight, one of Bill's favorites. After washing the potatoes, I put them back in a basket I kept in the pantry. I found a can of peanuts and munched on them while I thought about what else we could eat. I checked my reserve of oat bread, freshly made by my bread machine two days ago. It would work just fine. Weren't modern conveniences wonderful? You dumped in the ingredients and let a machine do its magic. My grandmother had taught me to bake bread, but that was a whole lot more effort. Slathered with butter, it would be perfect with the steak.

I made a small salad of lettuce greens and fresh juicy tomatoes while my mind focused on what I could only accept as a dream and what it might mean. Was the dark spirit Brandon? Or was this my subconscious working overtime with everything that had happened. I had no idea.

But I was reassured Aunt Harriett liked Bill. I had thought maybe my male companion compass was permanently damaged. That's M.C. compass, as Angie and I called it. I thought he was a good guy but doubted myself, based on my history. Maybe this time I'd found that special guy I could depend on and be there for. But what about the marigolds?

My cell phone pinged. I clicked on the text from Bill.

Have to cancel tonight. Sorry, hon. Got called in to work. Can we change to tomorrow?

I didn't have a choice. Bill was never late or canceled unless it was important or unavoidable. I knew that much about him. He must have been covering for one of the other guys.

Sure, I texted back.

He didn't usually call me when he was working since they were on call. I'd have to wait until he showed up on Sunday to find out what happened.

Breakfast with Angie, I texted. **Home after.**

Great. Sorry. Was looking forward to it. See you around noon, Bill texted.

I sent him a smiley face, and he pinged one back to me.

The potatoes and steaks would hold until tomorrow, or we'd eat out. The question was what to do tonight once I was off work. It had been a long day, and all I wanted was to curl up on the couch, find a movie on cable, and relax. Or I could go over my list of questions about the business.

I wanted to talk to Bill about it when we got together. I wandered over to my kitchen drawer with pads, pens, and assorted utensils and implements that had no other natural home. Digging through, I created a list of what I knew about the murder victim. And what questions I had about running a cab company. I laid them on the table.

My laptop was old but had an internet connection. I figured I might as well use it, and I had a few more minutes before I got ready for work.

I had finished powering up the computer when my phone rang. Dispatch.

"Trisha?"

"I'm here."

"I know you're on dispatch tonight, but Miss Merlot called and asked for you specifically. Sylvie said you could take the fare if you were okay doing that on your way in," the dispatcher said.

"Okay. No problem. What's the address?"

Dispatch read it off, and I wrote it down. "I'll be there as soon as I can."

I'd have to put off the research until later. Who knew what I might turn up that would be helpful? I'd only scratched the surface with my earlier check of Facebook at the office. Breakfast with Angie in the morning might leave me time to do a bit of investigating before Bill arrived, if I found any interesting tidbits about Mr. Brandon Jennings.

For now, I gathered my things and hit the road.

I wasn't sure why exactly Miss Merlot always asked for me, but I loved our fares. She was a hoot. She was a local celebrity headliner at the Corner Club. She wasn't as legendary or as flamboyant as Lady Chablis, made famous by John Berendt's book, *Midnight in the Garden of Good and Evil*, but she was a marvel.

The fare required the driver to go to the door of wherever she was, instead of merely waiting for her to come out, and knock. I'd picked her up several times from the club and other places and knew she'd be ready to roll. Today Miss Merlot was decked out in a fiery, red sequin, full-length gown with a plunging neckline. Her six-inch high heels matched perfectly. Flawless makeup and her dark brownish-black hair curled down her back—all defying the moisture and heat of Savannah.

"The club, please," Miss Merlot said as I opened the back door for her.

Once she was inside, I closed it and headed around the SUV. I turned the ignition.

"You're Harriett Reede's niece, aren't you?"

I swung my head around. "How do you know that?"

"Oh, I know lots of things. You should come by for a reading real soon. Cards, crystal ball. I do them all."

I'd heard that in addition to her female impersonations, Miss Merlot held séances and claimed she could speak to the dead.

"Okay."

"Lots coming your way that you need to be ready for, girl. Just saying."

My family had its quirks, but I'd never gone in for those kinds of things. We drove in silence until we arrived at the club. I got out again and helped her step down from the SUV.

Miss Merlot put her hand on my arm. "Your aunt passed recently. She hasn't crossed over. You watch out for signs she's here, you hear me?" She put money in my hand as she closed her hand over mine and shut her eyes. "Oh." She opened her eyes wide. "You've already seen her. She'll be checking in on you, now and then. You pay attention to what she says."

Miss Merlot smiled and sashayed across the sidewalk in front of the club. She turned and winked at me before she opened the door and went inside.

I closed my mouth, which had dropped open sometime during the exchange.

13

The mouthwatering smell of freshly cooked bacon laced with brewing coffee welcomed me as I walked through the front door of the local diner Sunday morning. There were several in Savannah, with differing motifs. The one where Angie and I always had breakfast was more traditional—booths with miniature jukeboxes, metal tables with matching metal chairs sporting red plastic-padded covers, and a long bar for patrons who stopped in for a quick meal or coffee.

Sunday mornings were always crowded, and whichever of us arrived first always secured our place. Angie was seated in a booth in the center row against the front windows when I arrived. As usual, she looked like she'd just stepped off the pages of a fashion magazine. In contrast, I'd chosen the fluff-and-go mode with blue jeans and a cap to cover my hair. At this early hour, I was lucky to be up and moving. I'd shower after I had a snack.

An Elvis tune was playing. Angie had used up whatever quarters she had picking all Elvis songs. She loved oldies, and the Beatles ran a close second on tunes she'd play. I liked oldies and Elvis too, but I wasn't the die-hard fan she was. I think the one thing she regretted was never seeing him in concert.

We each ordered eggs, bacon, hash browns, toast, and coffee. A twentysomething short-haired blonde, who could carry more food on one hand than I thought ever possible, served us. While she always asked for our order, she'd waited on us so many times she was writing before we even started our orders. Angie and I sometimes wondered how she'd react if we changed our choices, but we figured she'd take it in stride. Besides, we both loved having breakfast out.

"How's work?" Angie asked.

"Ugh. I worked dispatch last night. Long hours at the desk and we were so busy I didn't have time to do much research on the internet. Mark had an interesting call. Miss Merlot, no less. You know, the new Miss Chablis. Or maybe a wannabe. She had started using our services, so she doesn't have to drive to her performances in full makeup and gowns."

"Is she any good?"

"I don't know. I haven't seen the show. I might ask Bill to go to one." I brought Angie up to date on the murder.

She didn't have much to add and switched the subject, or so I thought. "You know, Cindi, Judy, and others are running in the Paint Coastal Georgia Pink Breast Cancer 5K Run next Saturday. Are you doing that?"

I hadn't planned to, but I mulled over the possibilities. It could be the perfect opportunity. "No, but I could. Is it too late to register?" I finished my hash browns and drank the last of my coffee.

"No, but you have to get sponsors. You know, they pay based on how many miles you walk or run." Angie held up her coffee to our waitress as she headed our way with a fresh pot of coffee.

"I might not meet the requirements, but I could try." I mentally ran through a list of who I might tap to sponsor me.

"Go online. You can check out the minimum amount and sign up if you're interested. I think it would be a great time to talk. If the ladies know this guy, it might come out in the conversation. We've all done this run in the past, and the conversation moves around a lot. Plus, we are all at different levels as to whether we wanted to walk or talk. I thought that might be a better way to talk to the girls than sitting next to one of them getting your hair done."

Angie took a sip of the newly poured coffee. "If you do this, you'll want to make sure you ask any questions early. A number of the girls will break off and run. Then we usually meet up at the finish and have drinks or lunch."

"Sounds like fun. You sure they won't mind me tagging along?"

"Nope. There's always a lot of different people. Not sure how much info you can get, but it might be worth a try." Angie crunched on the last bit of her toast.

Our waitress stopped by to check on us before she moved on to the next table. Our conversation moved on to men, and the upcoming competition Angie was going to enter, before we paid our check. She promised to confirm the date with me so I could come and watch her "do hair."

"Let me know what else happens and what kept Bill away last night. He seems like a great guy from what I can tell. Let's plan a night where we can have dinner again. I'll cook. And don't forget to register. We can talk later in the week about when and where we'll all meet for the run. And dinner." Angie turned and headed to her car on the south side of the building.

My car was parked on the other side. I needed to do some thinking about what to ask the other women next weekend. And find time to do a bit more research. I wondered if any of Angie's clients would know anything that could lead me to the killer.

14

It was early afternoon when I heard the knock. Right before the screen door creaked open, and as I poured myself my second glass of tea.

Bill walked in with a "Hi, hon. How're things?" He punctuated it with a peck on my cheek. He dropped the early version of the Sunday paper on the counter.

Heading for the refrigerator, he reached in for the pitcher of sweet tea. A black curly lock fell across his tanned forehead as he leaned down. Man, he looked good in jeans and the forest green work shirt. The regular gym routine kept him in great shape.

"Great. Work busy?" I asked.

"Yeah. I've already had two cups of coffee."

"Thanks for the text. I was looking forward to our date. Why'd you get called in?"

"One of the guys had a family emergency." He grabbed a tall glass and poured the drink. "I missed you too."

"Everything okay?'

"Yeah. He had to take one of the kids to the hospital. His wife was pretty scared. His oldest broke his arm. Lenny relieved me early this morning so he wouldn't lose all of his shift."

"You hungry?"

"What's on the menu?" he asked with a Cheshire cat grin.

"Funny. You know what I meant. I was thinking about Diamond Palace for lunch. What do you think?"

"That works. I could use a burger and fries about now, or maybe a steak or pork chops. And I wouldn't turn down a beer, either."

"Okay. Sounds like you're hungry." I laughed. "I need to finish doing my hair and change."

Half an hour later, I returned in a leather skirt and sparkly T-shirt to find Bill on the couch with the paper in various stacks.

"Anything interesting?"

"Not much. Just the normal news and the murder of the guy from your cab. Watch yourself when you're driving. You never know who is getting in your cab. You look like you're ready to roll. Or you want to hang out for a while?"

"Where's the article on the murder?" I should have known it would be reported.

Bill handed me the paper, and I skimmed the column. A few details I didn't already know, but not much else.

I looked up.

Bill was watching me. "What's all the interest?"

"He was in my cab. Can we talk about this after we eat? I had breakfast with Angie, but I know you're probably hungry. And a burger sounds good. Let me put my shoes on, and I'll be ready." It was time to gather my thoughts.

We headed out down Jackson Street, crossed at West Jones Street, and fifteen minutes later, we stood in line to be seated. My mouth watered from the aromas of the steaks and fries, but I was already regretting the leather skirt. Two o'clock and the air hung thick with humidity. My clothes would look like I hadn't bothered to dry them if I was outside much longer.

Diamond Palace had initially been a shotgun house. The main hall that gave the place its form was twenty feet long and three feet narrow. It was covered in historic photos of Savannah and old posters for beer, which patrons inspected while waiting to be seated. The place was a living history museum of the beer trade. Outside of the touristy historic district, most visitors didn't find it unless they knew about it from a local. The burgers were to die for, with a whole host of different Georgia beers to choose from.

Once seated, our waitress stopped off at our table. Bill ordered the bone-in center pork loin chop with a mushroom marsala sauce.

"Brown Ale Burger for me. With everything." I laughed. The hamburger was seasoned with Savannah Brown Ale and topped with jalapeño cream sauce. And to die for.

"We'll each have a Brown Ale, right?" Bill said.

I nodded.

"Be back in a jiff." Our server sashayed away. She had a cute figure and a huge toothy smile that got her lots of good tips.

"Hey, Bill."

I looked up. Bill's friend Dan and his girlfriend stood by our table. Bill rose to shake hands with the Dan. His girlfriend tossed her long blond hair as we nodded to each other. I didn't know her well, and we'd never double-dated with the couple. But Bill and Dan had been friends for years.

"We just ordered. Want to join us?" Bill asked.

"Nah. We're meeting my mom here. Another time," Dan said. "You working or playing Tuesday night?"

"I should be off, so plannin' to be there."

Bill played cards with a group of guys. An inexpensive game, he'd reassured me. My first ex-husband had turned out to be a gambler—in his business and outside of it. I wasn't wild about any kind of gambling. The group was mostly firefighters, and my brother sat in on a game every once in a while. Bill said his limit was a hundred dollars per night, and he hadn't lied to me as far as I knew, so I was trying to get comfortable with it. Besides, I had no right to tell him he couldn't at this point. Nevertheless, my antennae was highly tuned for addiction issues.

"Know anyone you want to invite?" Dan asked.

Bill's eyebrows rose.

"We'll need an additional person to replace the guy who was murdered," Dan said.

My ears perked up. "What guy?"

Bill hadn't mentioned anything along those lines.

"I'll let you know." Bill cut him off. "Talk to you then."

I kept my lips pursed, so my mouth didn't hang open.

Dan and his friend left for their table.

"What guy?" I asked.

"It was in the paper. The murder I mentioned and you read about? It was a guy we played cards with. I planned to talk to you about this after we ate. When you wanted to talk about what happened. Just not here and now."

"So..."

"The paper said he was dropped off by your cab company. I had already figured it might have been yours."

"Yeah. What about him?" I wasn't sure I wanted to get into all this here either.

"He's been at our weekly game for the last three weeks."

"What? You knew him?"

"Not really." Bill took a long drink of beer. "Sam invited him. He was a normal guy. Had cash, drank imported beer, and brought us all good cigars."

"Anything else you haven't told me?" My stomach was beginning to burn. This was where it all started. A small detail not told that led to more significant omissions.

"Look, I recognized his name from the newspaper article. Sam knew him. Dan must have talked to Sam. Until then, I didn't know for sure. And you wanted to eat first."

Our server arrived with our food, and I struggled to calm my stomach.

"Well?" I asked as she walked away.

"Look, it's not what you're thinking. I haven't been hiding stuff from you. But you always complain about Geoff."

"Geoff? What does he have to do with this?"

"There was a bit of an argument this past week. Brandon wanted to bet in the last hand but didn't have any cash. Since he came by way of Sam, we let him play with an IOU. Geoff won it. Only it turns out Brandon wasn't sure when he could pay and started trying to renege on the debt. And you know how Geoff is."

I did. I had seen his temper firsthand.

"So, what happened?"

"Geoff tipped over the table. Went after the guy. Just sort of snapped. I'd never seen him like that."

"Wow."

"Yeah."

"And?"

"Geoff got ahold of him. Was about to pound on him when Brandon whimpered he'd get the money to the loan shark. Geoff backed off, and they made arrangements as to the date and time."

"And you didn't think that was important to tell me? I've been questioned twice. They might think I knew about all this and didn't tell them. The dispatcher said Geoff picked up the other members of the flight crew. I checked the log last night when I was on dispatch. He was at the motel. He could have killed Brandon."

My brain was racing. It was probably the first time I'd ever let a Diamond Palace burger get anywhere close to cold. I felt like I'd been punched in the stomach. A whiff of fried onions did nothing to help. The beer burned down my throat as I sucked on it and considered what I'd heard.

"Whoa. You didn't tell me you'd been questioned. And I knew you'd react like this. I wanted to tell you at your house. I was gonna tell you when we got back," Bill said. "Why don't we finish the meal and we can go back to the house. I promise I'll answer any questions you have, although there's nothing else to tell."

I nodded, stunned that Bill knew Brandon. I took a tentative bite. Maybe this was for the best. If Geoff had killed Brandon, then this could soon be over. Could Geoff have driven back and confronted Brandon about the debt? Could he have killed Brandon?

My shoulders relaxed slightly, and my stomach growled. We ate in silence.

After paying the check, Bill and I walked back. I knew he was worried about my reaction. I had a choice to make as to staying mad or listening first. If I was going to listen, the gap we, or mostly I, had created had to be bridged. Plus, I wanted to give this relationship a real chance. I reached over and slipped my hand in his. He squeezed it.

As we stepped inside my house, Possum raced in front of us and around our legs, causing us both to stumble into the other. We caught ourselves and laughed. I was never more glad for her antics.

"Guess she's decided it's time I feed her." After filling her water bowl and putting out food, I poured us each a glass of sweet tea.

I carried them to the couch. Bill set his on the table and lifted his right hand to trace the edge of my face.

"I have a couple of questions."

Bill smiled. "I knew you would."

"How well do you know Geoff?"

He'd joined the Traveler's Taxi a couple of years ago. He'd been three years ahead of me in high school.

"He's an okay guy. Keeps to himself mostly."

"Don't you know anything else? Does he have a family, kids?" I asked.

"He's married. I don't know much else. We lost track after high school."

"That's it? You play cards every week."

I was rewarded with one of Bill's special looks. This one read, "you can't seriously be asking me this, can you?"

I persisted. Surely, he must know something that would be helpful. "How did he get involved in the games?'

"Long story but his cousin loans people money. Geoff came one night to collect from a guy who no longer plays. I didn't pay much attention to him. He was just a guy who does that kind of thing on the side for extra bucks. He stayed to play."

"He's a goon?"

Bill looked at me with shock written in his eyes. "Why would you use that word?"

"I'm not as naïve as I look." I laughed.

"Really? I can see the wheels turning in that cute head of yours. Geoff may have been doing his cousin a one-time favor. Leave this to the police. It's their job. You don't want to be messing with loan sharks and their enforcers if they're involved, which I don't know and neither do you." He paused. "Seriously, you need to listen to me on this."

"I am. I will."

How did I not know this? And if I didn't know, did Sylvie? What role did he really play at Traveler's Taxi? I was having a hard time comprehending all this and making sense of it. Brandon might have owed a lot of people money, including Geoff or maybe his cousin too. Was this a collection gone wrong? I didn't know much about loan sharks. I wasn't sure I knew anyone that did. Plus, how would I find out if there was a debt?

John might know or at least know about the loan sharks. I'd talk to him tomorrow.

"Do you think you should talk to the police? Or I could at least mention it to them if they talk to me again."

Bill considered my words. "Maybe. If you want to tell them, that's fine. But I'm not going to go in unless they're interested."

I nodded. I'd have time to mull over all this in the cab while I waited on fares tonight. For now, I concentrated on Bill.

We continued talking about our week. I realized I hadn't told him about my conversation with Sylvie.

"Sylvie talked to me about taking over the company. Maybe buying it. I'd like to get your ideas on the business and what I should be asking her about."

I saw a brief look of shock on his face before he covered it. "Who's been keeping secrets now?"

My cheeks heated up. "It just happened. She talked to me before our weekly meeting. I was going to tell you last night, but then you got called in. I haven't had a chance to tell you yet. And I didn't want anyone to hear about it at the Diamond Palace."

"Uh-huh. That sounds familiar."

I stared at him for a minute and then giggled. We laughed, and Bill kissed me lightly on the lips.

"My bad this time."

"Okay. Tell me what she said."

15

I related the conversation with Sylvie, and all that had happened after Brandon was killed. The knots in my stomach started to unwind. My intuition said to trust him, but I'd been wrong before—two times, resulting in two divorces—so I didn't trust myself when it came to men. But maybe Aunt Harriett and my sixth sense were right this time. It felt good to be talking about a possible future with him.

We moved into the kitchen so we could refill our big glasses of cold sweet tea. I found my notebook with questions and Possum decided to join the party. She insisted on trying to sit on my notepad. I ushered her off the table so I could write while we talked. She settled onto the floor beside me, where she stretched out

We had more things to talk through, but I decided to tackle the business questions.

"Okay. So, I don't know what to ask or even where to begin. Any ideas?"

"What have you asked so far?"

"Nothing much. I was so surprised. My brain froze. I'd thought Sylvie was calling me in to fire me or put me on probation for putting Brandon out of the cab."

"So, back to the business. There are a couple of things. You need to know what terms she's offering—price, how it will be paid, is she financing it, will she stay around to help you. All that kind of stuff. Then you need access to the books and need an accountant-type person to look at them with you if you don't know how to review that."

"Whoa. Slow down. I need to make a list. I don't know any of this."

Bill paused while I frantically tried to write down all he'd said.

In the end, I had him repeat it before we moved on. "How do you know all this?"

"I was a business major. I never wanted to sit behind a desk all day. Which brings us to something pretty basic. Being the owner means you have to supervise everyone. Hire and fire people too. But you will also have to be in the office a lot more. I know you like to be on the streets and have your freedom. Are you going to be happy doing all that?"

Good questions. All of them. I didn't have the answers. I raced to add these to my notes. "I'll need to talk to Sylvie about how much time she spends in the office. She used to drive a cab too, but she had Derek to carry the office load. They made a good team."

"You might need help with the office work. But it costs money. Derek and Sylvie likely have a business split, but you won't have that, so you'll have to pay an employee if you use help."

For a split second, I wondered if Bill and I could be like Derek and Sylvie. I dismissed it. Our relationship was too new. Even if it hadn't been, Bill liked being a paramedic, and he'd already said he didn't want to be in an office. He would be willing to help me, but the business would be mine and my responsibility.

"Those are good points. I'd hate being tied to an office every day too. I like driving. And I don't know anyone I could trust to help me early on."

"You could also talk to Angie. She runs her salon on her own. She probably has an accountant to help her with her books. Have you talked to her?"

I hadn't. I'd been so distracted with the murder I'd forgotten to tell her at breakfast. Angie was a great idea. She'd been in business for about seven years. And I knew she'd help me. To add to that, Bill agreed to go to the accountant with me when I was ready.

"I forgot. Angie's gonna kill me for not talking to her about this first." Realizing my choice of words wasn't so great, I backtracked. "Or at least she won't be happy she didn't know what was going on."

Bill laughed. "I don't think Sylvie would've offered this if she didn't think you could do it. And Angie's a good friend. I think you're going to find there are a lot of people who want to help you—if you decide to do it. But first, you have to decide for yourself. That means you need to think about what Sylvie does and talk to her about it."

"You're right. I'll set up a time. And I'll run by Angie's and talk to her too." I paused. "Tell me more about the poker games."

.

16

Early Monday morning, I plopped down on the couch to cool off from my run. Bill had left early Sunday afternoon so I could get ready for work. I wasn't comfortable with the fact he was playing cards with Geoff, my coworker and a part-time enforcer, no less. Bill knew I had problems with Geoff. Why was he part of a group that included Brandon?

I was probably overreacting. They were only playing cards. It did seem to be pretty casual from the way Bill described the games. Was this all a weird coincidence? It changed my whole perspective on things.

Maybe Bill wasn't who I thought he was. Or perhaps it was chance they all played cards. And did the cops know? Would they think I knew and was concealing that from them if they found out Bill played?

It felt good to relax. I'd headed out for an early-morning run through the tree-lined streets of Savannah, down Whitaker, and along the waterfront. I avoided the cobblestones on River Street. It was too easy to lose balance and end up with a turned ankle.

With a brief wave at the freighter ships sailing by, I'd headed back toward home along a route taking me away from the river and up

Abercorn by Colonial Park Cemetery and Lafayette Square, two of my favorite places to sit and think. At night the city was filled with shadows that grew and waved in the moonlight, and murky sounds not attributable to anything human nearby, that some had interrupted to be the dead rising to walk among the living. During the day, the city took on a more earthly feel, almost as if the otherworldliness ceded its hold during the daylight.

My pulse raced. October was such a great time of year—still green, generally less sticky from humidity, and cool enough to run, at least in the morning and late evenings, without becoming dehydrated from the heat. The air had been fresh without the thickness of the moisture it would hold later in the day. It cleared my head. And with each step, the sweat rolling off me felt like the stress and anxiety were sliding away too.

Until I felt something like a vine around my feet. I looked down and sucked in a breath. A bit of blackness had coiled around my right foot. I must have picked it up on the sidewalks in front of the cemetery. I seldom ran on them, knowing there were bones underneath. Which totally gave me the creeps.

And adding to that was my feeling the cemetery was alive at times —this, though, took it to a whole new level of craziness. And if it wasn't coming from the graveyard, could this be what Aunt Harriett warned about? I reached down to pull it off and it disintegrated. My skin prickled, and I brushed it all off. Then I ran home.

At the curb in front of my house, I'd removed my shoes, knocking them together to make sure the black bits were all gone. Then I'd done the same with my socks. And checked my legs—all clear.

Now, back home, cooling off, my heart rate was slowing. I closed my eyes for a minute.

"Trisha, girl."

"No," I mumbled.

"T, it's me. Open your eyes," Aunt Harriett said.

I tried to move away and escape the voice, but there was nowhere to go. I rubbed one eye and opened it, hoping this was a dream, but knowing it wasn't.

"Good. Now, pay attention. The angry presence is getting closer. Have you been watching for it? Seen anything? It's been following me. Probably thinks it can find you through me."

Talk about getting my attention. I stretched and opened the other eye. "Are you in danger?"

Aunt Harriett chuckled. "No, my dear, but thank you for asking. I seem to have lost the poor soul, but it will find me again. I'm much too well-known, if I do say so myself, and I can't hide for long."

I smiled back at her, knowing she'd only been "there" for a short time. And *poor soul* was what she'd always called those less fortunate than her. I wasn't sure if she was just saying that or if it really was a soul, or what else it might be.

"So, how can you talk to me? Why can I see you?"

"Well, dear, you know the women of our family have always had special talents. This may be yours."

I didn't even want to think about it. "What should I do? How do you know it's angry?"

"Oh, those kind leave little bits of a sooty material everywhere they go. They're easy to spot, but the black residue is tough to get rid of once it attaches to you. I'd need to go to a Cleanser, and my schedule is much too busy to fit anything else in. I think I can avoid it, but I'm more worried about you. Seeing it before it gets to you isn't always possible. Have you given any more thought about who this is?" Aunt Harriett asked.

What in heaven's name was a Cleanser? Was it like a cleaner for spirits? And if so, what did that mean? "There's the guy who was killed after I put him out of my cab. But I'm not sure why he would be searching for me. I didn't kill him."

"There must be a reason." Aunt Harriett paused, and the silence grew.

"Not that I can think of. I'm looking for my fare's killer. I have a couple of leads I'm following. But wouldn't it know and look for that person? Do you know if it's a he?"

Aunt Harriett laughed. "There isn't a he or she concept here. Things are a little less clear and much clearer at the same time. I choose to keep my earthly form, sort of. That way, you recognize me. But this spirit may be lost and knows it's searching but confused as to for who, or even who it was in its earthly form. If it's the guy you're thinking of, it may have latched onto the memory of you. It may have done that right before the event that caused his death."

Lucky me. A lost presence in search of his killer that wasn't sure why but wanted to find me. "Do you think it will try to hurt me?"

"I can't tell. That's why I wanted to warn you. Be careful. Finding the killer before it finds you could shift its attention to the other person," Aunt Harriett said. "It's the only thing I know for you to do to be safe."

Great. Now I needed to find Brandon's killer, but I had to time it right or risk a soot-shedding presence haunting me the rest of my life or worse. I shuddered when I thought about all the things that happened to people in horror movies. The last thing I wanted was to be on the run from something I couldn't see.

Aunt Harriett tilted her head as if she were listening—at least that was my best guess at what she was doing. The cloudy white shape was Aunt Harriett and her voice was clear, but there weren't all the details a person had.

"I hear it," she said. "I've got to go head it off if I'm going to stay ahead of it and not lead it to you, if that's what it's after. And I'll do my best to throw it off the scent and keep it from finding you until you're ready. Toodles."

"Wait. There was a swirl of soot near me. Could that have been what you're talking about?"

"It might be. My feeling was it hadn't found you, so it might just be swirling dirt in the wind. Mind you watch for more."

"Got it. I also need to know what a Cleanser is."

She was gone. A chill shivered through me for a brief second, and then it, too, was gone. I closed my eyes, and there was darkness. I struggled. My chest clenched as I felt myself being smothered. Bits of something filled my nose, and I sneezed. I sat up straight, and Possum's claws dug into my shirt as she hung on. Strands of her hair settled on me, and I realized those were what made me sneeze, not soot.

I relaxed and breathed. If the coldness had been Brandon's presence, it was gone now. I wasn't quite sure if I'd know it as its soot left behind, but I decided it had only been Possum's hair this time. And I wondered if the angry sooty presence was real and if it could hurt me. But Aunt Harriett sounded concerned, and that was never good.

Possum meowed, and I yawned. Picking her up, I rose and headed to the kitchen. At least this I knew how to handle. Time for Possum's favorite: Tuna and Cheese.

After Possum settled a face plant into her meal, I dialed Sylvie.

I asked her about Derek.

"He's home and resting, but I can't leave him alone. We have a nurse who comes in each day for several hours so I can take care of the business and whatever else we need."

I'd been so caught up in my issues, I hadn't even considered what all Sylvie was going through. She'd taken care of me when I was lost after my last divorce. The least I could do was help her now. "That's why I was calling, other than to check on you both. Is there anything you need or that I can help with?"

"That's sweet of you to offer, but we're doing okay. But I'll keep it in mind. Have you given any more thought to my offer?"

"Bill and I talked. I'd like to meet with the accountant to look at the books and ask questions. I'd like to bring Bill. His degree was in business administration, and he knows more about this than I do. It would be helpful to have him there."

"Great. I'm pleased you're so interested. I'll be happy to set it up. I have your schedule. Are there days when Bill can't be there?"

"He works a couple days and then is off a couple. We'd need to set it up once I know his schedule, if that works for you. I'll ask him about next week. And for sure, if you need anything, ask. You've done so much for me. I'd like to repay you if I can."

"I appreciate the offer. I'll call you or text you back with times once you get back to me about Bill's availability. Just knowing you're interested in pursuing this takes a load off my mind. I'm glad you have others to bounce ideas off of. I hated the thought of turning this over to a stranger who might make changes in how it was run, or who they employed. I'm much more comfortable you would protect and grow what Derek and I have built."

We talked a few minutes more and then hung up. It wasn't until I'd had a minute to reflect on what Sylvie had said that I realized a sale could mean I and the other drivers might not have a job. There were excellent points on my side—loyalty and steadiness, well, mostly. I was dependable, again mostly, and I worked hard.

On the other hand, I was somewhat involved in a murder investigation and was the least experienced of all the drivers at Traveler's Taxi. I had learned a lot and contributed to the overall success of the company. But would a different owner coming in think I was valuable enough to keep as an employee? Or was the loss of my job a possibility on top of everything else? Was buying this company something I would have to do to keep an income coming in each month? Could I do this, even with Bill helping me?

17

I spent Monday afternoon driving fares back and forth from downtown historic hotels to the airport. I drove past the Krispy Kreamery and The Tea Shoppe a couple of times, dodging the horse and carriage rides, and what the horses left behind. Mostly those were in the middle of the street, but I always kept a lookout for the droppings when I had a fare. Nothing much worse than a tourist grappling with shopping bags and stepping into the street, without looking. A collision ruined the day for everyone.

I didn't see a single squad car—one of those muggy day with breezes helping to cool things off. Almost as if the city were giving me a break by providing a reprieve from the heat.

I wasn't sure if John was on duty, but he wasn't getting coffee or tea at his regular stops. Since the police had talked to me twice, I wanted to ask him if they'd interviewed Geoff. If so, I wondered if they knew he was a part-time goon when he wasn't driving a taxi. Or about Brandon's gambling and the debt.

And what about the flight crew? I wondered if any of them could have killed Brandon. Josh and Ryan had always been polite, but you never knew. And while I was newer at this, I'd never had anyone want to put another passenger out. Maybe that was all planned.

Hours later, I continued to ponder this as I sat in my cab, waiting on the last Golden Wings Airways flight crew. Mark sat in his ride behind me. The flight crew emerged from the building, and we both climbed out of our cabs. There were two brunettes and one blonde flight attendant.

"Mark, why don't you take the pilot and copilot, and I'll take the flight attendants?"

He looked at me with suspicion. He was an even newer employee than me but had been a cabbie for several years. I could almost see the wheels turning in his brain as he tried to figure out what he was missing and why I would offer him the more lucrative fare. Pilots generally tipped better than the attendants.

"Seriously, my SUV will hold them, and you can take the other two in your cab."

The radios in our cars blasted. The dispatcher had a new fare for one of us.

"Mark, if you take those two, it will be quicker, and you can take the other fare as well."

Now his eyebrows shot up like fireworks. I could almost see the colors exploding in his head. For a minute, I thought they might launch right off his forehead. I couldn't very well tell him I wanted to question the flight attendants about Brandon.

"I'm feeling generous tonight. It's no trick."

I could see him consider it. I smiled a genuine smile, and he must have accepted I wasn't messing with him. Mark stepped forward, greeted the pilots, and began loading the suitcases in his trunk.

I greeted the three women flight attendants. They were all regulars, but I usually ferried the pilots so, while I knew their faces, I wasn't sure if I could put the right name with each one. Mark was back in his cab and moving forward before I'd finished loading their luggage.

Back in the cab, I asked, "How are you ladies tonight? Have a good flight?"

"Yes. Thanks. Smooth sailing and on time. And no drama, passenger or otherwise," one of the brunettes said.

"Great. I understand passenger drama, but what other kind is there?"

I couldn't believe I might not have to steer the conversation too much, *if* this was leading back around to Friday night.

"Oh, you know. There's always something stirring," the blonde said.

"You mean, like Brandon?" I took the leap, hoping I hadn't scared them off. I didn't have training in interviewing people, but she'd left the opening, and I was hoping she wanted to talk.

"Yeah. Was that you? What happened in the cab on Friday? The pilot told us, but you know how men are, they leave out all the good details. Brandon took Heather's shifts, and if we'd known, we'd have all ridden with you so we didn't miss all the excitement."

I laughed. So Heather had not returned to work. I told them my side of the story. "Was he always that rude? Or was it a bad flight?"

The women laughed.

"He was always on the make. Did he ask you to drinks after the flight, Taylor?" the brunette asked.

"Only once. I told him I had a boyfriend," Taylor said. "He asked you too, didn't he, Lisha?"

"I think he's asked all of us out, including Heather," Lisha said. "But yes, I told him I had a husband. I don't normally see him on flights, so I figured he'd never know differently. It didn't even faze him. He said my husband wasn't here, and it was, after all, only drinks. I couldn't believe it. I told him no way." Lisha turned to the third girl. "What about you, Kelsey? He ask you out too?"

"Yeah. I told him I had plans. He could be pretty charming, you know? But I heard he was dating a married flight attendant or some-body's wife. Maybe both. Depends on who you talk to. Me, I'm not into drama," Kelsey said.

"Huh?" Lisha said.

"Oh, I didn't mean you, Lisha. Besides, you're not really married," Kelsey said.

"In Savannah?" asked Taylor. "Maybe she had an angry husband,

and that's what happened to him Friday night. What else have you heard?"

"Well, I don't like to gossip," Lisha said.

Un-huh.

"I heard the woman had another boyfriend, or maybe it was a husband, as well," Kelsey added.

"So maybe a *ménage a trios* or a jealous boyfriend or maybe even a jealous girlfriend," Lisha said. "Brandon sure could pick them. Maybe he had more than one at a time."

"Did he date many married women?" I asked.

"I heard he liked the challenge," Kelsey said.

"Yeah, but I think he was partial to blondes. He followed Heather around like a puppy for a while, but I don't know if she ever went out with him, do you?" Lisha asked.

"Don't know. How's she doing anyway?" Kelsey asked. "Have you talked to her since she got sick? It's been over a week. Is she taking a leave of absence?"

I hated how the conversation was turning, but I couldn't see a way to refocus it back to Brandon. Although, if Heather had dated him, she might know helpful information about him. Finding out when she'd be back could be useful.

"Don't think so. She's a bit better. She took her dad's death really hard. She relocated to the DC area to help with his care. And I heard she was having health issues too. I think her dad took care of everything, so now Heather is taking care of her mom, too. I can't imagine how hard this must be for her," Lisha said.

I turned into Pondside, which I thought was one of the loveliest motel settings near the airport. The motel entrance was a half-circle as with most motels, but entering from the street on this side entrance meant you drove the farthest to the front door. It bought me thirty seconds at best.

Darn. Just when this was getting good, I was going to have to let them out. What a difference from Friday. I had time for maybe one more question. I was hoping if I expressed concern, they might volunteer more. "Do you know when Heather is due back?" I stared into the rearview mirror.

Lisha and Kelsey shook their heads.

Taylor added, "No. I don't think she can be off work too much longer, unless her dad left her money. Like all of us, she depends on regular paychecks."

"Makes sense." I'd probably mined this for all I was going to get.

A bit of yellow caught my eye. Near the curve before the parking lot, in the trees. I hadn't had a fare for Pondside since Friday night and hadn't been back. If I wasn't wrong, it was the kind of yellow fluorescent tape the police used for crime scenes. If it hadn't been for the newspaper, I wouldn't know where Brandon had died.

Once the women were dropped off, I'd circle back to see if I could tell where the tape was and then drive by where I dropped Brandon off.

At the front door of the inn, I retrieved their suitcases and pocketed a six-dollar tip. Small and less than I would have gotten if I'd taken the other fare, but I'd gotten a lot more in information. And if Heather was due to return to work, I'd see if I could maneuver my way into having her in my cab this week. She might know something, even if she wasn't in town when Brandon died.

I was a happy camper with any kind of tip. I shifted into drive and headed back around, glad I'd sent Mark off with the other fare so I could explore. The area around the hotel was dark, and I couldn't see much. I stopped by the tape and almost got out. A bit of wind picked up, rustling dead leaves on the ground and dirt. The clouds cleared for a bit of moon. Maybe it was my imagination, but a small funnel-like formation gathered more of what looked like black dirt and began to inch its way toward me. Aunt Harriett's warning came to mind.

The clouds covered the moon again. Was it a sign? I was sure it was nothing, but I couldn't see well. No sense in tempting fate. Daylight was needed.

Rounding the curve, I drove back to the general area where I'd let Brandon off. Not much was visible, with the only light shining from my headlights and the overhead one in the middle of the block. Nothing moved on the street. All of the dark, gray warehouse-looking buildings were locked up tight. Between the buildings were deep shadows of black where anyone could be lounging unseen. I drove down the concrete driveways between a couple of buildings. Either the tape was long gone, or nothing had happened here to tie it to the murder. Or at least the police hadn't found anything to mark off.

Since the hotel was where it happened, the killer could have been any of the guests or employees who thought Brandon was an easy target heading there. And if it was a random attack, I had no chance of solving this; but if not, maybe. What if this had been planned by someone who knew Brandon would be here?

I'd have to come back in the daylight to see more. I was pretty sure the cops had been careful. I figured it couldn't hurt and might be helpful to scout the area where he was attacked. Even with the tape, I might not figure out the exact area. John hadn't mentioned this important fact. I'd add one more item to my growing list of questions. The newspaper reports might even include that detail. I'd only scanned them. I'd double-check using the internet.

My thoughts returned to the conversation with the flight attendants. I had been at least Brandon's fourth choice for drinks, which told me all I needed to know about his character. Some women might respond to his looks, but I had dated a guy like Brandon. We'd broken up due to his cheating and I'd sworn I'd never date a guy who acted the same way again. It didn't matter. I wouldn't have gone anywhere with him.

I hoped the women I'd meet on Saturday might be helpful. Angie and I could steer the conversation better with the right questions at the Paint Coastal Georgia Pink 5K walk. One thing Angie was good at, if there was information to be gotten, she'd find it. And I'd be right there. I could always ask a question or two myself or nudge the conversation in the right direction. If there was knowledge to obtain or if any of the women had something to hide, I was pretty confident we'd unearth it.

Dispatch interrupted my thoughts with a call on River Street.

Late-night fare pickups from local bars could be interesting, and tonight had been no exception. Pulling over to the curb near a popular restaurant with a rooftop bar, the man and woman were leaning against each other, which was normal enough. Once they settled in the back seat and I turned around, I was hit in the face by the liquor smell on their breath. They both smiled at me, even as the woman edged closer to the man.

The man named a bed-and-breakfast inn about ten minutes away. I pulled away as he turned to the woman for a kiss. Or a lot of kisses, as it turned out.

I knew I shouldn't look, but not doing so could be so hard. I turned up the oldies station. Passionate moans and the rustle of clothes as the two moved in the back were hard to ignore, but I'd done my best.

As I pulled up to the B&B, I turned down the music and announced, "Folks, we're at your hotel," warning them they'd need to get out of the cab soon. That usually worked, but sometimes the couple didn't hear me until I said it a second time.

I parked and turned around to tell them the fare, and the woman laughed as she pulled away. "Pay the driver, honey."

From experience, I knew they might need a minute, so I climbed out and went around to open the door. The woman exited. The man grabbed his coat, which had come off, and handed me a couple of bills with a twenty on top. He smiled his thanks before the woman grabbed his hand and pulled him away. I didn't have time to check the payment. Those kinds of fares almost always included a nice tip. Plus, they were already halfway inside the hotel. I wasn't a driver who would chase people down if they shorted me.

Back in the front seat, I counted the money. A ten-dollar tip. I smiled.

18

I was so distracted after my shift I almost didn't notice John was waiting on my porch when I got home.

As I got out of my car, John walked up. "Trisha. Got a minute?"

"Sure. I've been looking for you."

"Well, as nice as it is to talk to you, we do have a few crimes to solve."

I balked at the sarcasm but held my tongue.

"Which is why I came by, unofficial like."

"I'm listening."

"When you picked up the flight crew, how did you know they were there?"

I knew my face screwed up in a weird, questioning way. John already knew this.

"We know their schedule. Two cabs are always at the airport for their flights. We get a call from dispatch if they're delayed so we can either wait or come back."

"And Friday night?"

"The flight was on time."

"So, no one called you? You didn't use your cell phone? And no one in the flight crew called you?"

"No?" I didn't mean for my word to come out as a question, but it did as wheels turned. What was John asking? Then it hit me. I hadn't told the police about finding Brandon's cell phone. "Oh, no. I totally forgot. When I dropped the pilots off, I found a cell phone on the floor of the SUV. I asked them if it was either of theirs, but it wasn't. I thought it was Brandon's, so I took it and left it with the desk clerk. That's what you're asking, isn't it?"

John nodded. "We're investigating all kinds of things. And preparing reports. Didn't Detective Stanley tell you to call him if you remembered anything?"

It was my turn to nod.

"Probably a good thing to do in the morning." He left. Only then did I realize I had forgotten to tell him about the poker game.

I called Detective Stanley once I was up and moving. He thanked me and reminded me to call anytime I remembered other details. I'd bristled at his tone and the implication I might be hiding things, although that's what I was doing even now. I hadn't told him about the poker game. Better to check things out a bit more before telling the cops. But I also knew he was doing his job.

Late Tuesday morning, I drove back to the intersection where I'd dropped Brandon off. In the daylight, I learned nothing more than I already knew. No police tape. Not on the sidewalk or the gray buildings. A few people loitered around. Mostly, it looked like the warehouse district it was. Just what I expected, but I didn't want to miss a clue, if there was one to find.

Afterward, I headed to the Pondside Inn. I reached the driveway for Pondside and then found my way back to where the tape hung. Mostly around trees, it seemed to form a broken semicircle. The trees looked to have been recently pruned, with leaves and debris all around. The circle included at least part of the pond that gave the inn its name. I almost laughed at the thought of the black swirl that had unnerved me the night before. There was nothing scary here.

I'd searched the internet after talking to John. The articles I'd found speculated on how he died and why, but there were more questions than answers. More items for my list. When I'd exhausted what I could see, I took pictures with my cell phone for reference.

In the early afternoon, I drove by The Tea Shoppe and then the Kreamery, in case John was there. I made a U-turn when I spotted the squad car at the donut place. I'd almost missed it because it was parked nearer the back.

Seeing John's shoulders drop as I walked in gave me my answer. John was a good cop, but I knew him well enough to know those small giveaways. I plopped down in a seat across from him. His partner was missing and likely waiting on an order, so I took advantage of him being alone by diving right in. "Anything new on the murder?"

John looked up and frowned. "Nice of you to ask. I'm good, and you? Or did you forget how to start a conversation?"

Clearly, I'd hit a nerve. "Sorry. I wanted to talk before your partner gets back. I didn't want to put you in an awkward situation of him seeing you talking to me about the murder."

John tried to hold it together and then laughed. "You really are something, you know that. It's a good thing I like you."

He took a bite of his glazed donut. "Nothing new I can tell you. We're working the case, interviewing people, dealing with evidence."

"Are you talking to Geoff?"

"I told you. We're talking to a lot of people. But yes, we already have."

"Then you know he works for his cousin as an enforcer."

"That's not exactly new. We're the police, remember. We know who does those kinds of things."

I sucked in my breath. Was I the only one in town who didn't know this? "So, does that cover grudges and debts owed?"

"You want to tell me what you know? Or are you fishing for information?"

I had hoped John would be a bit more interested. I wanted to approach this as more of a conversation where I steered it, but it was clear I wasn't in the driver's seat.

"Well, then you know about the fight?" I asked.

"I don't follow. What fight?"

"The one from the poker game? Geoff was there and got into an altercation with the victim." There, I'd said it out loud and even managed to make it sound like I knew the right words.

From the look on John's face, he didn't know about the fight. John took out a small notebook and his pen. "There are lots of weekly poker games around the city. Start from the beginning. Which poker game? Who plays? And what fight? When? Who was there? All of it. Don't leave out any facts you think we don't need to know."

John paused. "I can see the wheels turning. If I'm going to find who did this, then we need to know whatever you know. And now."

I relayed the little Bill had told me. I hated giving up Bill's name, but I hadn't been able to come up with any other way to explain how I knew. And I was almost certain Bill didn't have a thing to do with the murder. He had been working that night. I was still smarting about the fact Bill hadn't told me about the game and the fight, but I'd been over it enough to know I wasn't trying to get back at him. Geoff, on the other hand, was a different story. He could use a bit of shaking up.

John's partner, Josh Andrews, returned to the table about halfway through the first telling. He had questions as well. Then we went through it a second time—same stuff. I didn't have anything else to tell them, but I recognized this was all part of how they questioned people.

"So, will you check it out?" I asked.

John rolled his eyes. I thought only women did that, but he had mastered it too.

"Of course. We investigate all leads in these types of cases. I appreciate you letting me know about this. Seriously, though, leave this to us. I mean it."

I knew what he meant, but he wouldn't have known about the fight if I hadn't told him. And I had a few things I wanted to check out. Besides, I was getting pretty good at this.

My cell phone rang.

Dispatch again. Likely a fare. I looked at John, and he nodded.

Back in the cab, I checked in. The fare was on the other side of the historic district and a rush.

I pulled up to a historic building on Liberty Street that had been renovated to create apartments for Savannah College of Arts and Design students and other tenants. Dispatch had said the fare was named Daffy and she needed to be across town as quickly as possible.

Daffy turned out to be Daphne, although I guessed dispatch misunderstood her name from her muffled childlike high-pitched voice. I had to strain to hear her. "My car broke down, and none of my friends could get here fast enough. I have to be in character from the very start. That's why I sound this way."

I got out of the cab to help her. Daphne handed me one bundle of ribbons with yellow, pink, and green balloons attached. With the other bunch in one hand and a fabric-zippered pink bag in the other, Daphne walked down the sidewalk to the taxi, her tulle skirt swaying in the wind, while the balloons pulled upward as if trying to escape.

"I'm a princess. The little girl whose birthday it is wanted a cartoon princess, so I figure the voice and my dress will be exactly what she pictured."

I giggled. I wasn't so sure Daphne was what the child wanted, but I helped stuff the balloons inside the SUV, handing the ribbons back to Daphne once she climbed in the back seat. I'd had enough parties for Steph growing up to know that figuring out what a kid, even your own, really wanted could be frustrating at times.

Once we were all loaded up, we took off, and I zipped along streets I knew wouldn't be too congested at this hour. Daphne talked nonstop for the fifteen minutes it took to make the trip.

We arrived five minutes late. Daphne handed me the fare, whisked back a few stray blond hairs from her face, and gathered up her stuff. She thanked me as I helped her out of the taxicab but declined further help. The front door opened by what must have been the mom, whose face transformed from stressed to relaxed at the sight of the balloons and Daphne.

No tip. As frazzled as she had seemed, I wasn't surprised. Besides, she'd made me laugh, which was sometimes, like now, better than money. She'd also reminded me I hadn't heard from Steph. Calling her was next on my list of things to do.

19

My typical day off was Wednesday. I'd stopped by the office when my Tuesday night shift was over and the night dispatcher, Mark, had told me Sylvie's husband had been admitted to the hospital again. It had been a long night of driving, and I'd been on a call on River Street when the flight crew came in, so I couldn't get there in time to take the fare. The bars had specials going, and the streets were crammed with people, country music streaming out, competing with oldies and pop rock. This part of Savannah came alive at night.

I'd passed several walking ghost tours as I carried my fare to a hotel farther into the historic district. It was almost as if the luster and illumination that filled the city at night dimmed as you moved away from the main squares.

The fare had tipped well, but I'd wanted to see if the flight attendants might have any more information. Hearing Derek was back in the hospital was the end of a less-than-productive day.

Late Wednesday morning, I walked into the antiseptic-smelling hospital room and tried not to stare at Derek. I wondered why Sylvie hadn't called but figured she had her hands full. She looked smaller sitting by the bed that filled the room. The curtains on the windows were drawn as if to block out all light.

Derek had always been a thin man, but he looked positively skeletal. I pasted on a smile, hoping I had a bit more color in my cheeks than the stark white bedsheets and white walls.

"Hey, there. I hear you're feeling better." I was striving for a cheery tone.

Derek smiled.

Sylvie turned her head and hesitated. "Hello. Nice of you to come by."

The chill of those words was icy. I couldn't imagine what was wrong. Derek had a bad night, but he looked like he was on the mend. You'd never guess that from her greeting.

"How're things on the road?" Derek asked.

"Pretty much the same. Burning up lots of pavement."

Derek laughed. "I'll bet. How's Bill?"

"He's good."

Sylvie looked at me. "Could I have a word with you in the corridor?"

"Sure." What on earth was this all about?

We stepped around the corner.

"Derek looks like he's doing okay. I was worried when I heard he was back in the hospital. Will he be out soon?" I asked.

"He has some tests later. We'll know more then. But I wanted to talk to you about a different matter. Geoff was here earlier. The police know about his working for his cousin. Someone may have insinuated he might have a grudge against the murdered man or was enforcing a collection. Sound familiar?"

My face heated. I should have known she'd find out—time to own up.

"The cops talked to me again and asked if I knew of anyone who might have a grudge. Bill plays poker and was at a card game where there was a fight. Geoff was there, and he was the one who got into a fight with the victim. I didn't know if it was material, but after talking to Bill, we agreed they needed to know, since the fight was over a debt." There, I'd said it. Good or bad, I'd at least owned up to my actions...sort of.

"Didn't I tell you Geoff didn't do it?"

"Yes, but you didn't know about the fight."

"No, I didn't, but I did know about his working for his cousin."

"You did?"

"Of course. Geoff is an upstanding man, not to mention the husband of Derek's cousin. He came to me about it to make sure it wouldn't be an issue with his driving job. We came to terms. This information isn't widely known. We would have talked about it when we discussed the sale of the business."

"But how would I have known? Besides, Geoff's an enforcer, and the murdered guy owed money. It could have been him. Or the victim might owe other money that got him killed. I had no idea Geoff was family."

"No. What you don't know is Geoff agreed he'd only do collections where violence wasn't involved. He might threaten, but the deal is no broken bones. Otherwise, I would have fired him. I won't have my employees doing that kind of work on the side."

I thought back to Bill's description of the fight. He'd described it differently. Was it exaggerated? Or was there a difference if it was a personal debt?

Sylvie continued, "Plus, Geoff's wife has multiple sclerosis and why he has a part-time job on the side. If Geoff were to be convicted of a crime or even arrested for one he didn't do, his wife and children would be hurt. Geoff is trying to prevent that and pay for his wife's medical bills with the second income."

Oh, good grief. I had no idea.

"I can see from your face you didn't know. But there's no excuse for your behavior. I asked you not to go after him. I'm disappointed in you. How can you expect to run a business if you don't listen to what people are saying to you? And think before you say or act when you don't have all the facts."

Sylvie was silent for a few minutes. "I know you and Geoff are antagonistic to each other. If you want to own a company, you're going to have to learn to deal with men, especially men like Geoff. They'll try to run over you and undermine you. Finding your way of getting them to do what you need them to do without them knowing you are manipulating them is a key skill."

She paused. "We might need to put this idea of selling the business on hold while you sort things out about this murder. Give it time for the air to clear." She left that hanging in the muddied air as she turned and walked back toward Derek's room.

Maybe I'd gotten this all wrong. I wasn't sure how or why, but it sure sounded like Geoff wasn't the killer. But, with the cops insinuating I hadn't told them everything in the first interview, how could I not tell them. I didn't want to tell Sylvie that. Things would be even worse.

Besides, sifting through all this was the cops' job, wasn't it? And they would have found out about his other job and the fight during their investigation. I hadn't said he did it or even insinuated he did. He hadn't been arrested. I felt like a hippopotamus had just sat on my chest. I hated to admit it, but I hadn't listened to her. The only other person who'd ever managed to make me feel this guilty was Aunt Harriett. I had a feeling I was going to hear about this one from her too.

I wasn't sure it wasn't Geoff. He'd been in the area that night. He could have noticed Brandon wasn't in my cab. Or seen him walking to Pondside. Maybe things got out of control.

And Sylvie might be blinded by the fact Geoff was family. With all she had going on, who said he'd kept his word to her? Plus, Sylvie was dealing with Derek. Her attitude might be due to Derek's situation rather than me. But she'd put the brakes on the business deal too, so I had upset her. I wasn't helping. Instead, I was adding to all she was dealing with. I couldn't help thinking she might not know everything Geoff was doing. Or she might. It was hard to know.

If Geoff was the kind of guy I thought he was, who said he wouldn't take advantage of her distraction? Or that Sylvie wasn't blinded because she was dealing with an illness and medical bills. If Sylvie was right and it wasn't Geoff, then who else could it be?

20

Back home from the hospital, I plopped down on the couch with a glass of sweet tea. I stared at my phone, sure I had forgotten something. Steph. In my attempts at trying to keep in touch, I texted her sometimes midweek in addition to the Saturday calls. Not often or she'd say I too pushy, although all I wanted was to let her know I loved her.

I texted. **Hope you're having a great week. Love, Mom.**

No response. That could mean Steph was in class or not answering. Or I might get a response later when she had time and didn't have to explain to anyone it was a text from her mother. It didn't matter if she responded. I wanted our relationship back on track. This was my responsibility to fix.

I needed to get back to the situation with Sylvie. She was under a lot of stress. Groaning, I closed my eyes, willing my thoughts to slow down and relax. I dropped my head back against the pillows. My brain was running a million miles an hour, trying to sort through what I knew. I stared at the ceiling and tried counting the bumps on the popcorn texture. Losing track, I closed my eyes.

"That's not going to solve the problem."

I heard the voice but didn't respond. I knew who it belonged to. Another part of me wanted to ignore it, but that wasn't possible. I tried to open one eye enough to peer through my eyelashes while pretending I was still asleep.

"You don't think that will work with the dead, do you, my dear?" Aunt Harriett giggled. She moved to the couch and settled beside me.

It was the giggling that got me. I had heard her chuckle and laugh many times, but a giggle was rare. She usually saved a half-laugh for her men friends when she was politely responding. This was no half-laugh. It was a solid giggle of pure amusement.

"Oh, all right. You win."

"Honestly, my dear, competing with the dead isn't very smart. Competing with one who knows you as well as I do and is also dead, even less so. We may have our limitations, but not seeing people in their true light isn't one of them."

I opened my eyes and stared at this apparition. I ran my fingers through my hair to calm the wiry spikes and my nerves. What was in front of me was more the impression of her, all in white with flashes of color, rather than a single solid. She reached up and twisted the pearls around her neck, a habit I remembered from when she was alive. The pearls matched the clustered clip-ons gracing each ear. Aunt Harriett wore sensible heels, nylons, and a silky, flowing dress that screamed "date night." Well, at least an evening out on the town, but I wasn't sure what that meant wherever Aunt Harriett was.

All I could think of was a ghost was wearing nylons—or at least my aunt did by habit or effect. "Were you out on a date?"

"Don't look so surprised," Aunt Harriett said. "I'm a vital woman with a number of gentlemen callers. Why wouldn't I be out?"

Again, I wondered if she was real or a dream. Maybe I had a brain tumor and was conjuring people from my past. A scary thought. There were several I had no interest in ever seeing again.

"Be patient with Sylvie. She's got a good heart. And she'll watch out for you if you let her." Aunt Harriett was silent for a few seconds. "I need your help."

That caught my interest. How on earth could I help her? And how did she know about my conversation with Sylvie? I stumbled over my words. "What? How can I help you?"

She smiled at my confusion. "All will become clear. Just go with it for now. I'm looking for a spirit, a person from my past was supposed to wait for me. I can't seem to find him."

The thought of my being a ghost detective was more than I could deal with right now. I busted out laughing. "If you can't find a ghost, how can I?"

"I'm not sure, but I think between the two of us, we can find him. And I have a few ideas on how to start."

I realized as the words sunk in that I could very well be on my way to becoming like Great-grandma Sebelia—talking to lingering ghosts, which wasn't a bad thing. I just never expected I would be doing anything along those lines.

I couldn't deny Aunt Harriett the help, no matter what the cost. She'd been there through the many clashes with my parents and brother over what a "proper" Southern girl should act like and do. And she'd helped me pick up the pieces after each divorce. Finding a lost love, if that was what he was, was the least I could do.

She laughed with me. "I know. It sounds absurd. But I know for a fact he hasn't passed over to the next level, so he should be somewhere I can find him."

I gulped and took the leap. "Okay, assuming it's even possible that I can help, who is it I'm supposed to find?"

"Peter Mercer."

"Who is he, and what makes you think I can help?"

"You can see me. You can go places and do things I can't."

"Do all spirits or ghosts or whatever they are look the same?" I asked.

Aunt Harriett contemplated my question. "I'm not entirely sure, being so new to this. Have you ever watched how a plane goes through a cloud? You see the wing, and then the cloud obscures it for a second or two. That's what it's like. Wisps of white will cloud a place and then are gone. I appear solid to you, I think." She paused.

"Others seem more dense at times. Hard to say whether anyone sees them and, if so, if it's like what you see. I'm not sure if it's experience or choice."

"But maybe I can only see you."

"I don't know, but you can see more than most people. My confidence is in you. I'm asking you to try."

I nodded.

Aunt Harriett continued, "I've been to the cemetery and his family home."

"Why?"

"You know, the old stories of ghosts haunting those places are true. It's what happens with a few where they're kind of stuck here, so they gravitate to things they know. I can't imagine where Peter is, if not there."

"Okay. If that's the norm, then where else would he be?"

"That's what I need your help with. I know you don't know Peter, but you're a smart girl. I'd like to know if you have any ideas. It's important."

"Aunt Harriett, I don't have any idea where you should look. I wish I could help, but I didn't know him. Maybe if you talked about him, we could figure it out."

"I assume you know the history of the Mercers in Savannah?" Aunt Harriett asked.

"The Mercers?"

She nodded.

I dug into my brain, searching for the specifics. The Mercers had been a fixture in Savannah for as long as I could remember. The family home on Bull Street was now a museum. Jim Williams had bought and restored the house. The shooting of his assistant, Danny Hansford, had occurred there and was the basis for the novel *Midnight in the Garden of Good and Evil*. The family history was littered with politicians and artists. "Some of it. Weren't they involved in politics?"

"Yes," Aunt Harriett said. "Peter's father was very involved and very ambitious. His mother even more so. They were the poorer relatives, related to the family who owned the Mercer House at the southwest end of Monterrey Square. His mother never stopped trying to catch up to them."

"How did you know him?"

"His younger brother, Russell, and I were in the same grade in school. Peter was being groomed for office. All the right schools, clothes, and friends. We fell in love. It was all very secretive and fun. We both knew his parents wouldn't approve of me, but we were young and thought we could manage them."

I watched Aunt Harriett's face. She was miles away, reliving those memories with a glow of peace and contentment.

"It was a gentler, simpler time. Girls in white cotton dresses. Picnics and barbeques on the lawn. Sweet tea and sugar-rich Kool-Aid on the veranda as the games of courtship played out. We played croquet and badminton." Aunt Harriett laughed. "There were some surprised boys when a girl was mad. You had to watch your head for a badminton shuttlecock or croquet ball coming your way at a fast pace. Did you know his cousin was Johnny Mercer, who wrote the lyrics to the song 'Moon River'? I can't hear it without being transported back—the thrill of Peter taking my hand for the first time, if only for a brief moment."

She paused. "To see me, Peter always brought Russell with him. Russell adored and admired him. The whole family did. Then Peter was killed in a boating accident. Everything changed. Russell took it almost as hard as I did."

In the quiet moment, I had a thought. "Have you checked the marina, or where the family kept their sailboat? Don't spirits sometime stay close to where they died?"

"I knew you were one sharp cookie," Aunt Harriett said. "I think the family sold the sailboat after the accident, but the dock is there. That's a great idea."

Aunt Harriett turned as if she was listening. "Dagnabit. Three bells. I have to go."

What? I had no idea what three bells meant. What was it with bells, anyway? They were everywhere I went. I opened my mouth to ask, but Aunt Harriett cut me off.

"I'll just pop over to those places and check. Toodles." She vanished.

One of these times, I was going to have to make her sit and explain certain things to me.

21

After coffee and a shower Thursday morning, I drove across town in my Honda Accord to the apartment complex and building that had been in Brandon's online pictures. He had posted a ton of them, and it had taken an hour to go through all of them for relevant ones. I checked for the apartment complex name and a building marker I hoped was his, among the many pictures of him by the pool and tennis court.

I wasn't sure if the police had been there, but my guess was they had. If I was going to learn more about him or find a clue as to why this had all happened, seeing how and where he lived might help.

I followed a Toyota Prius into the sprawling apartment complex. What luck. They were opening the gate. I wasn't going to have to walk through the office, making up a story about why I was there or lying about wanting to rent an apartment. The development was populated with young professionals—not many cars this time of day and no amenities screamed it was for families. These were popular, but I'd never live in a modern building as long as I could live in the historic district. I loved the feel of old world and antebellum times.

Here, each building was tan with metal balconies or patios, cream doors, and cream trim. The buildings ran at angles to each other, with the roads running within them, edged with parking spaces on both sides. There had been a map at the front detailing the building locations, but I'd glided right past it. The corners of the interior streets were marked with the building numbers and progressed higher as you drove farther inside.

The apartment numbers on a building to the left started with 700. Brandon lived in the 1100 building, as far as I could tell from what I had found, or at least he had been standing in front of it. I continued forward, weaving around the buildings and the open green space with small oak trees that probably replaced the ones they had removed to build freely. I hated to think about all the old-growth lost each time a new development went up at the cost of progress. With Savannah's growth, people need places to live. I was glad the historic district downtown was protected.

Nice complex. The second- and third-floor balconies of many residents held late-flowering plants flowing like miniature waterfalls over the railings. Wrought iron patio furniture waited for drinks and a sunset. A stray beach towel swung in the light breeze. Between glances at numbers, I avoided a couple of walking residents, their dogs, and the occasional cat dashing across the pavement. No children here. Not a surprise, but it was during the week, and they might be at school. If any were allowed, that was. I was pretty sure Brandon's apartment would be in a separate area.

The clubhouse was in the center, and the sidewalk led to a pool. Ahead, I spotted an 1120 sign. I was in the general area of his apartment—time to park and walk the rest of the way. Before I moved into Aunt Harriett's house, I'd lived in apartments between husbands.

In this kind of large complex, there was always a group of singles living near the pool and at least one guy or girl with a unit that opened to the pool. Convenient for surveying who was there and sunbathing and it gave a quick exit to the outside—both to join friends or to a place to have drinks. I was betting Brandon was that guy. And if he wasn't, I wasn't sure what I'd do, but I'd figure it out. Or, at the very least, get an idea of where he lived. If he was that guy, then he probably had a key hidden nearby everyone knew about. Many of his neighbors would know and would have used that knowledge. I took a deep breath and climbed out of the SUV.

I followed a path leading in front of the buildings and looked for what I thought might be Brandon's unit between the buildings. Bottom floor. I counted the units from the end of the building on this side.

Next was locating the pool. I took a path leading between the buildings and, sure enough, the unit I wanted was inside the cluster. I rounded the corner of the building I'd been in front of, and, although it was October, a small group of hardcore sunbathers, also called partiers, were out in force for the early sun this morning.

I'd thought about my cover story. I knew I wasn't precisely Brandon's type, but he had asked me about having drinks with him in the cab. I thought if I said I had been here one night last week and lost an earring, no one would question it. But I might have to wing it.

I paused to count the units from the end, so I'd know which one was Brandon's, coming from the poolside of the building. After all, if I'd been here, while we might not have come in this way, it didn't hurt to know which one I thought it was. And anyone who might choose to help me would expect me to know. At least I hoped I was right, and my guess was all I could depend on right now. I was questioning myself, but I didn't normally do this kind of thing. I was a bit frazzled and excited, but anxious. I wiped my palms against my jean skirt to remove the sweat. I could blame the humidity, but this was nerves.

It had taken me almost an hour to decide on what to wear. I wasn't sure who might help, although I figured it was most likely a guy. I hadn't wanted my clothes to put off any woman who might help or might keep her from having her boyfriend help. I'd settled on a short blue denim skirt and a camisole blue denim vest with my Victoria Secret's bra underneath. I'd added open-toed sandals with a three-inch heel that flashed my atomic pink toenails. Pink in my hair with blue in between. I made quite a statement.

Hopefully, an alluring but nonconfrontational one. Was it enough or too much? I was about to find out.

My sandals clicked along the concrete sidewalk as I moved

forward. I strolled, scanning the units, and mostly ignoring the pool. I was hoping someone was watching.

"Hi there. You checking out the complex?" asked a tall sun-kissed guy.

I almost laughed. I shouldn't have worried after all. Although I was surprised to see this many people out during the week. What kind of jobs did they have? Maybe one like mine.

"No, I was here the other night. I'm looking for Brandon."

"Brandon?" he asked.

"Yeah, lives in one of the units along here. We had drinks in his apartment."

"You a cop, too?"

That was unexpected. "No. I was in the area and wanted to see if he found my pearl earring."

"Oh, sure," the guy said. "If it was there, the cops probably have it."

I stared at him, not sure what to say.

"Sorry to be the one to tell you, but Brandon's dead. Murdered. See the yellow tape there? The cops already searched it."

Darn. Was I going to fail even before I got to the door?

"I didn't know. We met at a party and hit it off. Came back here for a nightcap. You know how that happens." I gave my prettiest smile.

"Yeah." He returned my smile.

I shifted my weight and ran my fingers through my hair. Great. I hated this kind of pretense.

"Yeah," I repeated his phrase. "I'm sure you do."

He smiled a little wider, and I could see he was interested.

"Any idea if there's a way to get inside? Check for my earring. Wouldn't take me but a short time."

Wow. That almost sounded real. I was better at this than I thought I'd be.

"Hmmm." He stared at me as if he were trying to figure out if I was trustworthy or not.

"Brandon did keep a key. He was good about letting us use his apartment for ice and stuff."

Gadzooks! I had to control my excitement. I was in if I didn't blow it. But gadzooks? Where had that come from? Aunt Harriett had used that word. How much was she influencing me? I dismissed the thought and pasted on a smile as I tried to keep my cool. "That would be so great. I live across town, and I'm not over here often."

I wondered how thick I'd have to lay this on. "The earrings were a gift from my ex-husband."

His eyebrows rose even more.

"Not sentimental. It's the only thing I got from the marriage, and he wanted them back. I'd hate to lose them."

The guy laughed. "We'll need to be careful with the tape, but it's not on real tight. It even fell down the other night and we put it back up. Come on. I'll show you where he keeps the key."

22

I could hardly believe this was working. All those years of single living between divorces had paid off. I followed him down the path to the fourth unit. He reached behind a wooden chair and brought out the key.

"I'm Dave. There's a nail on the back. Put the key back when you're done. And I've got cold ones to drink if you'd like to stay awhile."

"Thanks. I'm Pat." I'd decided to keep the lies to a minimum so I could keep them straight. At least now I hadn't lied about my name. Well, not exactly, since the use of Pat would be a clue to anyone who knew me and heard it. But talk about cold: Brandon was dead, and Dave was hitting on me.

Dave's face said he didn't know if he believed me, so I added, "I'm sure it won't take but a minute. I'll lock up and replace the key when I leave—and make sure the tape is back up."

He walked back toward the pool as I unlocked and pulled open the sliding glass door—time to see if I could find out anything else helpful about Brandon. I wasn't sure how long I had or if Dave would be back. I'd have to be quick.

I flipped on the light and stared at the room. A brown leather couch guarded one wall. A plasma TV held court across from it. Two stuffed recliners with padded arms flanked the sofa. A couple of framed event prints hung on the wall. I walked farther inside and through a doorway.

A king-size bed crowned with beige silk pillows on the black bedspread dominated the bedroom. A side table with a lamp and a small chest of drawers completed the room. As in the living room, prints from concerts provided the only decoration. There was no sign of who Brandon was as a person in this apartment.

I opened the bedroom closet. Uniforms, dry-cleaned shirts, and jeans hung on the rod. Tennis shoes and two pairs of dress shoes littered the floor.

I wasn't going to learn anything here. It was as if he didn't exist. But he did, and I knew he had a computer because he had a Facebook account. After a quick search of the drawers, I realized whatever equipment he had wasn't here. The cops had likely taken it. I stared at the room. What was I missing? I'd gone to all this trouble. I couldn't believe it was for nothing.

"Hello. Still here?"

Dave moved around in the other room. I'd been here too long. Time to go.

"I'm in here. Just checking the floor."

"Bedroom, eh?" He grinned at me.

"Clean up those thoughts. I was in here the other night to use the ladies' room."

"Un-huh."

I laughed.

"Did you find it?"

I sucked in my breath. Find it? Great. Good thing I had my story before I got here. I'd almost forgotten what I'd told him.

"Not yet. We did have a drink. Thought I'd check the kitchen too."

I walked past Dave and surveyed the kitchen from the bar dividing the living room from the eating area. The kitchen was bare, except for a glass bowl on the bar, wineglasses, a bottle of rum, and plates in the cabinets. I glanced in the bowl. It was filled with coins, black and red round chips, and cigars with red bands. Looked like Spanish on them. Did they matter?

"I hate cigars," I said.

"Oh yeah?" Dave said. "Brandon loved them. Shipped the Cubans in special." He winked.

There was a regular shuttle between Savannah and Miami. Could these be Cuban? Maybe Brandon had been smuggling them in. How could I check? I'd have to palm one. It was going to be hard with Dave breathing down my neck.

I changed the subject to distract him. "No. It doesn't seem to be here. Thanks so much for letting me in." I moved my purse to my left shoulder and let it hit the bowl. The chips flew. "Oh darn, look what I've done."

I had to shield my face to keep from laughing and cheering. If I'd seen this in a movie, I'd have scoffed at how unlikely it was anyone would ever do that successfully. I couldn't believe I had managed it.

I reached across and started to gather the loose chips.

"Here. I'll help you." Dave moved closer.

"No, thanks. I think I've got it." I turned and blocked his view. I dropped the last chip, noting the black mask symbol. Huh? These looked like poker chips but not exactly. *Focus.* How was I going to take a cigar? Before I let the chip go, I wrapped my left hand around a cigar, willing the cellophane wrapper not to crinkle too loudly.

"All done." I turned away from Dave. I coughed as I jammed the cigar and chip into the side pocket of my purse, trying to mask the sound. Who decided to make cigars this long? The end was sticking out. How was I supposed to get out of here? I glued my arm to the bag and prayed nothing would fall out.

"I'd better get going if I'm gonna make it to work on time." I headed past him. I strode across the living room as fast as my heels would let me. Supermodels of the world look out. That was a runway-worthy move.

At the door, I stopped so he could open it for me. He gave me a puzzled look like I'd grown a second nose. I could hardly explain I needed him to open it because it was too heavy for me to do one-handed, and my other arm couldn't move because it was hiding the cigar.

"Thank you." I waited for him to me follow outside, lock the door, stick the yellow tape back across it, and replace the key.

"Last chance on that drink," he said.

"Sorry. Wish I could. I'll take a rain check, though." Steamboats would be dancing up the Savannah River before that happened. I hoped the cigar wasn't visible. I couldn't exactly check, right? How would I ever explain? "Thanks again."

He waved and headed back to his lounge chair in that easygoing stride that came naturally to guys like him. I headed back to my car, taking deep breaths to quiet my racing pulse. I didn't know how criminals did this. You'd have to have nerves of steel. Right now, I would have jumped out of my skin if anyone touched me.

I tried to walk calmly, but I kept looking around, wondering if anyone could tell what I had done. I hoped I wouldn't topple over in my heels or step wrong and break my ankle. Thank goodness there weren't any clouds in the sky. I was certain lightning would strike me down if there were.

Of course, there was still Aunt Harriett. I wasn't sure she'd approve, and I was certain she'd have a few choice words to say about it. A distraction before I became obsessive about this would help.

I shifted my thoughts. Did I know more? Not really, although the cigar might be a good lead. The poker chips were likely from the midweek night games, but I'd look at the one I'd taken when I had more time. There had to be a cigar expert I could ask. There was a tobacco shop in the City Market. I'd never been in there, but Bill might have.

What else? Brandon must have a computer. But where would it be? Maybe in his personal effects? More likely with the police. I could ask John, although that wouldn't do me any good. They weren't going to let me search on it. And they would be following up on emails and whatever else they found.

And they'd searched his apartment, although it didn't look like it was a crime scene. Maybe the police had marked it off to keep people out until they solved the case.

Hmmm. What else could I do, and what was I missing that would help solve this? Had John found the cigars? Were they following that lead too? They might be, but I could still check into them.

I unlocked the Honda, climbed in, and put the keys in the ignition. I looked forward to the drive across town. It would help me think but also calm me down. I would figure out my next step now that I had another clue.

23

Hours later I dressed for work. I felt the air in the room change. More of a twinge. Thinking I might be hypersensitive, I turned. And jumped.

Aunt Harriett stood before me. "Sorry, dear. I was waiting so I wouldn't scare you."

I didn't know if it was good or not that I was beginning to sense her presence. "I take it Peter wasn't at the marina."

"No, and there wasn't any scent of a trail, either," Aunt Harriett said.

"I don't understand, what trail?"

"Oh, I learned we all leave a thin trail behind. It lasts a short time before it disappears, but I now know what to look for. It's a bit like the wilderness trackers who can follow anyone, except it's in a different place, and you're looking for less obvious signs than broken branches or grass. Eddie is very good at it. He's been helping me with what signs are left behind as we travel. I mean, Eddie's an older spirit, been around more. Knows a lot about things like this."

"Okay." I didn't understand all this. "What does Eddie have to do with this? I have to be at work soon."

"Just a friend helping me. I'm helping him too. I know you have work soon, dear, but I thought you might have other ideas I could check out. So, where was I in the story?"

"You stopped where Peter died." I reached for my shoes.

"Yes. Such a sad time. I was heartbroken. No one except Russell knew the depth of my feelings for Peter. I had hidden them from even my closest girlfriend for fear his mother might find out. We knew everyone suspected, but they didn't know for sure. When Peter died, the only one I could share my deep grief with was Russell. Peter was the love of my life. When he died, everything changed."

"What happened?"

"It was a sailing accident. Nobody's fault, really. One of the lines came loose. Peter was hit in the head by a boom and thrown into the water. A boy went in after him. The others helped pull him into the boat and got him to shore, but it took too long. None of them knew CPR like they do now." Aunt Harriett turned away and for a moment I thought she might shed a few tears. Could ghosts cry tears like us?

I couldn't resist asking, "Weren't there adults on the boat?"

"Oh, no. The Mercers were a water family. Peter learned to swim when he was two, and Russell learned a bit later as well."

"Later? That sounds strange. What does that mean exactly?"

Aunt Harriett heaved a great sigh. "I guess it's not such a big secret. Russell was adopted. The Mercers had a ton of money, and with privilege came responsibility. When they heard about the disfigured boy, well, with their perfect son, they decided it was their civic duty to take him in and give him a home. Peter was raised knowing it was his duty to watch out for Russell. But Peter did more than that. Peter loved Russell like a blood brother." Aunt Harriett paused, and there were tears in her eyes.

"It was a different time. The Mercers' hearts were in the right place, but they had a certain place in society. A live-in housekeeper took care of Russell. But he wanted more, a family with lots of love and acceptance. They had the right idea, but it wasn't enough of what Russell needed.

"Russell was the one who wanted to go out that awful day. Peter didn't. But Russell wasn't allowed on the sailboat without Peter, so when the other boys wanted to go too, Peter gave in. Russell always blamed himself for Peter being there. And I think, in a way, so did the rest of the family. When Peter died, the Mercers were devastated. All their hopes and dreams died. Their idea of a successor didn't include Russell. Cousin Alan became the heir, apparent to the family ambitions."

I sucked in a breath. "How horrible."

Aunt Harriett looked at me. "It was the times. You shouldn't judge them too harshly. They made sure Russell was educated and went to college. When he wanted to go into business, they helped him start the tobacco business. He wasn't blood, and that was what counted to them. Or at least that's what the family thought. Truth be told, they would have been better off with Russell. Alan was a philandering, incompetent fool."

I laughed. "Tell me how you really feel about him."

Aunt Harriett laughed. "He was such a cad. So full of himself, he never realized the only reason anyone invited him anywhere was because of his money and family's position, which he succeeded in running into the ground."

"Would Peter have gone to see his cousin?" That didn't seem likely to me, but I couldn't think of anything else. "Or maybe a special place where the two of you used to meet?"

"I don't think he cared about Alan. But the other is a possibility. There were a couple of places we met. I've tried one of them, but now I know what to look for, I can try them again. I'll see if I can find any traces of Peter there," Aunt Harriett said. "It's so discouraging. I thought Peter would be waiting. I can't understand why he hasn't come looking for me. Surely he could feel when I passed."

Doubt shone on Aunt Harriett's face. I couldn't imagine how she must have felt, pining for a lost love your whole life and then not finding them waiting when you died. Had Peter been in love with her as much as she thought? I could see the thought had crossed her mind, even though she was fighting it.

"Daylight's burning. You've been a great help. I'm off." Aunt Harriett's jaw hardened. "I'll be back to brainstorm again if I don't find any hint of him."

I grabbed my keys and headed for the door. My shift started in thirty minutes.

24

I woke to sunlight on Friday. My shift had been busy last night with almost no time to think about things. I loved the fact I could sleep in most weekdays. It allowed me to run errands without lots of other people doing the same. I couldn't believe it had been a week since I put Brandon out of my cab. And I was regretting trading a day off with Mark so I could have dinner with Bill tonight.

Bill had to work the weekend, so changing my schedule had made sense at the time. I'd planned for us to go out to eat, but that was before I wanted to check back with the flight attendants. But dinner also meant I could ask him about the cigar, if I played this right, and we could also talk further about the business. Sylvie hadn't called, and I'd decided a text might be the best way to check in, kind of gauge how mad she was at me. Plus, I cared about Derek and hoped he was better.

Checking in on Derek. Is he doing better?

I shifted back to think. Coffee was next on my list, but I wanted to review things, so I lay back and let my mind wander. My cell phone pinged. Sylvie had texted back a sad face. My heart was breaking for her and Derek. I hated that I was adding to her burden in any way.

Seconds later, I felt eyes on me. "Aunt Harriett?"

"Yes, dear."

"Couldn't you announce yourself or make a noise?"

Aunt Harriett laughed. "Are you suggesting I ring the doorbell?"

"That would work. It would give me a bit of warning."

"It doesn't work like that."

"I have a bunch of questions."

"I knew you did. It's why I'm here. What do you want to know?"

"Well, I've been wondering. You know about the guy I put out of my cab. He was murdered."

Aunt Harriett nodded.

"I was thinking...and I feel responsible for what happened. Like maybe it's my fault he died." There, I'd finally said it. The knot that had grown to the size of at least a grapefruit, if not a basketball, in my stomach started to deflate. It didn't let me off the hook for what I'd done. I guess I needed to say it out loud, out in the open.

"Did you put him out with the thought he'd get hurt or die?"

"Of course not. I put him out because he was rude. And only after I'd asked him to stop. Even the other passengers asked him to tone it down. And the pilot told me to do it."

"Did you know he would be killed?"

"No, but it feels like I had a part in him dying."

"Well, you didn't earn any good karma points for letting your temper get the best of you or for not using your good judgment."

Geez. That didn't make me feel better.

"But you didn't kill him or set him up to be killed. That man did it all on his own. When the authorities figure out who was responsible, then you may know the why of it all. Do you think you will feel better if you know why he died?"

She'd hit on the exact point I was trying to work out. I wanted to know who but also why. And whether my putting Brandon out of the cab had contributed to his death. I'd been brought up to know the difference between good and evil. This lay somewhere in between, kind of like Aunt Harriett. I wasn't sure I could survive the kind of purgatory she was in. I recognized the gray in my life, but it was easier when things were black or white. Not always, but in this case I would've preferred everything to be more clear-cut.

"I don't think I'd feel better. I didn't like him, but I didn't want him dead. Just out of my cab. I'm more worried about, you know, Judgment Day." I paused.

"Trisha, we all have things in our past we wish we'd done differently. I'd be worried if it hadn't affected you. But you can't change what's happened. You can choose to make a different choice next time."

I could always count on Aunt Harriett to find the most important kernel of truth in any situation. I wasn't sure what I might do if there was a next time, although I might not get a chance. I was worried about keeping my job, whether I could clear my name, and if Sylvie had gotten over her anger with me.

Aunt Harriett interrupted my thoughts. "What's on the agenda today? Have you figured out anything else you need to check out?"

She was trying to distract me, and I decided to let her. I wasn't sure how I felt about being partly responsible for Brandon's death, but I'd work to find a way to make it right. For now, it meant following leads to find his killer.

"That's what I was thinking about. I went by the place where he lived, but there wasn't much there."

"Wouldn't the police have already investigated it?"

"Yes, they'd been there, but I didn't think it would hurt. Besides, I needed to take action. I won't see Angie and her client, who might have information on the dead guy, until tomorrow. I did find a few things, and I'm going to see if they lead me anywhere."

"Then be careful. You don't know what you might uncover. And if the black presence is Brandon, you may cross paths with him as you examine things in his life. A spirit goes back to what it knows or places resonating with it."

"Did you find Peter?"

"No. I have more places to check. I'll do that now. Keep thinking. I'll be back."

25

I almost dropped the pan I was holding when Aunt Harriett said, "Trisha?"

"I don't think I'll ever get used to you suddenly appearing. Maybe you could make the lights flicker."

Aunt Harriett's eyes pierced the space between us like a penlight as she giggled. It was great to hear the sound again, but I'd never realized a spirit might have light radiating outward.

"I did say I'd be back, but I'll see what I can come up with."

I yawned as I smiled, which must have created a loopy-looking grin on my face.

"That's not an attractive look, my dear. I've been everywhere I can think of, so I need your help again."

My eyes narrowed a bit as I struggled with the idea of how I might help her. "You mean like how to cross over?" I'd seen television shows where the star helped lost spirits.

"Not really. I'm not finding Peter. He's nowhere."

"That does seem strange. Maybe he crossed over."

"No. They'd know."

I wasn't sure who "they" were, but I was hesitant to ask. "What else can I do? I don't know that I would be able to see Peter and, even if I could, I wouldn't know him if I did."

"Well, if you can see me, then you should be able to see him. Besides, there are things you can do in the physical world that I can't." Aunt Harriett paused.

"Okay, I'm in. What do you need me to do?"

"I knew I could count on you." She smiled. "You'll need a sage smudge stick. Well, maybe more. Get a couple. Then you'll need a sterilized bowl and holy water."

I pondered this request. The smudge sticks, well, lots of people burned sage to purify a new home or cleanse an area of unwanted spirits or memories, so I could find them easily. I hadn't ever used them, but there were people who swore the burning aroma worked wonders.

The City Market shops in the boxy strip center were filled with souvenirs and fortune-tellers, all mixed in with the more normal offerings of the bakeries that made my mouth water each time I thought of their buttery treats, and the smells of the exotic spices from the ethnic restaurants filled with tourists each evening. The cobblestone streets carried the feeling of unseen life and powers that surrounded me each time. There were times when I heard the swish of long skirts covering petticoats, only to turn and see nothing. Just my imagination.

Jessica's Treasures likely sold the items. Her shop occupied a space between the restaurants and bars on River Street and the hotels on Bay Street. A gold mine for cabdrivers like me. Lots of tourists who had ridden the green and orange Old Town Trolleys hailed or called a cab after shopping when they were tired or pressed for time. The market area was more modern than the shops but had horse-drawn carriages for those who treasured the feel of what Savannah might have been like in the early days. The aroma of horse sweat and drop-pings always assaulted my nose during the summer months.

"I know sage purifies things, but why do you need the bowl and holy water? And where am I supposed to get those items?" I asked.

"Use an old bowl. Put it in the dishwasher with as hot a wash as possible. Then use gloves to take it out and wrap it up in plastic. You mustn't touch it with your fingers."

"Okay, I can do that. But the only holy water I know of is in a church. I don't think stealing from there would be a good idea."

"Don't be silly. We'll need fresh water—preferably from a stream, rather than out of a faucet. As natural as possible. You'll need to say a blessing over it."

I was skeptical, but what she asked was doable.

"Can you have those items today?"

I nodded.

"I'll be back tomorrow morning. I can show you the way."

"I have the breast cancer run tomorrow morning, and then I have to work. How about Sunday morning? But not before ten. I sleep in."

She frowned for a moment. "I guess that will have to do."

"So, where exactly do you want to go?"

"The family cemeteries."

"What? Why?"

"Sorry, I have to run. Will explain when I see you. Be ready." She disappeared with a crooked little smile on her face, leaving me wondering what she wasn't telling me.

26

Bill and I stood in the line snaking around Barnard Street, waiting for the restaurant to open. This area was off Forsyth Park, a vast green space filled with kids and families in good weather. There were homes in disrepair, but there was also a move to rehabilitate the area. I hoped they'd restore all the buildings to their former glory. Away from the tourist area, it was quieter but no less filled with the mystique of the city in the calm but shadowy streets lined with trees.

Bill had immediately agreed to barbeque for Friday night dinner. I'd heard the food was terrific, but they didn't take reservations. We'd been waiting outside near the navy metallic railroad car that served as the dining car. A bunch of us had sheltered from the heat and sun under nearby trees, which was slightly less stifling than the concrete sidewalk. I'd kept to my usual blue jean skirt, but humidity kept my silky green shirt glued to my back.

"Remind me why we're waiting here when we could be having a perfectly good steak and ice-cold beer at Paddy's Tavern."

I frowned. Bill was right. We were here because they had a cigar lounge in the expansion area off the main dining area. I'd wanted to ask him about cigars in a casual way without having to explain why.

"It's fun and different. And it got a great review, so everyone wants to eat here." I smiled my sexiest smile.

"Uh-huh. You hate trendy places. Why are we really here?"

I hated he already knew me so well. And thrilled at the same time. My heart swelled with joy, while the rest of me cringed in fear of being so intimate with a man again. I debated my choices and decided I'd melt in this heat if we hung around much longer.

My shoulders caved. "I wanted to ask you about cigars. I thought being here would be an easy opening for my questions."

Bill looked puzzled. "Thinking you'll take up cigar smoking?" He laughed. "Hon, I don't think it's quite the vice for you."

"Funny. I wanted to know about them and you and the guys smoke them at your card games so I figured you'd know."

He sat back and waited for me to continue.

"I'm not accusing you. I need to know about cigars—Cuban ones. Thought you might know."

I checked his reaction. His face had a stone quality I hadn't seen there before. The look was familiar. My second husband had worn it often near the end of our marriage. Not a good sign.

"I was going to check the internet, but I haven't had time. I figured you'd know. I wanted to know about Cuban cigars and smuggling. I knew the US had established relations with Cuba again, but I wondered about before—and whether you can have Cuban cigars in the states legally now. Or at least before the latest changes happened."

The look on Bill's face was priceless. He'd gone from irritated to confused to the wheels racing in his brain. "What's with the sudden interest? The truth."

My first instinct was to run. I was bungling this. I wanted to fix this but didn't want to explain the reasons behind the questions. Instead, I looked at the ground to give myself a minute. It was now or never. Relationships depended on trust. Bill had pretty good instincts.

"I'm checking out things that don't add up with the murdered customer I put out of my cab." I decided to try to be as truthful as I could.

"I thought you agreed to let the cops handle all this."

"Yeah, but I need to keep my job, and there's a big cloud hanging over me. Plus, it could impact the business, and maybe my buying it." I kept the part about the black spirit following me to myself. Bill might not believe me or that Aunt Harriett talked to me. It was enough that I was checking it out. I'd save those little tidbits for a better time.

"You know I don't like that. Somebody killed your fare. You could be putting yourself in real danger. Why would you do take such a chance?"

"I know. I thought if I could do a little bit to help, I wouldn't worry about it so much. Or feel so out of control."

I looked into Bill's eyes. "I'm not doing anything dangerous. Just checking around on a few things. I am going to tell the cops about whatever I find. Really."

"You need to stop. It's bad enough I worry about who's getting in the cab with you. You're fun to be with and have an honesty I appreciate."

My eyes widened and my heart almost stopped. I'd always been the one to tell Bill I worried about him being a first responder and all the bad things that could happen to him. I'd never considered he might be concerned too. That was good news. The bad news was I couldn't stop checking on Brandon's past. I'd have to make him see reason.

"It's a bit of research. I know the guy, Brandon, had cigars. I don't know much about what kind. I wondered if he might be involved in illegal activities, like smuggling in Cuban cigars. I don't think flight attendants make a lot of money, so maybe he did things for extra cash on the side."

That sounded very rational, didn't it?

Bill looked unhappy. He seemed to consider how to answer me. "I don't smoke them. I know there was an embargo on cigars for a long time. Now it's easier to get them into the country through internet sales. And they may be available in a port, or if not, they likely will be soon. Might be able to bring them in from Canada or Mexico, but I thought this guy flew the shuttle from DC."

"That's what he was on when I picked him up. It's not his normal route. I thought I'd see if it was possible. Might be worth checking out."

"I'd be surprised if that's the case with all the security at airports these days. And I think most flight attendants are like everyone else, honest people, but I guess there could be a bad egg. The police should and could check on. Not you. Promise me you'll let them handle it."

"I'll talk to John. He'll know what to do."

Bill nodded, accepting my answer. I hadn't promised what he wanted, but it was close. I pushed down the pang of guilt for not spilling the whole story. Things were too new between us. If only we were at the point where I could tell him everything and get his help. That kind of trust took time, and I wasn't quite there.

"Does that mean we can get out of this line and go have a steak?"

I grinned. "Absolutely."

"What else have you been doing to check out this guy that you haven't told me?"

I inwardly groaned. It was going to be a long evening.

27

I grabbed my ankle and pulled it to stretch out my quadriceps. Holding it, I searched for Angie. We'd agreed to meet near the check-in station at seven thirty. It was way too early for me to be up on a Saturday morning.

I'd already picked up my number. Since I'd registered so late, I hadn't quite met the minimum contributions, but I'd done the best I could. Bill and I had talked a long time the night before, but he hadn't had much to add on the cigars. He knew where the shops were, but that was about it. The best suggestion he'd had was for me to ask Angie. If my memory was correct, she was part of the owners' group for the historic district.

While I waited, I texted Stephanie to let her know I'd call her about eleven. Plenty of time to finish the walk and get a bite to eat.

After I texted her midweek, she had finally texted me back with a smiley face emoji. No conversation then. It wasn't much, but kept us in touch. If I wanted to catch up with her and talk, today was the day. I tried never to miss it and was hoping we were moving toward talking more often, but I'd already let her know about the breast cancer five-kilometer run.

"Hey there. You registered?" Angie asked.

"Yeah."

Angie was a dedicated runner and moved with the grace and confidence of one comfortable with her body. Behind her were two others.

"This is my friend Trisha," Angie said. "And this is Cindi, who I think you've met before, and Judy."

Cindi, with an *i* not a *y*. We'd only met once, at the salon, but I remembered it well. I never understood how anyone could have hair in Savannah that never frizzed. Or at least it never frizzed in public. I mean, how could that be? In a hundred percent humidity, Cindi's fine golden strands lay straight. Yes, I was envious. She was one of those women who could afford to have her hair and nails done every week as well as for special occasions, which was often. She had a handsome doctor husband and the two children, a boy and a girl. She had the dog and the Lexus. It was a perfect life. I didn't hate her. I envied her. Or rather, I craved life that looked perfect. My life wasn't perfect, and I suspected hers wasn't either. But hers looked that way, and I had never quite managed to come close to what she seemed to have—even for an hour. Certainly not at this hour on Saturday morning.

I didn't know Judy, but she looked like she fit into the same mold. One I would never fit into and, if I were honest, didn't want to. They reflected more of my mother's idea of what a woman was supposed to be. More women joined our group. We decided to walk the first mile or so. After that, anyone who wanted to run could head off. The first mile would be my best chance to learn about "Stone," which gave me less than a half hour to steer the conversation in a particular direction.

The first ten minutes were spent catching up on who was doing what. Angie must have noticed I was fidgeting because she turned the conversation in a different direction—families, kids, and dating. I half-listened as I waited for an opening.

"Hey, did y'all read about the guy getting killed by the airport?" Judy asked.

My ears perked up, and I about fell over.

"Scary. To think we were talking to him at the Masquerade Casino Night event, and now he's dead," Cindi said.

"Was that the blond guy? Brandon something," Angie said.

"Yeah. The one hitting on the blondes," Judy said.

"Creepy," Angie said.

"Yeah, I wonder why anyone would murder him," I said.

"I don't know," Judy said. "My mama said never speak ill of the dead, but I think he might have been dating a pilot's wife."

A pilot's wife. The police might have ruled out the flight crew too quickly. I'd have to check back on the pilots again. And I might need to mention this to John as well.

"I'm not sure that's right," Cindi said. "I thought he was dating a few women, all who thought they were his girlfriend. Could have been any number of them, although I'm not sure a cheating guy is enough to kill over. I think they'd drop him once they found out."

I had to agree with her logic. One more item to check out. Or maybe the husband could have done it. Coming on this run had been a good idea. I'd have to thank Angie later.

The conversation turned to what shop was having a sale. I zoned out. After a few more blocks, Cindi announced she was going to start running. Judy followed her.

Angie caught my arm and slowed her walk.

"Okay, spill it. Now that the girls are gone, you need to tell me everything. Don't leave out any details."

I brought Angie up to date, including the need to find out more about cigars, but leaving out Aunt Harriett showing up.

She was quiet for a minute. "I doubt he'd see you without me but we could try Russell."

"Who's that?"

"Russell Mercer. He owns the tobacco shop on West Bryan. Or one of his employees might be able to help us. That would be easier. Russell's a bit of a recluse."

I almost tripped over my feet. I wasn't sure what Angie would think about Aunt Harriett, but this was too good to be true. If this was the same man, I could scope out the guy for Aunt Harriett.

"How about Monday? How do you know this guy?"

"Oh, Russell's on the board for one of the charities I'm involved in. And in the owners' group, although he rarely comes to meetings. The charity board he and I are on arranged the Masquerade Casino Night the girls were talking about."

I vaguely remembered Angie mentioning the event. I'd also taken at least one fare to the airport at the end of the weekend. But I never attended anything like that. It was a bit out of my social circle.

"I'll call and see if he's available. If not, we can stop by and see if his employees can help you."

"Great. How about eleven?" That way, I could sleep in a bit and be rested up. And it was fun to have Angie involved in all this.

"Sounds good."

I smiled. Nothing like a good friend to help make things seem brighter.

"Ready to run?"

I nodded. We took off.

28

After I said goodbye to Angie, had a drink of water, cooled down, and caught my breath, I pulled my phone from my backpack to call Steph. A bit earlier than I'd said I'd call but worth a shot. Before I could dial, the phone rang.

"Mom. Why didn't you tell me about the murder?" Steph demanded.

"Whaa..." I was so surprised she had called me I almost dropped the phone. That was as far as I got before she cut me off.

"I mean, you know an actual person who was murdered! And he rode in your cab. Did you see him get killed? Were you questioned? What was it like?"

I was thrilled she was interested in something involving me. But less than excited that she wanted the details. Still, I couldn't blame her. I always liked reading murder mysteries and crime stories in the paper. She and I shared the same fascination.

"Gosh, I'm not sure where to start. The man was in my cab. He was pretty obnoxious. One of the other passengers asked me to put him out. So, I did. I don't know what happened to him after that. I mean other than he was killed."

"Oh."

"But I was interrogated at the police station." That might be a bit strong, but I couldn't help myself.

"Wow, did they handcuff and frisk you?"

"No. I was there because I was one of the last people who saw him. And they questioned me in one of those rooms with the glass on the wall like you see on TV."

"Was it a good cop/bad cop questioning?"

"Sorry, no. It was mostly questions about what happened. Then they let me go home."

"Oh. I thought maybe it would be more interesting."

I could tell she had lost interest and was about to hang up. I couldn't contain myself.

"They let me go, but since I'm already involved, I thought I'd do a bit of digging on the guy. You know, check out where he lives, see what's on the internet, similar sort of stuff."

My tongue was going to be sore from biting it. A part of me was screaming that I had no business telling Steph any of this, and the other part was a mother desperately wanting to reach out and connect with her daughter. Shameful? Maybe, but I missed our talks and her company. I also wanted her to be safe. I'd tell her only the things I knew wouldn't put her in danger or scare her.

"Cool. Do you need any help? What have you found out so far? Is it dangerous?"

I smiled at her enthusiasm. At the same time, I knew I was about to burst her bubble. "Not much so far. Mostly background stuff. You remember John Davidson, right? My friend from high school. He's on the case. I'm going to turn over whatever I find to him. I don't know who killed the guy, but it's the cops' job to find the perp."

I'd thrown in the perp cuz I'd heard the term on TV.

"I have a few ideas of things I don't know that they will know to ask. I'm trying to help, but not get in the way and not make a dumb move, if I can help it."

"Oh."

"But I'll let you know if I find out anything." I hoped that would keep her interest.

Steph didn't reply.

"I could update you as I know more, if you like. You would be in the know for what I give to the cops."

"Okay. Let me know when something good happens, or you find out new information. Before it hits the paper. I mean, I should know what my mom is involved in before the rest of the world, don't you think?"

Ugh. Here I'd called every week for the same thing and gotten no real response. I didn't know if Steph got the irony of all this, but I certainly got it. My mother and I hadn't talked much at Steph's age either, but it had more to do with our differences in women's roles in life that were changing as I grew up and her age. My mother also disapproved of multiple marriages. And all the other things she thought I'd done wrong in my life. I guessed that every generation of moms and daughters had their issues. I wanted ours to be over soon so we could go back to having a great relationship again.

"I've gotta go, Mom. Don't do anything crazy, okay?"

"Bye, hon. I'll be talking to you." We hung up. I was exhausted from the run and headed home for a nap before heading to work. Saturday nights were always busy, but I was happy to have talked to Steph, even if I didn't get to ask her much about her week.

You never knew when raising kids. I was trying to save my job and keep ahead of an angry spirit. Who'd have guessed that might help me with Steph. If doing a bit of investigating helped with our relationship, it was one more reason to keep doing this. I'd call her midweek rather than texting to see how she was doing. She might not be there, but it would be worth a try. I wanted to be sure she wasn't getting in deeper with all the Goth stuff she was already into or something worse. In the meantime, I was running from one ghost and talking to another. Crazy was relative in this situation and appeared to run in the family.

29

Sunday morning came way too early. I waited, coffee cup in one hand, the other hand on the cool granite counter to steady me, staring at the floor. I decided that having my back against the cabinets would make sure, this time, Aunt Harriett didn't take me by surprise. I watched the digital clock roll over to ten.

And she arrived.

No poof, no air movement, just a white swirling mist settling into the figure of my aunt, sort of like when you flew through clouds that looked solid from the ground but were wisps when you saw them outside the plane window.

"Morning, dear. Was that better?"

I took a breath and smiled.

"Don't get used to it. I can't always schedule when I need to talk to you or can show up."

"It's okay. I wanted to see how it might work."

"Did you get what I asked for?"

I nodded and pointed to the country table holding court in my kitchen. I had a container of water. Jessica had been in her shop when I arrived and knew what I needed after I answered a lot of questions. There was a science to sage smudging. She'd ended up selling me the basics, five clumps. I was sure there was a technical word for it, but it looked like clumps of brown dried herbs to me. No magical powers that I knew of, but then again Cousin Iris might have known more. I could see Aunt Harriett, but I had no talent with herbs, as far as I knew.

"Great. Now we need to take a road trip, as you would call it."

"Where are we going?"

"A bit east. Toward Tybee Island. I'll direct you as we go."

I had a vision of a ghost riding shotgun that sent giggles up from my stomach, only to have it turn into a reality once we settled into the Accord. As unreal as things were, I trusted her and was glad to have time to ask more questions. "Is this my gift?" I turned over the motor and began backing out of the driveway. When she didn't answer, I glanced across the beige seat and could see she was puzzled. "You know, like Great-aunt Agnes's cures or Cousin Iris's foretelling of events. Will other ghosts want to talk to me?"

"You mean, will you be crazy like Great-grandma Sebelia? She didn't actually talk to spirits, you know. She couldn't bear the loss of any loved ones. Her way of dealing with things was going to the cemetery, where she thought they could hear her."

What a relief.

"But you may be like your great-aunt Maude."

"How?"

"She was born with the gift of sight. When her mother figured it out, she told Maude to hush up about it and never tell anyone. It wasn't until she was sick that she told me. Thought I might inherit her gift once she died. I didn't, but I think I'm the only one she told later in life. She always regretted ignoring all the spirits, from what I could tell."

Aunt Harriett let me stew on this for a short distance. "I don't know the extent of this for you, or if our bond will be strong enough so I can reach out to you when I know you are threatened. We'll have to see. It may be that now that you've seen me, you'll see others.

There are quite many of us roaming the earth. Looking for loved ones, confused, or trying to make things right."

Aunt Harriett was silent while the implications sunk in. "It would be a great service to them if you can help them. Provided you can see and hear them."

I sucked in a breath and almost choked. I reached for the insulated metal water bottle I kept in the console between the seats and drank. "Let's see how this goes first. I've only begun to get used to you being here. A lot of other ghosts with problems isn't what I need." I had no idea what this might mean or how I might deal with all of what was happening. I could barely conceive of owning a cab company. What would being a ghost helper mean? That could be a full-time job in a city with so many buried from the Civil War who might be wandering around. The last thing I wanted was to be like the character on TV who was continually being haunted by them and their problems.

"I completely understand. I wouldn't foist anything on you. You know me better than that."

Hmmm. Not sure about that one. "So, where are we going?"

We'd already traveled out of the downtown district, and I took the highway ramp onto Route 80.

"Keep on this road for a while. I'll let you know when to get off."

"What are we doing?" I tried a different tactic. The bowl, water, smudge sticks, and a clean hand towel were on the same front seat as Aunt Harriett, almost clear as day among the pale whiteness. Except now, Aunt Harriett was shimmering so she resembled a mother of pearl. I wondered if spirits gave off a different look when they were excited.

I checked my mirror. No other cars were around, which was great. I figured most people would think I was talking on my phone or singing along with a song. Or they'd think I was crazy talking away as if there was another person in the car with me. Little did they know.

"So, you've got me for the morning. Where are we going? I know it's connected to the family, but I don't know this area, so I can't even venture a good guess."

"I knew you were one sharp cookie. I've been to the dock, which was a good idea, but no luck. We're headed to where the Mercers lived back then."

"Do they still live there?"

"No, but there's an old cemetery." Before I could ask more questions, she said, "Turn off at the next exit, then go left at the stoplight."

I followed her directions as we headed down James Road. This part of the Isle of Hope was unfamiliar to me. The two-lane road was lined with trees. There weren't any houses that I could see. All I knew for sure was we were headed toward the Wormsloe Plantation, which was at the southern end of the island.

"Slow down. We're near the turnoff. There's a driveway to a house nearby. We need to go a short way past it."

I slowed to twenty miles per hour, which was okay because we'd left any traffic behind a while ago.

"There. A foot or so before where the new group of magnolia trees begins."

I could almost make out a weedy gray gravel trail. I turned right. We bounced along through the potholes on the two tracks, which were a bit more worn than the green and brown grassy center. I wished I'd driven the SUV that would have taken the bumps better.

"All the way to the end. It's a short distance. There's a circle there to park and turn around."

I obeyed. Two minutes later, I was parking among the trees in a shady spot. A small area to the right was cleared and what must have been a family cemetery, long neglected, was fenced off with a rusty metal half-fence, almost as if whoever this belonged to had only half-tried to protect it.

Gathering up the required elements, I climbed out. There were about ten headstones. There were sandstone remnants, worn and crumbly from the humidity and moisture. Most were granite markers, and, while obscured by weeds, the chiseled markings were clear. "I assume we're looking for Peter's grave, right? And that you know where it is?" I stepped over the metal fence.

"Yes. It's in the far right-hand corner."

Ten steps and I was standing over an engraved granite marker flat against the ground. "Wasn't this family wealthy? I would have thought they'd have elaborate headstones."

"That's what I remember too. But there aren't any here. Although, I haven't been out here in over thirty years. I was hoping you could answer that question."

"Okay. That should be easy enough to track. Is Peter buried here or not?"

"I don't know. There is a bit of residue from his body. I can sense it, but not much else. But it does not matter. I have it on good authority that sometimes spirits need their burial place cleansed. Otherwise, they can be trapped."

"And who might the good authority be?" I wasn't sure I wanted to know.

"Others who have been where I am. They have a lot more experience at this, so I have asked around. And Eddie is helpful. Did I tell you he is looking for his sister? She is missing too."

Great. "What do I do?"

"This would be better at midnight. I don't suppose I could talk you into coming back then? No? Okay. Take out the bowl. Careful you don't touch the inside part. We don't want your earthly essence mixing with the water and herbs."

I could feel her watching as I laid the bowl on the ground by Peter's marker.

"Now, you need to bless the water."

"How? Is there something special I need to say?"

"No, just a general blessing."

"Please bless this water for use on this earth. Bless Peter Mercer's family and Peter. Bless my family and me. Please bless Aunt Harriett and Eddie in their searches." I looked over at her.

She nodded. "Now, clear the weeds around the marker. Then pour the water into the bowl. Pour a bit of the water on the gravestone."

I finished the tasks and looked to her for guidance.

"Now, wipe clean the marker." When I was finished, she said,

"Pour more water on the marker so it cleans it further. The next step is to pour the water on the dirt where the grave was. Just a few drops here and there."

Emptying the bowl, I almost dropped it as a new deep-throated growl said, "What do you think you're doing there, girlie?"

30

I turned around to face a gnarled older man in full camouflage, holding a .22 rifle, pointed at the ground, with his finger on the trigger. His mouth looked stained from chewing tobacco, and his skin was tanned to the point of being cracked leather that matched his brown hiking boots. He must have come from the woods, although I'd not heard even the crack of a twig.

"It's a long story."

"Always is when youngsters are up to no good. I've got time."

My back and shoulders straightened. I was hardly a youngster. Truth, or as close to it as possible, was going to be the best plan. "My aunt Harriett died, and she asked me to cleanse a grave for her. I haven't had a chance before today. I wanted to honor her request."

He studied me for a minute. I held my ground.

"Family obligations. They're important. But this isn't your family."

"No, but she knew them when she was a young girl, and Peter was her boyfriend."

He stared at me, considering what I'd said. "Who'd you say your aunt was?"

"Harriett. Harriett Reede."

"I remember her. Ran after Peter like a dog with a stick too big for his mouth. Never saw what was right in front of her. His family would never have allowed them to marry."

Aunt Harriett huffed. "I know him. Henry Rollins. He doesn't know anything. But he was willing to eat my peach pie. That was good enough for him."

He continued, "Cleansing this is nonsense. Won't bring him back. Besides, the family moved the graves when they sold the property. You'd be better off leavin' things be. If you're a Reede, you know your family history. Don't go messin' with the spirit world. Or is it already too late?"

"You're Henry. You seem to have liked her peach pie."

"Damn it all. If there was one woman who would've come back, it would have to be Harriett. But if she's here, ask her how many times I asked her to marry me."

I had to give him credit, he was more astute than I realized, and I hadn't guarded my reactions to his words carefully enough. "Aunt Harriett said four."

He laughed but quickly became serious. "I loved Harriett. She was one hell of a woman, but you be careful now. Spirits have their own rules. I've heard they don't always tell you what you need to know. Best you be getting on now. And tell Harriett she should move on too. Best for everyone, including her."

"That is such a bunch of hooey," Aunt Harriett said. "Don't listen to him. I would never hurt you. You are, or well, were, my blood kin. That matters above all else."

"I haven't smudged the grave yet," I said.

"Do it quickly and then leave. The new owners don't much like people wandering around. You're trespassing on private land."

"Aren't you too?"

"I have permission. In return, I watch out for the grounds and run off those ones shouldn't be here. Seeing as you're related to Harriett, I'll forget about you being here this once. Don't come back. This here's a one-time opportunity, so to speak." He began to laugh again.

I didn't like the tone of his laughter, but I nodded and watched him head back into the woods. "What do you think?"

"Peter was buried back here. The headstone is gone, so his grave may have been moved. I think you have more than enough sage for us to smudge the area too, as a precaution, don't you think?" Aunt Harriett smiled.

I nodded. The smudge stick began to burn as I brought the lighter flame to its end. A waft of sage and smoke rose from my hand. Aunt Harriett had me wave it over where she thought Peter had been buried. Then the surrounding area until she was satisfied we'd purified this as best we could. I said a final blessing before I gathered everything up and headed back to the Accord.

Once settled inside, Aunt Harriett asked, "Can you find out where else the Mercer family could be buried now?"

I didn't need research to know where the graves were likely located. Every cab driver in the city knew the Mercer-Williams house and the Bonaventure Cemetery. A short three miles east of downtown Savannah, the cemetery lay on the Wilmington River.

The Mercer family plots were near the back. It was a popular tourist destination, formally having been a plantation. Moss-covered trees, similar to those in the historic district on the squares, colorful azaleas, and statuary drew many tourists.

So many that the Bird Girl statue from the movie, *Midnight in the Garden of Good and Evil*, was replaced with a replica and the original moved to the Telfair Museum of Art downtown.

I backtracked to Savannah, detouring to the Bonaventure after I stopped for more water. Would we find Peter's grave there, and if we did, would Peter's spirit be there too?

I usually let my fares off outside the cemetery by the small gravel parking lot. The wrought iron entrance marked where the roads inside the Bonaventure became more like gravelly one-lane trails surrounded by grassy areas, with blocks of family plots, markers, and statues farther in. People stopped and parked, so you had to go around them. I didn't know the cemetery well enough to maneuver in the less-traveled areas. I headed in on the main road, following signs to Section H, where the Mercers' plot was located. I parked and walked deeper into the cemetery. There were tourists taking pictures as Aunt Harriett and I approached. I hung back on the path as she wandered among the headstones and grave markers. I couldn't tell if Aunt Harriett was reading them or sensing anything. The carvings on the statues were so delicate and intricate. I could see why so many people were drawn to wander here.

"Trisha," I heard her call.

She was in a far corner, standing before a small engraved stone, seeming more grayish-blue in the shade sheltered by moss-covered live oak trees.

"I found it."

I walked through the stones, making sure to step around the actual graves, knelt, and swiped my hand across it to clear the debris so I could read the words. *Beloved Son*.

This section was less well maintained and, although it was sad, I was glad there were fewer people around. I repeated the ritual with the water and sage. I saw a tear on Aunt Harriett's face, but it could have been what was again white mist swirling. Except, now she was no longer shimmering.

When I finished, I asked, "What now?" I'd thought maybe we'd see Peter erupt after if he'd been trapped.

"I don't know. Sometimes the spirit shows up when it's called. Other times it can take days. I think I'll stay here a while and see if he comes."

"I'm sorry, Aunt Harriett. I know you must have hoped he'd be here."

"Go on now. I know you have things to do. I'll check back on you again."

"Could I have done this wrong?"

Aunt Harriett looked around, checking for what only she could see or know. "No, but if Peter's bound by a spirit or there's another power at work, then he might not be able to show himself. If that's the case, we might have to take stronger steps."

I wasn't sure what those might be. I thought about telling her I was to meet Russell, but she was lost in thought and starting to fade. Henry might have been right about not messing with spirits, but I couldn't let Aunt Harriett down. The problem was, I wasn't sure I could do what she might need.

31

I settled onto the wooden bench in Johnson Square to wait for Angie, glad the weekend was over. Sunday night had been chaotic, with lots of people traveling. We'd had the regular groups leaving town, but there were lots of cars on the road as well. That made for a treacherous evening when nothing went right. The flight crew had ended up with other cabs while I was across the city.

As I settled on the wooden bench this Monday morning, a slight breeze with the barest hint of tobacco blew the leaves of the live oaks, sending whispers all around me. I thought of Aunt Harriett. I hadn't given much credence to ghosts in the past and certainly not in this square. It might have been the absence of the Spanish moss here. I'd heard the legends about how Nathaniel Greene was buried there and how, while living, he hated the moss so much he had his slaves pick it from the trees at his plantation. After his burial in the square, the moss quit growing from the trees. I was sure there was a scientific reason, but I hadn't researched it. I rather liked the thought a dead person could cause it, although ghosts were more easily imagined with the moss.

A bark startled me. A dog was snapping at a bit of black on the sidewalk before it disappeared. It looked up at me and then wandered over to nudge at my toe, investigating the bottom of my shoe. His long tongue scraped the sole, and I silently wished him a happy meal.

"Digger."

A longing look for another lick gave way to his owner's call.

As I watched a family struggling with a map, I thought about my conversation with Bill about the cigars. He'd been right about what shops were around. And that Angie knew the owner of the Savannah Tobacco Shop. But then, Bill was usually right. It could be annoying, so I almost hated to ask him things. The cigars had been a different story. I knew Bill loved cigars, and I had been surprised he didn't know the owner. Bill was the kind of guy who walked into a shop and walked out knowing everyone there. What kind of recluse was the man? I couldn't imagine owning a shop for over thirty years and not being there every day, especially when he lived over the shop. I hoped the employees knew a lot about cigars or, if not, I figured Angie could talk her way into the owner's apartment. If I were a betting woman, which I wasn't, I'd lay odds on Angie.

Russell Mercer. An old and familiar family name in Savannah, but it told me nothing else about the man. Angie had said he had a physical deformity. That didn't tell me much. With no other close relatives, he was the last of his line. Aunt Harriett hadn't told me much else about him. She was more focused on his brother, Peter.

What kind of personality did he have? I needed information and how to approach him. I had tried to reach Aunt Harriett after giving her time alone at the cemetery but realized I'd never asked her how to do that. A whisper calling her name hadn't worked. Neither had yelling for her in her old room.

"Hey, daydreamer," Angie said with a laugh as she approached. "Readying yourself for battle with Russell?"

My cheeks heated. I stood and stretched. "Yeah. You know me. I like to have my approach planned out. But I don't know anything about him. Were you able to reach him?"

"No. He doesn't always answer his phone. And he has no voice mail or message center. He's a bit old-fashioned. But, as I said, don't worry. And don't stare at him. He can be very self-conscious with new people."

"Are you going to tell me why?"

"He's very short and slight. More so than others. You'll see. I've never asked what caused the defect—and he doesn't talk about it. We might get lucky, and one of the employees will be able to help us."

I straightened. "Okay, let's head over."

The store was two blocks over. The sun warmed my back and eased part of the tension in my shoulders. Being out of the cab and on my feet felt like a vacation.

As we crossed the street, I heard the strains of Santana's "Oye Como Va" and knew we were close. My eyes widened as I realized the music was spilling out of an all-glass storefront with open doors. My perception of a dark smoky backroom shop couldn't have been more wrong. The shop was light, airy, and extremely clean. And the electric guitar and drumbeat of the song, well, it made me want to dance through the kaleidoscopic reflections. Anyone who played Santana in their shop couldn't be too difficult, could they?

Angie touched my arm. "Are you going in?"

I grinned. "Yep. Just loving the sunshine and the historic build-ings today."

A college-aged guy worked the cash register, finishing up with the customer in the shop. His eyebrows rose when he saw us. "Help you ladies?"

Where to start?

"I was given this cigar. It looks Cuban, but I'm not sure if it's real."

The guy frowned.

"I'm looking for an expert who might know," I continued.

"I don't think I can help you. I've only worked here for a couple of months."

Angie stepped forward and flashed a brilliant smile. "We had hoped there might be an employee here could help us, so we didn't have to disturb Russell. Russell Mercer, the owner," she continued in response to the puzzled look she received. "Is he around? Could you let him know Angie Kokett is here and would love a few minutes of his time?"

Angie continued to smile, and I wondered if anyone could ever refuse her when she turned on the charm.

The guy looked uncertain.

"I have a shop in the historic district too. I've worked with Russell on several matters relating to owners' issues. Besides, we've known each other for ages," Angie said.

I almost laughed at Angie's Southern drawl of the word "ages." If it wasn't clear how long she'd known Russell from the words, it was from her exaggeration. I wished I could manage to pull that kind of act off.

"We're not supposed to call him unless it's an emergency," the guy said.

"Please. I know Russell would want to know I was here," Angie said.

I believed her, and I could see she was wearing the guy down. I wanted to help but was afraid I'd destroy the moment if I added my pitch.

"I'll take full responsibility for the call," she said.

The guy turned around and reached for the phone. "Mr. Mercer? I have a lady here who's asking to speak to you."

The guy listened.

"I know, but she says she knows you," he said, his voice tapering off.

"Angie Kokett," he said with a certain defeat in his voice.

"Sure." His face brightened. "I'll send her right up."

I was amazed. Angie had worked her magic again.

"I know the way. We'll need you to unlock the downstairs door," Angie said as the clerk started to give her directions.

We moved to the back of the shop. The young man stepped forward to unlock an ancient wooden door.

"Thanks again for all your help." She gave him another dazzling smile as we began to climb the stairs.

Behind us, the door closed and Angie said, "Don't forget what I told you. No staring."

"I haven't forgotten. You won't let me." I huffed. "What's with the door?"

"Russell collects things. From his travels. He's a bit security conscious."

That was an understatement. If it hadn't been for Angie knowing him, I might have turned and left.

32

At the top of the staircase, there was a small landing, then a door. Angie moved forward and knocked. I steeled myself for whatever was behind the door. The last thing I wanted to do was embarrass myself or worse, Angie, after she'd gotten us this far. I had two things riding on this meeting.

The door opened. I lowered my gaze. A miniature man stood there in what I could only describe as a black velvet morning coat, paisley vest, and trousers—stylish for the last century. The man couldn't have stood more than four feet tall. He looked to be in his late sixties, but his stature made it difficult to tell. He was so slender he appeared emaciated, but without wrinkles. And his skin was white and almost translucent. But that couldn't be right, could it?

The shop appeared prosperous, and the cut of his clothes, while not current century, was expensive. I caught myself staring at the oyster shell buttons.

"Russell." Angie stepped forward to plant a kiss on his cheek. "So good of you to see us on such short notice."

Russell accepted her kiss and smiled at her.

"And this is my friend Trisha." She turned to me.

I stepped forward and offered my hand. "It's nice to meet you. My thanks as well for seeing us."

I smiled and pulled my gaze away from Russell. Angie met my gaze, and I could feel her approval that I wasn't staring.

Russell opened the door wider. "Come in. I was about to have tea. Would you like a cup?" He moved from the doorway.

We followed him into the next room, which had all the trappings of a Victorian parlor. This man lived in a different era, or tried to. As I looked closer, I saw the mantel and shelves held current books and what looked like mosaics and Middle Eastern pottery. Had Russell traveled all his life, or did he live his life through purchased items and the framed photographs from foreign lands hanging on the walls? Was he always a recluse or only in Savannah? I'd have to ask Angie. Or maybe Aunt Harriett knew more than she'd told me, like Henry had said in the cemetery. She hadn't prepared me for all this. Then again, I hadn't told her I was seeing Russell today.

I explored the room while Russell and Angie left to make the tea. A flash crossed an ornate mirror, and I looked around to find Russell and Angie returning from the kitchen.

"May I have the honor of pouring?" Angie asked.

Russell appeared pleased. Angie filled the porcelain cups. We sipped our tea in silence for what seemed like minutes but was likely less.

Russell set his teacup down. "Now, to what do I owe the pleasure of your company today?"

I didn't think anyone ever said that outside of the movies and had to stifle a giggle. This man was an expert. I was asking for his help. Offending him wasn't on my list of things to do. Plus, he might be able to help Aunt Harriett.

Angie turned to me. "Trisha needs some expert advice. We thought you could help."

"If I can," said Russell. "What's this about?"

"I have this cigar I'd like to know more about." I removed the cigar from my purse and handed it to Russell. "I think it's Cuban, but that might be illegal, right? It may be a fake."

"Is the person one you care about? Or who cares about you?" Russell asked.

I was sure the surprise showed on my face. I wasn't prepared for questions like this. "No. More of an acquaintance. But I'd like to know about him." That was true, as far as it went.

Russell smiled. "I'm familiar with this label. You can purchase a package of twenty-five of them for about ten dollars on the internet."

I tried to process what he was telling me. "You mean he changed the label on a cigar so it would look like it was Cuban?"

"Exactly," said Russell.

"Wouldn't most people know the difference?"

"Did you? What made you suspicious?" he asked.

"I don't know the difference, but I do know Cuban cigars are illegal. Or at least I thought they were. That's what made me ask," I said.

"Do you mind if I unwrap this?"

"No. Please do. I'd like to know what kind of cigar this is."

Russell's slight hands painstakingly unwrapped the label without tearing it. He removed the cellophane just as carefully. He raised the cigar, turning it around in his fingers.

"A true Cuban has a solid chocolate color and very few veins." Russell lifted the cigar and passed it under his nose.

I held my breath, then tried to breathe as I watched this man pondering the aroma.

"Do you know the history of cigars?" Russell asked.

I groaned inside. I wanted to know where it was from, not a history lesson. "No."

Russell laughed. "And you don't want to, I think. Here is the condensed version."

He watched me as he took a sip of tea, until I nodded for him to continue.

"When Cuban imports were outlawed, a number of the cigar makers immigrated to Nicaragua. The climate and dirt there are ideal for growing tobacco. Those people took with them the expertise to make excellent cigars. Nicaraguan cigars are considered superior to Cuban cigars by many."

"Are you saying this is a Nicaraguan cigar?"

"A man who changes a label on a cigar is of a certain ilk. He may be a man who is trying to put on airs regarding things he may not be able to afford. Or one who buys them to resell for profit. Then again, he may be a man who can afford the best but chooses not to spend the money."

That almost sounded like Aunt Harriett. How tightly connected to this family had she been? He was clearly of the social class she'd have grown up in.

Angie cleared her throat, and I realized Russell was waiting for an answer from me.

"Sorry. I was thinking about what you said. I think he was the first kind. You see, he was murdered, and I am trying to find out why," I said.

"Perhaps someone guessed at the difference? Killed him for the deception. Or he sold a cigar to a party who learned they had been cheated?" Russell asked.

I pondered this. "Maybe. I think he may have given cigars to people who would not have known or wouldn't have cared enough to kill him." I considered his words. Selling the cigars didn't make sense. Brandon would have had to move a lot of them to make it worth his while, and it would have been hard, involving help.

Russell lifted the cigar again and drank in the smell. "What you have said about the man confirms what I think. The cigar is Nicaraguan. They can be legally purchased, and, except for a knowledgeable connoisseur like me, it would pass for Cuban. Of course, it's difficult to know. Even I could possibly be fooled, although that is unlikely. I have spent my life around tobacco and cigars."

I stared at him. Not because of his size but of his self-assurance. As he sat on the couch and talked, he'd grown to six feet tall in my eyes. I had no doubt he knew what he was talking about. Brandon wasn't a smuggler. While he may have had activities that got him killed, this wasn't likely the cause. I'd ask John, but I had a gut feeling this was a dead end.

Darn, I'd thought for sure the cigars had been involved. And that

Brandon had been killed either for smuggling them or for not selling them quickly enough to pay off his debt. They didn't appear to be related to the murder at all, other than to show more of who Brandon was.

"I believe you," I said.

"You're unhappy with that answer," Russell said.

"No. I wanted to know. But the answer means I need to look in another direction for what I need to know."

Russell gave me a quizzical look.

"It's a long story, but I appreciate your help. And you have a lovely home. Are all these antiques from your travels? And the pictures, are they from there too?"

Russell smiled. "Yes. I've been lucky enough to travel the world. And many of the photographs are from those trips. Others are family."

"Brothers or sisters?" I asked.

"One brother. Sadly, he died when I was young. I miss him terribly."

"I'm sorry," I said, knowing he was Peter's brother.

"And you, my dear." Russell addressed Angie before I could ask more. "You've been uncharacteristically quiet. Is there anything I can do for you?"

"No. You've been most helpful. I can't thank you enough. Let me know if there's something I can do for you," said Angie. "I know you must have a busy day, so we should leave."

Angie and Russell rose. As they moved toward the door, I followed them.

"Thank you for the tea." Angie air-kissed both of Russell's cheeks.

"I appreciate your time," I said.

As we exited, Russell handed the cigar back to me. "It's an excellent cigar. Give it to a smoker who would appreciate it.

"But," he added, "don't try to fool them. They'll be happier if you're honest with them."

I wasn't sure if he was talking about the cigar, but I knew it was good advice.

33

Angie and I hugged goodbye, promising to get together soon, and I headed home. I pulled into the driveway as my cell phone buzzed. I checked the caller ID. Steph. She'd called on Saturday, but that was about the murder. Twice in one week was unheard of these days.

"Steph? Is everything okay? Don't you have school this morning?"

Steph had a way of looking down at her feet and dragging one in front of the other when she was struggling with how to deal with me. I imagined she was doing that now.

"It's Stephanie. And everything's fine. I'm on my lunch break. Nothing has to be wrong to call."

"Sorry. I forgot. I'll try harder not to call you Steph. I was surprised you were calling. We already talked on Saturday."

"I know, but I was curious how your investigation is going."

It was a relief we had connected again and she wanted to talk. Even so, I felt guilty for telling her about it.

"I'm at a standstill. I've talked to the people I could think of, but the leads I had haven't panned out."

"Well, what haven't you looked at?"

"Hmmm. I have been thinking about this in terms of what I know and following those leads. That's a good thought."

"So?"

"Give me a minute. I know Brandon dated a lot of women, but I hadn't followed up on who he might have been seeing before he died."

"That's a good idea. It's always the jealous boyfriend or husband on TV shows. Maybe there's one of those here, and he found out about the guy messing with his wife and came after him."

I laughed. It sounded like a TV mystery. Much better than dealing with a loan shark or worse.

"I'm serious. Don't laugh at me. I'm hanging up."

"No. Wait. I was laughing at me. One of the flight attendants I've talked to mentioned he might be seeing a married woman. I haven't had a chance to follow up on it. Your saying that made me remember it. Talking to you is helping me."

Silence reigned. My laughter had also covered the uncomfortable truth that my daughter was a teenager and a smart kid. I'd known that, but, in one quick minute, I'd seen her differently and knew I had to stop treating her like a child.

"I mean it, Stephanie. You're smart and cut right through to the important factors. I sometimes forget how much you have grown up in the last year."

"Thanks, Mom. Gotta run. Let me know if you want to talk more about other areas to investigate." She paused. "And, Mom, if you call me Stephanie, I'm gonna think I'm in trouble. Talk soon."

Steph hung up. I stared at the phone, holding back tears. We'd taken a big step forward in mending the relationship that had become so strained with my last divorce. What I hated was the fact it was a murder investigation bringing us together.

34

I walked into my bedroom and debated taking a warm bath. I was still sticky from the early-morning humidity and decided on a quick shower. There wasn't anything I loved more than soaking in bubbles and vanilla bath oil, but I was so stressed I knew I wouldn't enjoy it. After rinsing off, I slipped into blue shorts and a gray T-shirt. I'd change later for work.

"Trisha."

I groaned. I wasn't sure I could deal with Aunt Harriett today. If she knew I'd met Russell, she'd want all the details. I feigned not hearing her, thinking maybe she would leave. She didn't.

"Oh, all right. You win." I turned around and stared at the form before me. I couldn't be sure, but I would have sworn Aunt Harriett was becoming more solid. She was dressed to the nines again. "Were you out on another date? It's not even happy hour yet."

"Yes. Time is irrelevant to us. Besides, that's not the point. We need to catch up."

"Can't we do this some other time?"

"No. I haven't found any signs of Peter. I wanted to see what you might have found." She paused, and a look of comprehension came over her face. "You met Russell."

It was more a statement than a question. I had no idea how she had figured that out but nodded.

"What did you think of him?"

"He was very knowledgeable." I gathered my thoughts. "He stared at me for a long time when we met. Angie had warned me about his size, so I didn't react or stare at him, but it was weird when he stared at me so long. I don't know why."

"That would be my fault."

"Yours? Why? I know you knew him, but why would Mr. Mercer stare at me?"

"Mr. Mercer? I never thought of him that way. Mr. Mercer was always his father. We've already talked about the family history. I guess now is as good a time as any to talk more about Russell."

I wasn't sure whether to urge her on or not. I knew my aunt only as an older woman who dated but never married. Her love for Peter explained a lot. My father's statement that she was too independent and picky couldn't have been more wrong.

"What happened? I don't understand," I prompted.

Aunt Harriett's shoulders slumped. "I didn't realize Russell had a crush on me. I guess I should have. And I never knew how to help him with the other children. His size and ailments set him apart. By sharing my feelings of loss for Peter, I thought I was helping, but he misunderstood our relationship. I tried talking to him, but he insisted we could make it work. That he could make his mother understand. I knew he couldn't. Even if he wasn't a true Mercer, he carried the name."

Aunt Harriett stared into my eyes. "You see, having had Russell around us so much, I knew him better than he thought. Russell grew to be a good man. He was adept at withstanding storms, but it was because he was flexible, not because he stood firm. I knew that if he had to confront his mother and father, he would bend. I'm not sure he ever really understood why I said no. I hated to hurt him, but I always thought it was kinder than the alternative. You look very much like I did at your age. Hasn't anyone ever told you that?"

Of course. I had forgotten. There had been cryptic remarks and comparisons over the years. Very few pictures existed of Aunt Harriett from her younger years. I wasn't even sure who had those now. I silently vowed to find them. We let the silence hold court. The man I had met was confident but had cloistered himself above the cigar store. Aunt Harriett had created her own life, but without a husband or children.

"Has Russell always lived over the tobacco store?"

"Good heavens, no. Russell found a proper Southern girl his mother approved of. They married. It didn't last long. No children. Russell came to see me not too long after. He finally understood what I had been trying to tell him."

Aunt Harriett paused.

"Russell tried to convince me he was a changed man. His father had died, but his mother was dependent on him. I knew that even if he were different, his mother would make my life a living hell. I turned down his advances for the same reason I had before."

"How sad. For both of you."

"Yes. Russell is a good man. He has his physical limitations, but his heart is in the right place. I never loved him like Peter. It wouldn't have been fair to either of us."

"Have you been to his cigar store or his apartment upstairs? I wonder if Peter might visit him, especially if they were close."

"Maybe. Russell has always done things a bit differently, lived a bit off the track. Most likely because he was afraid people would treat him differently due to his physical stature. I heard he fully embraced the New Age concepts, had psychic readings and the like."

"His apartment had a lot of foreign objects. Lots of candles, antiques, and what looked like collectibles that might be related to the occult. Would he have been the kind of person to go to séances or try to talk to Peter?"

"He was always superstitious, so I would think yes."

"You know, at one point, I saw a flash in a mirror. Russell and Angie came out of the kitchen at the same time, so I thought it was only a reflection. What if Peter was there?" I squeezed my eyes shut.

Things were getting more complicated by the moment. "If I can see you, could I see Peter?"

"Very possibly, my dear. It may have simply been a play of the light, but I think I'll pay Russell a visit and see what he's been up to."

"But if he can see Peter, won't he be able to see you?"

"Yes, but that's exactly what I want. If Russell knows where Peter is, then I want to talk to him face to face so I can gauge his words."

I wanted to bite my tongue, but the words came out anyway. "Do you want me to go with you?"

"No. I have to do this alone."

35

Two hours later, I finished my computer searches. I'd done quick searches for the pilot names. I always greeted them by first names, so their last names didn't come easily. Searches about Golden Wings Airways helped me find them.

Searches on Facebook showed happy family men—with wives and children. Birthday parties and backyard cookouts. Anniversary celebrations. Neither family looked like affairs had been an issue, but I knew better than anyone you could put on a happy face, even while the walls of your marriage were falling apart.

I figured it was unlikely either of the pilots' wives was behind Brandon's death. Both wives had small kids at home. It would have been almost impossible for them to travel to Savannah and kill Brandon without lots of planning. Even then, having a sitter for the kids and being back before their husband returned would be quite the feat. Killing Brandon in their hometown while he was there would have been a more likely choice. There might be a motive. I couldn't completely take them off the list yet.

On the other hand, the pilots might have killed him. Based on the pictures, it was hard to imagine their wives having an affair with a guy like Brandon. The timing would be tight too. They arrived together but would have gone to their separate rooms. One of them could have doubled back and met Brandon near the pond. Difficult. Plus, I suspected John and the police might already have checked out these angles. I added that to my list to ask John next time I saw him.

In the meantime, I planned to talk to the flight crew if I caught their fares tonight. I was hoping I'd get lucky and draw the flight attendants in a talkative mood. I shut down the computer. It was time to get ready for work.

I WAS in the middle of sliding my leg into my jeans when I heard it.

"Dammit! Hurry up and turn around."

I almost didn't recognize the voice underneath all the anger. I'd never heard Aunt Harriett use a curse word before. She was a proper Southern lady, and, in her world, they didn't cuss. I couldn't imagine what I was in for, but I knew I had to move more quickly. There was no telling what would come out of her mouth next if she was swearing.

"I'm dressing. What's wrong?"

"Russell." She let the name hang in the air. "He's known where Peter was the whole time," she huffed. "And Russell knew I was looking for Peter."

"What? Why would Russell do that?"

"Exactly what I asked."

I stared at her. "What did Russell say?"

"That's the problem. He didn't. Who does he think he is? Now he's ignoring me. As if I don't exist."

Well, she kind of didn't, but I knew better than to argue the point.

"I don't understand."

"I don't either. You need to get dressed and go over there and find out why. I'd do it myself, but Russell sees ghosts, so I'm not scary enough. And he put in earplugs when I started to yell at him. He didn't even care when I knocked his pictures off the wall." She paused. "If I knew how to hit him, that might get his attention. I'll have to have Eddie teach me the art of moving physical objects imme-diately."

I smiled. I couldn't help it. The idea of Aunt Harriett hitting any man with her hand or anything else, let along Russell Mercer, was more than I could handle.

"Stop right there, young lady. I'm serious. A whack to the head with my purse would straighten Russell right up. Don't forget yours."

I lost it and started to laugh. It was too much. I struggled to control it. "I'm sorry, Aunt Harriett," I gasped between giggles. "I can't imagine you hitting anyone. You always told me to be a lady. You set an example for me to follow."

Aunt Harriett watched me, frowning. Slowly her mouth relaxed. She grinned. "Well, what I meant to say is you should always be a lady until it's time not to be one. And then you might have to whack them into shape. But you do it with style, my dear. That makes all the difference."

Ohh. My eyes misted over as I realized how much I had missed her.

"Oh, stop. No getting sentimental on me. I need you to get over to the cigar shop and find out where Peter is—or at least what Russell is up to so I can find Peter myself."

Aunt Harriett disappeared. I closed my eyes and stretched and rolled my head around to get rid of the kink that had shown up in my neck. I opened my eyes. Possum was sitting in her usual spot. I finished dressing and looked around for my leather handbag. I wondered if I'd need it.

As I walked down the hall, I wondered how she had found out Russell was hiding something or if Russell had simply told her outright. If so, why would he do that? Was he holding a grudge for her rejections?

If Aunt Harriett knew Russell knew where Peter was, why couldn't she find him as well? Why couldn't things be easier? If Russell could ignore Aunt Harriett, he might refuse to see me or even open up the door. He'd probably guess why I was there. There had to be an excuse I could use to get me inside so I could grill him. But what?

I reconsidered my outfit. Maybe a skirt was called for. I believed in the old saying that you got more flies with honey than vinegar. I suspected Russell would see right through me. But even with that, would he be intrigued?

It was worth a shot.

I turned around and headed back to my closet. I emerged in a short denim skirt and light green knit top, carrying my work outfit with me so I could change later. For Russell, I drew the line at high heels. He'd be suspicious enough without those screaming my intentions at him. I'd figure out a reason for the drop-in visit on the drive over. I didn't have any more questions on the cigars, but maybe I could talk to him about seeing ghosts or his love of antiques.

36

I parked my Accord a street over from the store. As I was walking, I heard a car slowing and checked behind me. A police car. One with John and his partner. They stopped.

I walked over to the open window. "Hey. What's up?"

"Thought that was you. What are you doing out here?"

"An errand to run that couldn't wait." Not precisely a lie since Aunt Harriett had insisted.

"What's new? I know you're checking around. Anything we need to know about?"

"Well, your timing is great. I was going to call you later today, but hadn't had a chance yet." I proceeded to tell John about the cigars. Not the trip to Brandon's apartment. I fudged a bit on how I knew about the cigars.

"We do have those in evidence but hadn't checked them out yet. Who did you say you talked to?"

I gave him Russell's name, pointed the store out, and made a mental note to tell Russell the police might call him. Although he might assume everyone knew he was an expert if they called.

At the front door of the cigar store, I paused. I wasn't sure what I'd say or what would persuade Russell to see me. Maybe I'd say, "Hi,

Russell. Remember me from this morning? Well, I'm here about a different matter. Aunt Harriett says you're keeping Peter from her. Why is that?"

It didn't sound right.

How did I get myself into these things? I was only trying to make a living and have a good life with a good man. It wasn't fair. A black cloud hung over me, I was deciding on buying a company, and I trying to keep my job. And the police hadn't cleared me yet, so I could be a murder suspect, for all I knew. Then there was Aunt Harriett. But Russell believed in her, so I figured I'd use that.

"Is Russell around?" I asked the same clerk from earlier.

"I'll let him know you're coming up," the guy said.

Interesting. I was on the approved list. At least for now. I wasn't sure I would be after our conversation. I bounded up the stairs.

Russell opened the door as I hit the landing. "So, twice in one day, to what do I owe this honor? And so soon?"

"We need to talk."

"Ominous. Mysterious. I like that in a woman." He laughed.

I moved past him and rolled my eyes. Men. Sometimes you just wanted to strangle them.

I sat down in the closest chair.

"Oh, do sit down."

He appeared to be enjoying this, and I had a suspicion he knew why I was there.

"How are things with Harriett?" he asked.

My eyes narrowed. I hated it when I was trying to be sneaky and never had a chance. I liked to think I was good at reading people and handling these types of situations, but here, Russell was way ahead of me. What had Aunt Harriett been up to, and what had been said between them that she hadn't told me? I'd have to ask her on the next visit. For now, a new approach might give me better results. I decided to be honest—up to a point. "She's a bit confused. She's under the impression you're keeping Peter from her."

"She's right."

I stared at him. I hadn't expected him to be so direct. Or honest. "But why?"

"Because he's my brother. He promised he'd always be here for me."

"Yes. But that doesn't explain anything."

"Sure, it does. Think about it. I've lost my parents. I don't know if my friends are real or people like me because of my money. Harriett died. Peter loves me. He always has. He's the only one I can trust."

"You're holding him hostage for a promise he made as a boy?" I couldn't believe it. Nobody did that. Kids made promises all the time they couldn't or didn't keep. That was part of being a kid. I'd done it lots of time. I'd had good intentions. But you grew up. Changed.

"I lost the older brother who looked out for me. I know my parents treated me well, but they're gone now. When Peter died, it was hard. I found out the other kids were friends with me because of Peter. Do you know how hard that is? To be different and to find out people were pretending to like you?"

"I don't believe it. You had no friends?"

"No. Everyone turned their backs on me. They wouldn't talk to me. No one sat with me at school. I finally asked my parents to have a tutor. They agreed when they saw how miserable I was."

"People don't know what to say when a person dies. Kids in particular. Maybe the other kids didn't know how to talk to you."

"They should have tried harder. How would you feel if everyone stopped talking to you?"

It must have been awful for him. I tried again. "You went to college, didn't you? Didn't you meet friends there?"

"Sure, I met people. They were all nice to me because of my family name and money. I've never had any true friends. That's why I can never let Peter go."

"But what about Angie? She cares about you. I know. She told me. And there must be others like her."

"Angie is nice to me. Nicer than most. But we only see each other for charity events, so it's the same thing. She's nice to me for my money and what I can do for the charity."

I had to clench my fists to stop from slapping this guy. "Angie is the most generous person I know. She'd give the shirt off her back to anyone who needs it. And she's got more than enough connections with her famous director brother. She doesn't need to use you! She's nice to you because that's who she is. And she doesn't say she cares about you if she doesn't. I'm not a liar. Neither is she." I breathed in slowly to cool my anger. How dare he?

Russell watched me. When he spoke again, his voice was almost a whisper. "She's lucky to have a friend like you. I wish there were people in my life who'd defend me, no matter what."

"You could if you'd let a few in. You're pushing everyone away." My anger receded. "You're afraid." I stared at him, waiting for any kind of reaction. "You can't have friends unless you're willing to let them be your friend."

Russell's shoulders fell. "No matter. It's too late, anyway. I'm too old to make lasting friendships. I have Peter. I'm not letting him go. He promised."

"I'm so confused. I don't know what that means."

"You've probably heard people promise they'll be there for you forever?"

I nodded.

"Well, when Peter and I were kids, he knew I was having trouble making friends, with school, and with pretty much everything. We made a promise to each other that we'd always be there. Pinky swear and all. We were going to do the blood brothers thing, but Peter said we had done enough to bind each other forever."

"But he died. Didn't it die with him?"

"No. Peter showed up in a dream and then as a spirit. That's when I began to see ghosts. The point is the bond between us remained in place. Peter is here with me and will be until I die. He goes with me when I travel."

"So, he can't leave this building?"

"Not exactly. He can come and go, but he and I both agreed he wouldn't do anything that would violate his pledge."

"But you could share him. It's not like Aunt Harriett wants him for only herself."

We sat in silence. Then it hit me. "There's more to this than the promise, isn't there?"

Russell smiled a sad little smile.

"You were jealous of them. You're not worried Peter won't be there for you. You don't want Aunt Harriett to have him again."

Russell didn't have to say a word. I knew. My heart went out to him, even as I felt like I was disloyal to Aunt Harriett with those feelings. I thought human relationships were complicated. I thought things got less difficult when you died. I was wrong. How could this be? And how could ghosts be tied to an earthly promise? Unless, of course, they wanted to be. Was there more here? I decided to try again.

"Can I talk to Peter? I'd like to hear what he thinks about all this."

"No. He understands his commitment. He doesn't want to talk about it to you or Harriett or anyone else."

"Why? What can it hurt? I have to report back to Aunt Harriett. She's not going to be satisfied with this."

"Tell her whatever you want, but you can't talk to Peter. I won't help you. Or her."

I sat and stared at Russell. He was unwavering. This wasn't going to work. I'd have to tell Aunt Harriett that Russell wasn't the way to Peter.

I rose from my chair. "*Thanks* for your time. I think you're wrong about a lot of things."

"I know you think you know. But it's my life."

He was right. I walked to the door. Peter had been a popular boy and, while his parents weren't alive, I wondered if there were other relatives or friends still living. There had to be. Or, for that matter, there could be more who weren't alive but were hanging around with unfinished business in the earthly realm. Aunt Harriett would have to find one Peter might be connected with. She wasn't going to be very happy about any of this.

37

She descended on me as soon as I got into my Accord.

"Russell won't let anyone talk to him." Better to get it out right away, like pulling a Band-Aid in one quick move. The pain was immediate but faded quickly.

"What do you mean he won't let anyone talk to Peter?"

I'd heard the phrase "fit to be tied" all my life, but I'd never understood it until now. Aunt Harriett was undoubtedly all that. I could swear her eyes had turned red, and if I got too close, flames would flare out and burn me. It made me wonder where exactly she was. But that was crazy. Although she had a temper when you got her riled up, Aunt Harriett was a good person.

I relayed what Russell had told me.

"Well, that's just nonsense. Russell doesn't think it will work, does he?" She paused, and I could see she was thinking. "Peter can't be with him all the time. I wonder where he goes when he's not there? Sounds like I have more investigating to do on my own. Need anything before I go?"

"Yes. I don't understand most of this. Can you answer a few questions?"

Aunt Harriett's head turned. Did she have a date? Her white

gloves, pumps, familiar pearls, and flowery dress suggested she did, but I was beginning to wonder if it was more like a uniform. But a date with who or what or where? It was a bit overwhelming to try to sort out.

"What is it, girl? Spit it out. What's got you so uptight?" Aunt Harriett smiled.

"I'm trying to understand why you're here. You're not helping me by flitting in and out all the time before I have a chance to ask any questions."

"There's not much to tell."

I waited. I knew my mouth had tensed into a pout Aunt Harriett would recognize.

"Okay. You have my attention. What do you want to know?"

"Are you a ghost? Have you been to heaven? Is there a heaven?"

"That's a bit hard to explain. You know about the light and the tunnel, correct? Everyone always talks about that."

I nodded.

"Well, if you go all the way to the end, then your soul passes over. I didn't get that far. For those like me, we stop along the way—in the Gray."

I stared at her. She had a look on her face that said, "Okay, now I've explained it, can we move on?" I wasn't ready.

"What's the Gray? How does it work?"

"Think of it as your world is laid out. You've got the main city, where lots of people live, and then there are the suburbs. Then there are the neighborhoods. Some are good and others are seedy. In the Gray, the shade is what identifies where you are."

Huh? No one ever talked about stops along the way. "I don't understand. Why would you be in the Gray?"

"I'm in the lighter Gray. I decided to stop for reasons of my own. I was not quite ready to be released from the world. Others are tortured souls who are afraid of the light. Poor things. They don't realize the light would embrace them and heal them.

"For now, they're stuck in the dark Gray. Others were unwilling to let go of their worldly natures and remain, wandering in the middle sameness. I think I'd almost rather be in the deepest darkness if I weren't here. That sameness is a desert of lost souls."

My mouth was edging closer to the floor by the minute. I'm sure I looked like a possum in headlights—frozen in place, afraid to move, not having any idea which way to turn or what to do next.

"Is it like a circle around the light then? With one end lit, and that spreads out into the dark?" I was having trouble with the visuals on this.

"No, dear. More like a straight line. The tunnel leading to the light is a line. From there, it fans out into gray, then darker and then to the blackness. Think about a meadow fanning out as far as the eye can see."

"And what's in the blackness?"

"The lost ones. Deeply troubled ones. I don't know, maybe much worse things. No one talks about it. No one seems to know. Maybe the Supreme Council knows, but if they do, no one talks about it."

The Gray. Blackness. A Supreme Council? I wasn't sure what to believe. I'd never heard of such a thing. Or had I?

"Is the Gray like the Purgatory the Catholics believe in?"

"Oh no, not in that sense. This is not a place of punishment or purification. I have it on competent authority you leave everything behind when you fully step into the light. No, this is more a place a soul chooses to remain for a period of time. And unlike when you die on earth, here, once you decide to move on, you must apply to the Supreme Council first."

My mind was spinning. I had soooo many questions.

"Okay, but why would anyone want to stop off?" I could barely believe I was having this conversation, much less asking these kinds of questions.

"Lots of reasons. A loved one in need. Wanting to watch over a child as he or she grows. Not wanting to let go of a wrong or anger, or of a love. You can't take that with you, and it takes a soul time to sort things out. It's like most things in life. Some can deal with things more easily, and others cannot."

"And the Supreme Council?"

"Oh, they are souls that have passed over but desire to be of service to those who haven't made the last steps. There's also the Lower Council—mostly those were psychologists, social workers, or psychiatrists in their earthly incarnation. They help many to find their way. It's their way of continuing to give back and keeping one foot in the earthly world for others."

She stared at me. "They have special permission to go 'between,' whatever that means. I'm in the process of learning all this, you see. Generally, once you pass through the tunnel and step fully into the light, you cannot return to the Gray."

I laughed at a vision of a cloudlike couch with spirits lying there talking to another lifeforce. The *New Yorker* cartoonists had nothing on me—except I had no artistic bent and who'd ever believe it or think this was funny? More likely, they'd think I was a nutcase.

"Do you live in a neighborhood, or what?" I was trying to relate to this so I could comprehend what she was telling me.

"Heavens, no." Aunt Harriett laughed with a sound like bells chiming. "Nothing like that. It's not that structured. We gravitate to the shade of gray we are most attracted to. Then we create our own space. I have a very nice Victorian as my 'home.'"

I shook my head. This didn't make much sense.

"Trisha, dear. It's not important that you understand where I am or what I am—only that I'm here for you. Trying to make sense of it all will make your head swim. I know. I live it. Mostly, I feel like a minnow—brand new, in water that's all murky where things tend to swirl around. Then other times, it's as clear as the Caribbean coastal waters and makes sense."

Hard for me to imagine. But I could identify with the chaos and murkiness of life. My relationships were a lot like that. I was hoping I'd made a better choice in Bill this time.

"Enough of all this for now. I'm late for a date, and I have to investigate a few things. We'll talk again later."

I started to protest. And then she was gone. I wished I could do that. It sure would have gotten me out of trouble on more than one occasion when I'd stuck my foot in my mouth. I wanted her to stay longer and explain things in more detail. I wasn't sure I understood the Supreme Council, the Gray, or what the blackness was. I had a lot of questions. If I could figure out what else to ask. I'd have to think about all she'd said and make a list for next time. And while I was at it, I'd listed questions and tasks for my investigation.

For now, a place to change clothes was next, and then I'd check in for work. I couldn't wait for this Monday to be over.

38

Dispatch had told me business was slow, so I decided I'd run by The Tea Shoppe to change. In the parking lot, I gathered up my jeans and waited, hoping John would stop by for a cup of tea so I could ask him a couple questions I hadn't asked earlier. I'd about given up when a cruiser rolled by. I watched him find a parking spot up the street from me. I got out as he did. He veered over my way, while his partner headed inside.

"Let's get this over with. Are you waiting for me? I told you to let us handle this."

"I know. I wanted to ask a couple of questions. Then I'll leave you alone. Okay?"

John's face was impassive. I took no answer as permission to go ahead.

"Any new information on Geoff and the loan shark? Did Brandon have unpaid gambling debts?"

"The investigation is ongoing, and we're looking into all it. Don't go there. The guys involved aren't anyone you want to mess with."

I wasn't sure that was true but decided I'd take a different route. I chose my words carefully. "Brandon was dating different women. I heard one was married. Have you considered a jealous boyfriend or husband might be involved?"

Not bad. Better than my normal slash-and-burn blunt self, who might have demanded the information rather than asking.

One of John's eyebrows raised. He folded his arms across his burly chest. "And who might have told you that?"

Thinking I might have struck a nerve in the investigation or that they didn't have this lead, I wondered how to find out exactly what he knew. Honesty, or close to it, might be the best route. "Look, I need to solve this, so I don't lose my job."

John let the silence hang. I understood this game. I could wait him out but decided to raise the stakes first.

"And it's not public, so you can't say a word to anyone, but Sylvie has talked to me about taking on a different role with the company. But it all hinges on not having this hanging over me like a thundercloud."

John's arms came down. "We know the victim was a player. He'd dated a lot of women. There were those who weren't so happy with how he ended it. We have a list to get through. I have to get back to work. My partner's got our drinks. I need you to tell me what you know now. Or we can do it at the station. We probably have them on the list, but we need to make sure we cover all the bases on this."

John appeared serious. Given Sylvie's reaction to talking about Geoff, I was pretty sure she would blow a gasket if she knew about this conversation. I didn't see I had any choice.

"One of the flight attendants told me she'd heard Brandon had dated a pilot's wife. I don't know if it was the wife of one of the pilots I dropped off that night or one of the airlines' employees. She was pretty vague about it."

"And you didn't think it was important to tell me?"

John had a slow burn of a temper. His temperature gauge was fast approaching medium-high.

"We were in the middle of the street when I saw you. I forgot to tell you this when I was telling you about the cigars. Besides, I only heard about this during the five-kilometer run Saturday morning. It's been a crazy Monday."

John frowned, let out a deep breath, and looked like he was trying not to yell at me. "Who else have you told about this? I know you're trying to figure this all out. What else have you done to follow up on this?"

"I haven't told anyone, but there were several of us in the group. And the flight crew mostly lives out of town, so I haven't figured out how I might check this all out."

John took out a notebook. "Start from the beginning and tell me everyone who was talking in the group. I'll need to make sure they're on our list."

After ten minutes of being grilled and going over the list three times, John seemed satisfied I had told him all I knew. I'd tried to keep Angie out of it, but John now had her on his list too. I doubted she knew anything else, but I'd warn her to expect his call. One of her rules was she never shared any gossip she heard from her clients. I'd ended up telling John about the charity ball. John was pretty good at directing his conversations with people, and I figured maybe the women wouldn't realize it was me they could thank for putting them on the list of people to talk to in this investigation. At least, I hoped. Angie was another matter. She'd know.

Angie's shop was closed on Mondays, and she typically didn't answer her cell phone. Texts were always better, so I sent her one as I got back in the SUV. **Had to tell John about our conversation. He's probly gonna call u.**

"Car Nine. Customer downtown hotel on River Street. Can you pick up?"

"Ten minutes away. Which hotel?" I asked.

Dispatch gave me the name, and I pulled out of the parking lot. I'd mull over what else I could do in the meantime between fares.

39

Three fares delivered, and my SUV idled at the light, giving me time to reflect. John had tried to steer me away from the Geoff angle. If they hadn't cleared him, that meant he was a possibility. I wondered who he worked for and how I might find out. Then it struck me. Everyone knew I needed this job to pay bills. What about additional cash I didn't have or needed for a costly repair? I wasn't a good credit risk for any bank. My family and I didn't get along well enough for me to ask them for money, not that I ever would. What if I posed as a person needing a loan? The idea might work. But I'd need to make sure I got to the right person.

A horn honked behind me, interrupting my thoughts. I headed toward the airport, where I'd be in a queue of cabs and could think while I waited.

At the airport, I was fifth in line for the next fare. I shut down the engine and stared ahead. Who would know who had loaned Brandon money? And who would he have asked?

Geoff knew, but I couldn't ask him. The other guys he played poker with might know, but I didn't know any of them, except for Bill. Would Bill tell me? Probably not unless I tricked him into it. That didn't feel right. He'd have to be my last resort to find out who all he played cards with. It might give me an additional name to check out.

Even then, he might not tell me.

Other coworkers? Maybe. There were a few I knew were struggling to make ends meet. Mark was the one I knew best. I'd check the schedule and see when he was on dispatch. I could stop by and have a quiet talk with him. I'd have to be careful how I worded this to make sure it was the same loan shark.

My thoughts shifted back to the flight crew. I wasn't optimistic about the pilot or copilot being involved, but it never hurt to try again. And the flight attendants might know more if we talked again. I'd try to be at the airport tonight.

I was next in line for a fare. I'd run by the office between customers, or when we weren't too busy, then I'd fire up my computer later for more researching. For now, I could start planning how to steer the conversation with the crew, depending on whether I had the pilots or the flight attendants.

Loading the luggage in and closing the doors, I rounded the SUV, climbed in, and started the motor. The couple was staying at a historic hotel down by the waterfront. I pulled away from the airport.

My shift was busy with tourists looking to be taken to local restaurants or the airport. As the evening got late, I circled back to the airport and got in line. A flight came in, and everyone wanted a taxicab.

Darn. I had hoped it would be quiet. I picked up a fare for a hotel on the waterfront and headed into town. I made record time and got a big tip, although I didn't think the lady let go of the armrest the entire time. She almost jumped out and kissed the ground. I raced back to the airport and found the line of cabs five deep, which was short. The line moved a bit, and by the time the flight crew arrived, I was second in line. Perfect. For the first time in days, things were moving my way.

I loaded the flight crew's luggage in the back and closed the SUV door. I had two of the same women from the last time and one other slender blonde woman who'd been on previous runs. I'd have to sort out who was who again. I climbed in and started the motor. The women were all talking about sales at a local store in their home base and what bargains they had each found.

I couldn't figure out a way into the conversation, so I listened. Rounding the corner to the hotel, I'd about given up when the blonde, Lisha, asked, "Hey, have you heard anything else on Brandon's murder? I haven't been back for a week. Have the cops found who did it?"

I wanted to hug her. "Not that I know of. I think they're looking into everyone who knew him. Have any of you been questioned?"

Lisha nodded. I looked in the rearview mirror, and the other two women nodded as well.

"I wonder if they questioned the pilots. I heard Brandon might have been having an affair with the pilot or copilot's wife," the second blond attendant said.

Funny, I could swear I'd seen her before, other than in my cab. Now that I could watch her in my rearview mirror, I saw she had a peaches-and-cream complexion and dark brown eyes, with a habit of pushing her blond hair behind one ear.

"No way, Heather," Taylor said. "Josh's wife just had her second baby. And Ryan's wife is six months pregnant. I can't imagine either one of them would do that. Or that Brandon would."

"I don't know. They say pregnant women glow. Maybe Brandon was attracted to one of them," Lisha said.

I realized this flight attendant was the one Brandon had replaced the night he died.

"Unlikely," Heather said. "Brandon didn't have a death wish. Josh and Ryan would have killed him." I heard a breath suck in as she must have realized what she had said. "I didn't mean anything by that. Just, you know, Brandon wouldn't do that."

Lisha reached out and patted her arm. "We know what you meant. I don't think it was Josh or Ryan either."

Turning into the hotel, I wanted to ask more questions, but the women turned the conversation back to the logistics of their flight the next day. I parked and helped them out of the SUV. The conversation had been helpful but hadn't resolved anything. What I needed was concrete evidence.

All in all, it had been a good day. I hoped that meant the rest of the week would be too and things were starting to turn around.

I even allowed myself the smallest glimmer of hope the latest calls meant Steph might be willing to start weekend visits with me or move back in. I'd need to resolve whatever was going on with the black spirit first. No way would I put her in any danger if I could help it.

40

I was watching the coffee drip into the pot as I tried to get my brain to work when I almost jumped out of my skin.

Aunt Harriett's translucent nose was almost in my eye. "There you are. I need to talk to you."

Like I hadn't realized that. I swallowed an inappropriate retort and struggled to focus. "Can you wait until I have a few sips of coffee?" My head swung around to a strange little man I had caught in my peripheral vision. "Whoa, what's he doing here?"

"Michael. My new friend." Aunt Harriett grinned.

I knew he was a ghost. He was too transparent to be anything else. I wasn't used to strange men seeing me in my comfy, feel good, looks-be-damned pajamas. Not even a grandfatherly gray-haired man, with what looked like blue-green eyes, in khakis and a polo shirt. Those eyes took in everything at once, almost with an expectation of danger. Or maybe he was the intense, nosy kind.

It was kind of like my mother used to say about going out in old underwear. Only here, I had to be careful about going to bed and wandering around an empty house when I thought I was safe from being seen. All that had gone out the door with Aunt Harriett's entrance. It was inherently unfair to have to worry about what PJs I wore when no one was around. And what had happened to Eddie?

"You could have warned me. We haven't even been properly introduced. Although Aunt Harriett has talked about you." That wasn't true, but a white lie could be good in awkward social situations.

Aunt Harriett rolled her eyes.

I smiled. The next time my mother or other person complained I rolled mine, I was gonna point to Aunt Harriett as the responsible party for teaching me that move. I remained silent and crossed my arms. I could be as stubborn as she could.

"Michael is my new friend. Having been on this side longer, he knows more about dark spirits—he's watching my back. And he's experienced with the Council. Meet Trisha, my niece."

Michael nodded at me. His form was stiff and looked like he was a bit intimated by either Aunt Harriett or me or both of us.

Before Aunt Harriett could continue, I said, "I'm barely awake. You haven't explained what the Council is."

"It's like a bureaucracy. You know, like the DMV, only a hundred times worse. Or maybe a Supreme Court, with emphasis on Supreme. I now understand why humans can't get things done without massive red tape."

I almost choked on my laughter at the picture of a fading in and out panel of robed judges. I was having trouble grasping all this but decided I'd pin her down on this more when she and I were alone. "What's so important?"

"Dear, you need to listen. The Council."

I hated it when anyone was condescending, even Aunt Harriett. "I got that. But I don't know what you are talking about. Plus, it's early, and I worked late last night."

"Sorry, hon. I lost my train of thought. You know we older folks do that sometimes."

I groaned. Playing the feeble elder was a favorite game of Aunt Harriett's. It worked for her lots of time. This one wasn't one of those. I stared at her and waited.

"I know. I know. It's a group that decides important things. Very much like the Supreme Court but more on an individual level." She looked as if I would understand the significance of all this. When she got no reaction from me, she continued, "Michael knows all about this. He's been trying to find his wife. And now he's trying to help me find Peter." Aunt Harriett paused and turned to Michael. "Oh, I'm jumbling this all up."

Michael smiled at Aunt Harriett. "The Council handles a lot of issues. I'm looking for my wife and sought help there. I wanted to find out if she was bound to a human or if there were other obstacles. I'm waiting on an answer," he said, as if I would understand what that meant.

I didn't respond, just waited for more of an explanation.

"In your aunt's case, we think Peter may be bound to his brother. If so, Peter or your aunt could request the bond be broken. It's not done often, if at all, but it may be possible. It's a very hot issue as to whether any of us should ever be able to break our earthly bonds," Michael said.

Now, this was beginning to make more sense. Except, I didn't understand it at all. I couldn't go before the Council. "So why are you *here*? Shouldn't *you* be taking this up with the Council?"

"I am," Aunt Harriett said. "But it would be helpful if we knew where Peter is." She paused. "That's where you come in."

"Me? I don't get it."

"I think Russell is holding him, so he has to remain close by, because of a bond between them. If that's true, then if you set up a group of your friends to watch him, we might get a clue from Russell or see Peter."

My mouth had dropped open. No way I wanted to talk to my friends about Aunt Harriett. When were we supposed to do this?

"Really, dear, it's simple. You're very perceptive. I know if anyone can find Peter, you can." Aunt Harriet's smile was beaming.

I could be a pushover, but this was a bit much. "Aunt Harriett. I have a job. Besides, how will they see Peter? And how do I explain what they're looking for?"

"You're smart, my dear. You'll find a way. I'm counting on you," Aunt Harriett said.

"But why don't you get your friends to help with this? Wouldn't they be better at this than me?"

"Michael and I will both be watching for Peter. But we can't do it by ourselves. And I'm trying to get to know more about who are on the Council. They aren't public figures, so finding out who is currently on the Council can be a challenge."

"Sounds a lot like dating."

"I guess it is," Aunt Harriett said. "We'll have to organize this. We should arrange shifts. When will you be able to be there?"

I hung my head. I couldn't believe she thought this could work. I had no better idea to offer. "I'm not sure. I'll have to check my work schedule. But there must be a better and easier way. Why don't you let me think a bit about this?"

Aunt Harriett began to fade.

"Have you seen the black swirly mass again? Or know if it's the murdered guy?" I had no idea what to call it or if this kind of thing had a name.

"I've seen a glimpse or two of it, but I've been moving too fast for it to latch on to my trail. If it were anywhere close, I'd have been here double-quick to warn you. It hasn't left enough of a trail for us to confirm who it is, but I have a kind of ghost detective who does this kind of thing working on it. Any luck on solving who might have killed your fare?"

"All my leads seem to be drying up. But I keep searching. Any chance you can check out things where you are?"

Aunt Harriett considered this. "Probably not, unless there's a relative who has passed but remains in the Gray. Do you know who his parents are or other ancestors?"

That was a thought. "Not right offhand. I'll do more searching and have new names when you show up again. Any idea when you think you'll be back?"

Aunt Harriett laughed. "No. And not sure who I will have with me, so you might want to remember that. Catch you later."

I groaned. I figured I'd better get my shower while the chances of Aunt Harriett returning with another ghostly presence were slim. Then a quick search on my computer and a check-in with Sylvie on how Derek was doing. If she wasn't still mad at me, I'd talk to her a bit more about buying the company. I'd left that last part far too long without asking her the questions Bill had helped me with so far.

41

Our schedule showed Mark's shift tonight started at seven. Since I'd be working, I'd have to plan my dinner break at a time when I could stop by the office to speak to him. That was okay. Being Tuesday, we'd had lots of fares for the evening diners and those flying out on late flights, but there were always slow times during the workweek.

Around nine, I dropped off a hotel fare and called in for a break. Normally I'd grab a quick bite, but tonight I was planning to see whether Mark could help me.

I parked outside our office building where there were few other cars. Sylvie's BMW convertible was missing from the parking lot. Without her there, I could talk to him easier. I'd texted her earlier. She'd replied with a sad smiley emoji, so I didn't call her to ask more questions about the whole company purchase thing. I let myself in and glanced around. "Hi, Mark."

He was talking on the phone to one of the drivers and lifted his hand so I'd know he heard me. I'd called in my break, so he already knew I wasn't on the clock. No one else was there. He hung up the phone.

"To what do I owe the pleasure?"

I laughed. "My computer at home is slow. I need to run a quick search. Hope you don't mind me stopping by." This wasn't all quite true, but most of the drivers stopped by at times to use a computer, so it was a believable reason to be here.

"Nope. Breaks up my evening."

"I also have a question I think you might be able to help me with."

"If I can. What is it?"

"It's kinda embarrassing. I'm a little short this month. I don't want to ask Sylvie for an advance. I'm wondering if you know of anyone who does short-term loans."

Mark frowned. I could see he didn't like the way this was going.

"It's only for a week or so. I have a project at the house I need to fix right away. I'd ask my family, but they've been unhappy I got it when my aunt Harriett died."

"What about Bill? I'm sure he'd help you."

I'd forgotten he knew about Bill. I thought I'd been quite clever with the whole house thing and how I couldn't ask my family.

"I hate to ask him. We've been dating a little while. I don't know if it's been long enough for me to ask anything like that. He's my last resort. I think I need to solve this one on my own."

Mark pondered this. "Well, there's always Big Louie. But he can be mean when crossed. Plus, if you don't pay him, he'll send a different collector. A few others like Big Louie. Can't you take out a loan on your own, like on your car?"

"I get all that. I would never shirk on a debt. Plus, my car's not worth much." I looked at my shoes as I tried to gauge if it was too quick, then decided to go for it. "Is that who Geoff works for? Off duty?"

Mark looked surprised, and I wasn't sure if it was because I knew of Geoff's other job or that I would mention it.

"Yeah." It was drawn out like he was trying to decide how much to say.

"I know he does that. Bill told me he was chasing a gambling debt at a poker game one night."

Mark's shoulders relaxed. It might have been that he didn't want to be the one to tell me about Geoff's other work. Or it might be he was afraid of Geoff's temper or the family. I certainly was.

"I'd think twice about all this. There must be an alternative."

"I hear you. I've been working on other solutions. Just haven't found one yet."

In trying to figure out what Mark's reaction was to all this, I realized I had missed the most essential part. I now knew who Geoff worked for, and I could ask Big Louie if Brandon had owed him money. He might not tell me, and chances were good he wouldn't, but I was doing better with finding out what I wanted faster than I had expected.

"It's a bit of an emergency, so I need to move quickly. But I'll think about what else I might do. In the meantime, how do you get in touch with Big Louie?"

"He has a restaurant down on West Broughton, Italiano Eatery. The office is off the kitchen. If you're going to do this, ask for Louie before they seat you. And be careful. He's not anyone to mess around with."

I thanked Mark as the phone rang. He turned to take the fare information and pointed to me. I nodded and headed out the door.

42

I'd missed the flight crew again last night. It was almost like I wasn't supposed to talk to them. After talking to Mark about the loan shark, I was glad to have a different route to explore.

At West State and Montgomery Streets, I parked my car and walked the block and a half to the Italiano Eatery. I'd done a bit of research after my shift last night. It wasn't part of City Market, but close enough tourists could find it—within walking distance of the Chatham County Courthouse and what remained of Liberty Square. I could see the American Legion Flame of Freedom that graced the small strip of land, which was once combined with its neighbor, Elbert Square, before US 17 was built through the middle.

Big Louie didn't advertise, but I'd learned he also specialized in bonds for those who couldn't go the more typical route with a bail bondsman. I looked around. Early afternoon meant there was a mix of tourists wandering in search of other shops. Hints of fresh bread carried on the slight breeze. I'd been to the bakery, and their pastries melted on your tongue, only to reappear on your hips or thighs. The galleries all opened at about ten, but the real business didn't start until lunch, when travelers went in search of a meal and came back after seeing the artwork. The process would repeat for the evening rush, and live music would entertain wanderers in the evening.

I took a breath to steel my nerves and wondered again if this was a good idea. The restaurant was a standalone new building—but built in the Victorian style to meet the historic district requirements. Painted navy and white, with plentiful parking nearby, I could understand the draw of the location. Big Louie's business must be doing well. How cliché that Big Louie's office would be in an Italian restaurant, although it was effective. Given Mark's comments about finding an alternative and Geoff working for Big Louie to get his money back from people who didn't pay, the whole idea of this put me on edge. Why had I thought this was a good idea?

A notice outside announced that Eddie DeLuca was the chef. A guy with the same name had been in my high school class. I wondered if he was Louie's brother, since the restaurant was owned and locally run. I remembered he'd wanted to go to culinary school, but no one had taken him seriously at the time.

The aroma of garlic and herbs assaulted my nose as I stepped inside. I was transported back to Aunt Harriett's kitchen as she cooked spaghetti sauce. She wasn't Italian, but her teaching me to cook was a favorite memory. At two in the afternoon, the hostess wasn't yet on duty, so I walked past her station toward the kitchen. I almost wished I were here to eat rather than talk to Big Louie.

A waiter pushed through the kitchen door, his arms full of white linen tablecloths and napkins, frowning when he saw me. "We're not open yet. Come back at five."

"I don't want a meal. I'm here to see Big Louie."

I could see he was trying to decide if I was legit or a cop.

"Most come through the back door."

"My first time here. I was told he had an office off the kitchen. I need to talk business with him."

Behind him, the kitchen door pushed open a couple of inches and a voice rang out, "Show her in."

The waiter set the linens down on a nearby wooden table for four and turned to his right. I followed along through what looked like a steel-reinforced solid brown wood door blending into the paneling. I didn't even want to think about why.

"He's down the hall, second door on the right. Knock and then go right in." The waiter turned around and left me alone in the hall.

I followed his instructions and took another deep breath as I knocked, turned the knob, and entered the office. I wasn't sure what I expected, but this wasn't it: a normal-looking office, complete with a mahogany desk that had an inbox, stapler, and notepads, two beige guest chairs, plants by the window, and a bookcase full of ledgers. The man sitting behind the desk stood. Tall and lanky, he looked like he could be seven feet tall. He was spaghetti thin. I wondered if he was athletic. He would have been perfect for a basketball team. I wasn't tall, but I'd been fast in high school and played guard on the women's team. He was older, but I'd have remembered him if he'd been on the squad.

"Not quite what you expected? Have a seat."

I continued to look around and saw a small computer monitor showing the dining room and front door. A second one focused on a small door that was possibly a back way in and out. Now I knew how he'd seen me coming and authorized admission to his inner sanctum.

"What can I do for you today, Trisha?"

I knew he caught my surprise by the slight smile at the corner of his mouth. He was skilled at keeping people off-balance, and if it were possible, I was even more wary of this man.

While I knew his brother slightly in high school, I didn't know Big Louie at all. How on earth did he know who I was? And if he knew my name, what else did he know? It explained why I'd gotten past the first waiter. He'd known who I was all along.

"Yes," he answered my unspoken question. "I know who you are. That's my business. I don't know why you're here, although I can guess. But humor me. I love hearing the stories."

"I'm here to talk to you about a loan."

"Why? There are better and safer places to ask for money."

Huh? I'd thought he'd jump at the chance for new business. My plan to open with that and then steer the conversation had backfired on me. Improvising wasn't my strongest tactic, but it was my hand to play. "Well, I need cash for a short time. I thought this would be a good way to take care of that."

"Still didn't answer my question. Do you have a car?"

"Of course."

"Is it paid off?"

"Well, yes."

"You can get a loan with the title for a short time. Might be a bit cheaper on interest than my going rate or not. It's easy to get. No background check, no hassle."

"I need my car for work. If I lose it, I won't have any income."

"And you think I'd be easier to work with if that happened?" He laughed. It was an ugly laugh that said, are you really so dumb? "Assuming that's true, didn't you inherit a house?"

Okay, now I was impressed. He couldn't have known I'd be here today. Did he keep tabs on everything in the city? Or everyone? I couldn't imagine I'd show up on his radar.

"Yes, but I don't have time for a bank loan. And my brother would kill me if he knew I took out a loan for short-term things." I couldn't believe he was trying to talk me out of this. What kind of loan shark was he?

I could see he was studying me. "Okay. How much do you need?"

"Two thousand dollars." I'd decided whatever I asked for should be high enough to pique his interest but also low enough so he thought he'd get it back. I had no intention of actually borrowing the money, but I wanted him to know I was serious, or at least think so.

"That's a lot of money for repairs. How long to repay?"

"A month. I'll make other arrangements but need to fix the hole in the roof before it starts to rain."

"And a credit card won't work?"

"I'm almost maxed out, and the limit on my card is too small to handle this. I'm working on increasing it, which should be approved, but I need the roof fixed before it causes any damage. You know October can bring rains or a hurricane. As soon as I have the approval, I can repay you." I was surprised I was doing so well here. I hadn't stumbled over his questions, even though I hadn't expected most of them.

"Okay. I can do that. But I don't think that's why you're here. Why don't you stop wasting your time and mine and tell me why you're really here?"

43

I'm sure my face went white. I hadn't seen that coming. "Wha...?"

"You're the driver who put the fare out, the one who got killed." The amusement played on his face as I struggled to control my reaction. "Yes. I read. In my business, I need to know what's happening in my town. And I pay attention to news about people who I have loaned money to. My people tell me you've been nosing around."

His people? My shoulders drooped a bit. I might as well be straight with him. He already knew anyway. I wondered if Mark had told him. Or maybe Geoff. I'd have to be more careful in the future about what I said and to who. "You're right. I wondered if Brandon had gambling debts that might have gotten him killed."

"Not me. He owed me money, but killing him would be bad business. Besides, Brandon paid his debts. His payment might be late, but he always paid." Big Louie paused. "So, why is this any of your business?"

"I put him out on the street and now the cops are hassling me, and my boss wants this cleared up so it doesn't affect her business." It was true as far as it went. I didn't see any reason to tell him more than he knew.

"You were the last to see him." It wasn't a question.

"No. The killer was. That wasn't me."

"But you're the last one to see him alive."

"No. The killer was. I left him alive by the side of the road."

"But you're responsible for him being there. And you were close enough to circle back. I am sure you're high on the cops' list."

"They've talked to me. But the guy was a jerk, and the pilot wanted me to let him out before the hotel. Besides, I had every right to put him, or anyone else, out of my cab if I didn't feel safe or if they were obnoxious."

"And I have a business to run. Brandon owed me thirty thousand dollars, plus interest. If you hadn't put him out, I think he'd be alive and able to repay me. That makes you responsible for his death. And responsible for his debts. I doubt Brandon has an estate to collect from, even if I tried. I don't lose money, so the way I figure it, you owe me the money he should have paid me."

I gasped. No way did I have that kind of money. "That's not my debt. I didn't borrow money from you."

"I don't care. But since you're so set on finding his killer, here's what I'll do. If you find the killer and give me the information, your debt will become the killer's debt. I won't even make you collect it. And you're off the hook if the cops figure this out. Whoever killed Brandon is the responsible party and should pay me back. But if you or the cops can't find whoever did it, then someone has to pay."

My mouth was hanging open. I couldn't believe this.

"And I'll go one step further. If Brandon's estate has money and if I can get paid in full, you'll be off the hook."

I didn't see how the last part was possible. Recovering from his estate would require a claim. I doubted there was evidence of the debt owed. At least not anything that would be enforceable. "This isn't fair. I'm not going to be responsible for someone else's debts. I have my own to take care of."

I paused and sucked on my bottom lip, trying to slow my beating heart. In a flash, before I could stop myself, I said, "Besides, my coworker, Geoff, who works for you at times, was the other driver that night. He could have killed Brandon. Maybe for you, maybe by accident. How do I know you're not trying to pin this on me when it's your fault?"

His eyes narrowed, and the air in the room thickened before it was sucked out in a vacuum where nothing moved or breathed. His hand moved, and I had a vision of him drawing a gun and shooting me. While I thought my imagination was running too far, I couldn't be sure, but realized I had probably stepped in it, big time. Why had I thought this was a good idea? When would I learn to control my mouth in moments like these?

A full two minutes elapsed before Big Louie spoke. "I'm going to chalk this all up to your ignorance and let it pass. You only get one of those. You understand?"

I nodded.

"You have exactly one week to find the killer or bring me the money. Or bring me a deed to your house to settle this. I don't care which."

I could barely feel my legs and wondered how I was going to get out of there.

"How's your daughter? I hear she's living with her stepfather. I hear he's doing well financially. Maybe he'll give you the money to settle this. You wouldn't want to do anything that hurts your chances of your daughter coming back to live with you, would you?" He paused.

"Leave by the same door you came in. Don't come back without the money or the information. And stay away from Geoff. He's not the killer. He's under my protection and employ. Although I'm sure he'd be happy to pay you a visit if he hears what you've been saying behind his back, off the clock. And you can bet I'll send him or worse to collect if you aren't back in a week."

I forced my legs to move so I could stand and walk back to the door with as much dignity as I could manage. I thought I might be sick.

I hurried as best I could to my car, stumbling in places as my eyes filled with tears of frustration, fear, and anxiety. For once, the feeling of a steamy wool coat of humidity felt good. I had no idea where to start or what to do. My mind was racing in five directions. I wouldn't figure out a new plan until I calmed down.

My back straightened and I swiped at the tears. No one threatened my family, especially not Stephanie. Resolving this whole situation and protecting her was now top priority. He'd probably thrown that in to knock me off guard, but I'd never take the chance. And now he'd made me angry. My face heated, and my body tensed at the thought of anyone hurting Steph.

I would have loved to talk to Aunt Harriett or Bill, but I knew both would lecture me about what I'd done. I wasn't ready for that. Would anyone listen? My mind blanked and then cleared. Angie might just be the ticket.

I punched in a text message. **Need to talk ASAP. Can I come by?**

44

Sure. At home.

The answer came back in a text before I was settled in the car with my seat belt on. I started to breathe a bit easier. If nothing else, it would be reassuring to talk it through.

I fumbled with the key, turned the key, and checked twice for traffic, not trusting myself to see a car coming before pulling away from the curb. I hoped Angie could help me make sense of this before anything worse happened.

I stopped at a red light and let go of the wheel. I'd been gripping it so hard I hadn't realized my hands were shaking. From fear, frustration, or anger, I wasn't sure. I had no way of knowing if Big Louie would make good on what he'd said, but I had no intention of finding out. I drove more slowly to Angie's, knowing that being upset meant I wasn't paying as much attention as I usually would be. On Bull Street, I parked and walked the block to her Victorian house. Unlike mine, hers was in immaculate condition, with a manicured landscape I knew her gardener cared for each week. Hers had the same gingerbread arches and spindles my house had. Instead of a purple façade, hers was mustard yellow, with cream molding, much like the

Asendorf House or Gingerbread House on Bull Street several blocks away.

I raised my hand to knock, and it opened immediately. It was a sign Angie knew how upset I was that she answered so quickly.

"Come in. I put a pot of water on. You need tea. Then you can tell me all about whatever it is."

I breathed. There was comfort in having a longtime friend who knew you so well she simply accepted that you needed a shoulder. And was there to listen. I sat at her butcher block kitchen table. The light wood was a sharp contrast to my aunt's antique table I seldom used. We'd had family dinners around it that had been full of laughter and conversation. I couldn't imagine a meal without Aunt Harriett. Maybe getting a new table was the solution. Or I'd figure out how to make new memories differently. For now, Angie's table was a welcome change.

Angie walked to the table with a china teapot. She poured steaming water into each of our matching mugs, and I wrapped my hands around mine. The warmth helped with my shaking hands.

Angie let her tea steep and added a tiny bit of sweetener. "What happened?"

I relayed my encounter with Big Louie.

"What did you expect?"

I was shocked at her abruptness and lack of sympathy. It must have shown on my face.

"He's a loan shark. I'm your friend, but this wasn't your smartest move."

I stared at her and then began to laugh. "You're right. I've done dumber things, but this one is right up there on the list." I stared at the table and took a drink. "I guess I've been so worried about my job and clearing my name, I didn't realize I could make it worse."

Angie smiled. "Now you know. What do you plan to do next?"

She was distracting me, which I appreciated. I was calming down, starting to think more clearly again. "I don't know. I've tracked down the pilot and copilot family information, but it isn't promising. I can't see either of them killing Brandon."

Angie looked puzzled. I realized she might not know Brandon could have been having an affair with one of the pilot's wives. I brought her up to date on my theories, reminding her of what the women said at the five-kilometer race about who he might have been dating.

She nodded. "What about the company?"

"I talked to Bill. He had good ideas on questions, but I haven't had a chance to talk to Sylvie. And I wanted to talk to you too, since you own your own company."

"Get a good accountant to help you value it and make a business plan. How will you finance this?"

"Sylvie said we could work it out."

"Get help on that too. An attorney too. You may need both. I can help you with referrals if you'd like. But first, you need to look at the books and see if the business has enough revenue for you to pay the bills, employees, and whatever financing you need. It also needs to make enough for you to live. You need a budget too. And I know you hate that. Your ex-husband is a good businessman. Have you thought about talking to him?"

I hadn't. We didn't have children together, so we had no real reason to talk, other than about Steph now that she was living with him. He had a local business, but I wasn't sure I wanted him to see any signs of weakness on my part. On the other hand, he was good at business. At the very least, he might have good advice to offer me. It felt good to make a plan and be distracted from my conversation with Big Louie.

"Good idea. I'll think about it. Bill gave me a name of an accountant."

"And if the worst happens, talk to me first. There's no reason for you to lose your house over all this. What else can I do?"

My eyes filled with tears that I fought to keep from streaming down my face. I swiped at them, grateful to have such a good friend. "I need to think about all this. Thanks for listening. I need to do a bit more research and then work."

Feeling better, I took a better look at Angie. She had on a little black dress and heels that sparkled. "You're dressed up. I didn't realize you were going out," I said.

"Stuart's in town shooting location shots. We're attending a gallery opening. Which reminds me, I've got to find the tickets."

Angie rose and moved to her credenza. "Where are those tickets?" She rooted around in her Coach purse.

I hid a smile. Far be it for me to say anything. My jam-packed shoulder bag was twice the size. There was no good response to that kind of question.

Angie removed her calendar, then a hairbrush. Next came her face powder compact and then a pair of square black-rimmed sunglasses with crystals glittering in the light. I stared at them. I'd seen them before. My arm tingled. Where? I racked my brain, knowing this was important.

"Darn," Angie said. "I know I have them in here."

I reached over and picked up the glasses, trying to keep my voice steady. "These are different. Where'd you get them?"

Angie looked up. "Oh, those. I keep forgetting to leave them here. Don't let me put them back in. I have real sunglasses on the entry table. Can you get those?"

"Sure. But where did you get them? They don't look like anything you would buy. Or wear, for that matter." I moved to the entry and retrieved her other sunglasses.

"You're right. They gave them out at the Masquerade Casino Night event last month."

"Really. When was that?"

"A couple of weeks ago. Didn't I tell you? I helped organize the event. Good for business development."

"Right." Angie attended a lot of functions I wouldn't be invited to, much less have an outfit appropriate to wear. "Was it fun?" I asked.

"It was okay. I don't gamble as a rule. It was all for charity, but it's not the kind of event I enjoy. And Judi's friend, Heather, who I'd never met and was nice, was there. It was strange, though. At one point, in like midsentence, Heather turned white and said she had to leave. Cindi told me later that Heather saw her boyfriend there, and he was nuzzling up to another woman. I felt rather sorry for her. You know, we've all had a similar kind of moment when we realized a guy we were dating wasn't who we thought he was."

I stared at Angie. What was I missing? The hair was now standing up on my arms. And then it clicked. I knew who could have approached Brandon and gotten close enough to kill him that night.

But why? There had to be more to the story. Parts were missing. This person wasn't supposed to be in Savannah the day Brandon died.

Hmmm. Maybe that had been wrong. Perhaps we were all supposed to think the person wasn't there. How could I figure it out? There'd have to be a car, but it could have been borrowed. I had no way of finding that out. Or it could have been a rental.

I didn't have a lot of chances to stop by the rental office, but I dropped off customers for rentals on occasion. I racked my brain and came up with the one person I knew who worked for a car rental agency. Tanesha.

We weren't close but I'd been impressed with how Tanesha handled the few customers I brought in. We'd traded referrals. This, though, would be different. I wasn't sure if she'd help.

I'd have to think of a good reason why she should look it up. This would require her to check on rental cars and who rented them on a couple of days. But hey, like I always said, "if you don't ask, you surely won't get it." Why not ask? All the car rental agencies were housed near each other, and I decided I'd stop by tonight. If she was working, I'd see what I could find out.

45

"Earth to Trisha." Angie stared at me with a quizzical look.

"I'll explain later." I gave her a quick hug before I ran out of her door. I started planning a mental checklist as I turned the key in the ignition. With two hours before I had to be on duty, I headed to the office, where the computer was faster. It reminded me that, once this was all settled, I might need to upgrade the home computer Steph complained about. Mike had the latest technology, and I couldn't compete.

As I pulled into the building parking lot, I realized I might run into Sylvie. If I did, there might be questions. That, plus the fact we had a lot of open questions about the business transaction, gave me a good excuse if anyone wondered why I was there. Parking in an open spot, I took a breath to calm my nerves. Things didn't add up. Pieces were missing. At least my research might help eliminate a few possibilities.

Inside, quiet reigned, except for Mark, who was in dispatch. He smiled and waved. I suspected he was the one who told Big Louie I was coming.

I walked over. "How's it going? Busy?"

"Not too much."

"Is Sylvie in?"

"No. You just missed her."

"Darn. I needed to talk to her. Oh well, I'll catch up with her tomorrow." I paused. "Guess I'll do a bit on the computer before my shift."

Mark accepted this, so I walked across the room to a table with a computer on it. Until I knew for sure whether I could trust him, it made no sense to let him know what I was doing or why. Too bad. Mark was a wiz on computers and could probably complete my search in half the time. I waited for a search engine to come up and began researching the Masquerade Casino Night event. Lots and lots of pictures. Lots of masks and the sunglasses I'd seen at Angie's. I knew I was on the right track.

I logged off the computer and headed outside. I'd see if the flight attendants might talk about the pilots tonight—if I managed to be in line to pick them up. And I'd check out the rental car part of my theory. Between fares, I could call to see if Tanesha was working tonight. If Uber or Lyft had been used, I had no idea what else I could check.

Sunshine hit my eyes as I drove out of the office parking lot. I pulled down the visor, slid my sunglasses on, and headed to town to pick up the fare Mark had assigned me. I was on a roll and wanted to be sure I did as much as I could while my luck was running hot.

46

The night was busier than I expected and it was eleven thirty by the time I had a free moment. The car rental place was closed. Disappointed, I headed home. Once there, I kicked my shoes off and fixed a big glass of sweet tea. Possum had other ideas and apparently thought feeding her was more important than my need to settle in on the couch. Two sips of tea later, and Aunt Harriett materialized in front of me.

"You have to come quick. Peter's at Russell's," Aunt Harriett said.

I stared at her, not knowing where to begin. "Okay. First, we need to figure out a new way, so I have a warning. I almost dropped my drink. Second, how do you know he's there or that he'll be there when I get there?"

"We'll work on the first one later. Right now, we need to get there before we lose Peter again."

I waited for more to come.

Aunt Harriett frowned. "If you must know, we've been on ghost watch. At least that's what you would probably call it. You were right that mortals wouldn't be very helpful in watching. Unless, of course, they can see ghosts." She let her words sink in. "A spirit, however, can sense another soul if they know what they're looking for. Michael and I created a phone tree of sorts."

"A phone tree?"

"You know, back when there weren't cell phones. People used to set up a phone tree for emergencies. The one on the top called two people, and those two people each called two more. Well, we have a support group for spirits who are searching. We all volunteer for watch times, then we send out a signal when we spot the one we're looking for. The spirit on duty is the one at the top of the tree and sends one signal starting the chain reaction. The spirit needs to continue to monitor so it can send any updates. Don't ask me why. That's the way it works. Each spirit reports to those on the branches below until the one who needs to know is notified."

"Someone called you?"

"Of course. I wouldn't be here otherwise. Michael is there now, making sure Peter doesn't leave. You need to get there. I want to be sure you're there in case we need your help with Russell in this physical world."

I had no idea how I might help, but I could see Aunt Harriett wasn't going to take no for an answer. I dragged myself off the couch and looked for my shoes.

Fifteen minutes later, I had parked near the tobacco shop. It was late in the evening and the street had plenty of parking. I could see lights on upstairs but had no idea how I was going to get in. Angie and I had gone through the shop, which was closed and locked up tight.

"Around the corner, dear. There's a late-night call button by the back door."

I must have looked surprised.

"We've been scouting this place for all contingencies. You didn't think I'd get you out tonight without a plan, did you?"

Well, I did think that, but I wasn't going to tell her I thought this was a fool's errand. I wondered how much of a plan there was.

"Go ahead, push it."

"Okay. I don't see why you need me. Can't you go inside and see Peter?"

"Yes, but he might disappear, making it even harder to find him. Or Russell could make us leave or ask Peter to complain to the Council. If he did, the Council might forbid me to return, sort of like an earthly restraining order."

This was getting stranger and stranger. "It's pretty late. Russell might not let me in."

"Nonsense. He likes you. You look very much like I did at your age. I wouldn't be surprised if he didn't have a crush on you. Ring the bell. All he can do is say no or not answer."

I was torn. One part of me wished he wouldn't answer, and the other part wanted to help Aunt Harriett.

"Hello. Can I help you?"

"Hi, Mr. Mercer. It's Trisha Reede. I know it's late, but I need to talk to you. Can I come up?"

After a couple of seconds of silence, I heard the click of the lock on the door. I was in. I ran up the stairs and Russell met me at the door.

"I see you brought family with you," Russell said.

"She insisted. You know how Aunt Harriett can be."

Russell laughed. "I do. We go back a long way, as you know. Come on in. You and whoever else is out there."

As I walked into the apartment, I saw a wispy figure I didn't recognize, but I suspected it was Peter. Aunt Harriett's entourage had been right in thinking he was here.

"I knew it." Aunt Harriett's haughty smile radiated her triumph.

"Harriett, stow it," Russell said.

I almost laughed, except that Aunt Harriett's face had grown dark with anger.

"You ungrateful little prick," Aunt Harriett said. "Why are you doing this? We took you everywhere we went as kids."

I was glad my tongue was attached. I would have surely swallowed it at Aunt Harriett's use of the word prick if it hadn't been. I'd heard her swear, but this was a new one on me. Russell's face was now equally as dark. Peter slunk back into the shadows of a corner. I wasn't sure who he was hiding from, Aunt Harriett or his brother.

"And you hated every minute I was there. You always wanted Peter for yourself. If you think I wasn't aware when you tried to ditch me, you're wrong. I remember every time," Russell said.

"We wanted a few minutes of our own. But you never allowed it. We wanted to be a regular young couple without a tagalong brother."

"He was *my* brother. I never had anything else, and *you* wanted him. You had your friends and your sisters. You could have had any guy you wanted. But no, you had to have the only positive thing I ever had in my life."

Aunt Harriett looked stunned. I don't think she'd ever considered Russell as other than a nuisance back then.

"Russell, we've talked about this before. We were teenagers. We were in love and exploring what that meant," Aunt Harriett said quietly.

"Well, I never had that. No one wanted me. Look at me. Would you ever have considered going out with me?" Russell's look demanded an answer to the one question he must have hated to ask.

"No. But not because of your size. You were too young. And I liked to have fun. I wanted a boyfriend with a lighter personality. You were dark and much deeper than I could ever be. Besides, you did marry."

"She was after the family money. Left me when she discovered I wasn't the main heir. You're saying all this to get Peter back now."

For the first time, Peter stepped from the shadows. "No. She was frivolous and silly back then. It was what drew me to her. I didn't have to deal with anything serious. We could just have fun."

"I miss the easiness," Aunt Harriett said.

"Well, too bad. Peter made a vow to me. He can't break it."

Aunt Harriett looked at Peter.

"He's right," Peter said. "Before we went sailing that day, he made me promise I'd never leave him...no matter what. I had no idea what I was doing, but it doesn't change the fact my words bound me. It was almost as if he knew."

Aunt Harriett considered this. "You could approach the Council for a release."

Peter remained silent. I stared at him. Conflict played across his face. Confusion. And then a decision. Perhaps he'd decided it had been long enough. "I already did."

"What? Why would you do that? I thought you loved me," Russell screamed.

After a few seconds, Peter answered, "It's not a matter of love. I have always loved you. I always will. You're my brother. Nothing can ever change that. But I've been tied to you and unable to control my destiny for almost sixty years. Can you even imagine what that's like? You and I both know that wasn't what the vow was about."

Russell remained quiet. I couldn't tell if he was angry or defiant.

"It doesn't matter. You're tied to me. I'm not letting you go."

"I see you haven't changed in all these years. Still that petulant little boy who wants his way," Aunt Harriett said.

"Yes, but this time you're stuck with what I want. You should have listened when I said I loved you. We could have been together and shared Peter," Russell said.

"I did listen. You didn't listen to me. Your mother would never have accepted me," Aunt Harriett said.

Russell stared at her in silence. "He's mine. I won't let him go."

"At least until death," Michael said. "The vow dies with you."

47

It was the first time I'd heard Aunt Harriett's friend speak since they'd arrived. And it was like all the air had been sucked out the room.

I hadn't even remembered he was there. But I realized it was one of the most significant statements of this meeting. Almost ominous and foreboding in the way he said it.

"Look," Russell said, "she's already replaced you with a new guy. Can't you see what she is? I'm the one who always loved you."

"Michael's a friend. Trying to help me."

Peter said, "Russell, I'll always care about you. But I wish you'd let this go. I'll be there for you, no matter what happens. You've got to know that."

"No," said Russell. "I'll never let you go."

"We'll see," Aunt Harriett said.

I had to admire her. It didn't look good, and I didn't see a solution. Neither did Peter, from what I could tell. He'd slunk back into the corner, and I wondered whether he was worth all the trouble Aunt Harriett was going through. I couldn't put my finger on what didn't seem right. I stared at Peter and wondered if he had approached the Council or just said so. I couldn't see why he would lie, but he'd been a kid when he drowned. Did that mean he had or had not approached them? And what was the decision?

"You'll have to leave. All of you."

Aunt Harriett held her ground, but Michael reached out to touch her, at which point they both disappeared.

"I'm sorry we bothered you. I don't think I understand all of this," I said. "I need to help Aunt Harriett. You understand. She's family."

"I do, but you see, I lost the only real person who loved me when Peter died. How can you expect me to give that up?"

"I'm sorry. I don't know your family, but I know that even though I have differences with mine, if I needed them and was willing to ask for their help, they would be there for me. I wish you had had the same."

"Thank you for saying that. I thought when I met you that you reminded me of Harriett. Now I see that you're quite different. In a good way."

Russell paused. "It's late. You should go. Tell Harriett to let this go. I won't change my mind."

I turned to the door.

"But you're welcome to come back. Or if you need more help with the cigars, I'll be happy to help with that."

I wasn't sure I ever wanted to come back. The whole situation was a mess, similar to my life. The murder. The black spirit. Aunt Harriett's problem. Well, the last one wasn't mine. More like I was an on-call assistant. If I could solve even a small part of all this, I'd feel better. I headed down the stairs. It was time I found out who killed Brandon and why, then I'd see if I could come up with any new ideas on solving Aunt Harriett's problem.

48

I'd arrived home dead tired from the confrontation with Russell. Aunt Harriett had stormed around my kitchen before Michael had convinced her to leave. I'd dove into bed and slept late.

The whole thing had been bizarre, and I wasn't sure how to help Aunt Harriett. Instead, I'd concentrated on picking up customers and dropping them off. Tanesha was supposed to be working tonight.

The SUV in gear, I headed to the rental car building after my last Thursday night fare. I parked in front, turned off my headlights, and squinted. I could see one person behind the counter. It looked like Tanesha, but I couldn't be sure.

When I called earlier, the sales representative said she was working the late shift. It was almost closing time, and I knew there wouldn't be a lot of people around. How was I going to do this? If it wasn't her, I could act surprised and try to find out when she was working again.

If it was her, it wasn't like I could walk up and say, "Hey, I'm trying to figure out who killed the guy I dumped out of my cab. And yes, I know that's the cops' job, but I feel a bit responsible since I was one of the last people to see him. And, oh, by the way, I need you to check to see if a certain woman rented a car that night and violate probably about all of your company's rules by telling me." I must be nuts to think this would work.

I thought I could appeal to her sympathy, because I was somewhat responsible for putting the guy out of my cab. Or her sense of right and wrong. But I wasn't sure what else might work. I'd worked with her before, but this was a begging mission for sure, and I expected my knees to take a beating.

I took a deep breath and swallowed my apprehension. As I headed across the pavement, I tried to think of what I could use as an opening line. I was a complete blank. Aunt Harriett came to mind. She could ooze charm like mud coming up between your toes. Silky smooth where you wanted to settle in and wiggle around. I figured that was my best bet.

I opened the door and stepped inside. Cold air blasted from the air conditioner, and goose bumps rose on my arms and legs. Every muscle clenched as I tried to adjust to the change in temperature. So much for silky smooth.

Tanesha looked up from the counter and smiled. "I'm about to close up. How can I help you?"

"Hey, Tanesha. How are you doing?" Great. She doesn't remember me. Not Aunt Harriett-like at all.

"Oh, hey, Trisha. How're things? Been a long time. I didn't realize that was you. I'm about to close up shop."

"Sorry. I know I'm late, but I have a couple of questions if you have time." I was trying to figure out when my cool approach went out the window, although I suspected it hadn't even been there to start with. Oh well, there were days like that.

A furrow creased across her brow. Her smile disappeared. "Okay. But I've gotta close out, and I haven't had a break for hours. Can you watch the desk for me while I take a quick bathroom break? Just tell anyone who comes in that I'll be right back. Once I've closed up, we can talk."

I couldn't believe it. I might be able to do this. "Sure. Happy to. I'll come around the counter and sit here. Take your time."

49

I was not a whiz at computers but mine was so old I had learned my way around the system. Plus I'd temped a few jobs where I had to learn fast. Tanesha headed to the back, leaving her computer on. I reached over the counter, stretching to touch a key, keeping it active until I saw her go around the corner. Then I flew around the counter end and went to work. I knew the last name of the ill flight attendant, Heather, was Sanders, and I knew the general time period. If she'd been in town that day, she would've had to borrow a car if she didn't want anyone to know she was here. Or take Uber or Lyft or even a cab. I was betting she might've rented a car instead.

I typed in October 15. Then I scrolled through, looking for Heather's name. Nothing. I started to sweat as the screen flickered. What if the computer crashed? How would I ever explain what happened? The computer screen steadied. I said a silent prayer of thanks. I scrolled down the list for the day before. There it was—a Ford Focus.

So she wasn't out of town that day. And it sounded like her sick excuse might not be real either. I clasped my arm to my sides to keep from jumping up and down. I was right. Heather had been in town that night. She could have been the one Angie mentioned—the one who saw her boyfriend with another woman at the Masquerade Casino Night charity event.

I also bet she was the one at the Pondside Inn I saw in the dark glittery sunglasses. No one wore those kind of glasses at night unless they didn't want anyone to know who you were. If she was at the inn, then she could have killed him or saw who did. I wasn't sure why, but I was pretty sure I was on the right track.

I shifted the screen back to where it was when Tanesha left.

Just in time, as Tanesha rounded the corner.

"Thanks so much. I can't leave the desk unattended. Now, what was it you wanted to talk about?"

I swallowed hard. In my excitement, I'd forgotten to figure that out. "Oh, you know, we haven't seen each other in a while, and I wanted to catch up. I was on my way home and nearby. Thought I'd swing by and see if you had time for lunch next week."

"Lunch would be great. How about next Wednesday?"

"Sounds good. I'll leave you to close up. I'll give you a call, and we can decide on where."

Tanesha turned back to her computer. I walked outside. I climbed into the front seat and beat the steering wheel with excitement and pent-up nerves.

I caught my breath and turned the key in the ignition. Maybe I should tell the cops about this? They probably knew about the pilots, but I was betting they hadn't checked Heather's story. While I could tell them, I wasn't sure they'd care. And how to explain that I knew Heather had rented a car. Maybe I should figure out whether Heather had a reason to kill Brandon other than jealousy. Then I might have news the cops would listen to. Now I hit the steering wheel in exasperation. I would have to wait another day to test out my theory.

50

I sat in the Accord, wondering if this was a waste of time. I'd been circling the arrival lanes, trying to time it right. The flight crew from the last Golden Wings Airways shuttle should be exiting the terminal any minute. I hoped Heather was on this run. I wasn't sure why I was here, but I had a feeling.

An opening door caught my eye, and uniformed figures exited the building. I strained to see who they were. As they walked closer, I saw Heather with the other flight attendants. The crew separated into the first two cabs. I followed the second one. Cabs were so common in traffic that I didn't think anyone would pick up on the fact I was following them.

The cab took a similar route to the one I would've taken to the hotel. In the parking area, I found a space where I could watch the front door. All three women went inside the Pondside Inn. I waited.

Ten minutes later, Heather walked out. She'd pulled her hair back and changed into blue jeans and a black shirt. She walked to a row behind me and climbed into a Ford Focus. When had she rented it? After she had pulled onto the road, I started the engine and followed. We wound around Savannah. At eleven thirty, there wasn't much traffic, so I hung back as I'd seen on TV. I watched the shape of the taillights as I stayed several cars behind her so I wouldn't spook her by following too closely.

As we turned onto the interstate, I guessed we were heading to Brandon's apartment. What on earth was she going there for?

I expected the whole place to be marked off with the yellow police tape. There wasn't much there, as I had found on my last visit there. What had I missed? Or was this a visit to the scene of the crime? They always said the killer returned, but this was his apartment, not where he died. I'd have to watch out. The last thing I needed was to get caught following her or being with her. But, at the same time, I hadn't heard from Aunt Harriett. Was she okay? Or devastated by Peter's actions? And what about the dark spirit she warned me about? Was I any closer to finding out what it was after?

I followed Heather through the open gate of Brandon's complex and turned left when she went straight. I circled back and parked near the apartment. It was dark as I watched, but I thought I could see her rounding the building that would take her to the back of the apartment and the patio. If I was right, she knew where the key was and could let herself in. If the cops hadn't found it and taken it, that was.

I hurried across the parking lot and peeked around the building. A cool wind brushed against my back, and goose bumps prickled my arms. No one else seemed to be around as I watched Heather make a turn and walk onto a patio. I walked up the path, keeping an eye out for others.

As I approached, I could hear people in the pool area. The sliding glass door to Brandon's apartment was open, and a light was on inside.

My stomach churned.

Now what? I'd only thought to follow her. I had no idea what to do now that I had.

I stopped at the corner of his patio and tried to see inside. The curtain had been pulled halfway across the door. I could see movements in the shadows. I thought Heather was in the kitchen. I felt another cool breeze. Was that the wind?

Be calm. It wasn't like Brandon had been killed with a gun or anything.

Was Heather armed? If not, was I strong enough to fight her off if I confronted her and she attacked?

A breeze wrapped around my feet. I looked down. The lights from the apartment lit the area a bit more than the dim lights around the pool area. It looked like there was a swirling black mess, but I couldn't be sure. Was this Brandon?

I danced around, trying to escape it, but it almost clung to me. I wasn't sure what this was, but I wasn't going to stand around to find out. I preferred dealing with things I understood, namely the living. Where was Aunt Harriett when I had questions for her? I took a step and almost fell over a wicker accent table.

I steadied myself. This only worked if I wasn't injured.

I walked to the door and stepped inside.

51

Heather was standing by the kitchen bar. "What are you doing here?"

I stared at her. "You can talk to me, or you can talk to the cops. They already know you were in town when Brandon died. They're looking for you."

Her eyes narrowed. "You don't understand."

I waited. She was partly right. I didn't know what had happened, but I was sure she was involved.

"So, tell me. Make me understand. Why did you come back here?"

She held her ground. The cops might have to sort this one out. There wasn't anything else I could do.

"You know, you're not the only woman that's ever had relationship issues. Look at me, a couple of ex-husbands. My track record speaks for itself."

I saw the smallest twitch in the corner of her mouth, and then two tears escaped from her eyes.

"So. Tell me about it. Why are you here? There must be a good reason behind all of this."

"Yes. That lying cheating asshole. He ruined me," Heather said.

"I don't understand." Ruined? What did that mean? She looked healthy. Hurt, but then most women by the age of twenty-five had at least one bad breakup. You dove into the ice cream, or whatever your comfort food was, and spent the weekend watching sad chick flicks. A pity party didn't usually mean coming after the guy, no matter what he'd done. Maybe she hadn't had anyone to talk to about all of this.

"Tell me what happened," I said.

Heather rolled her eyes and shook her head.

"Look, I know it's painful. I know you don't want to talk about it. But sometimes that's the one thing that helps. I know about that part."

Heather considered what I said. Her shoulders sagged. She dropped her gaze. "I thought he was the perfect guy. Good looking, intelligent, and funny. I knew he flirted and had been a bit of a player before I met him."

Heather must have seen my disbelief. "I know. I was naïve to think he'd changed. But he did all the right things. He was attentive and affectionate and gave me small gifts to surprise me. I thought he cared."

"When did you learn he wasn't?" I asked.

"I think I knew at the Masquerade Casino Night event. I wasn't supposed to be there, and I didn't know he was going. He'd never said a word about it. We were going to move in together but, at that point, we were living in different cities. I was working on getting my home base moved to Savannah."

She glanced at me as if to check that I wasn't going to judge her. I nodded.

"I went with Cindi and another woman. I was staying over with a friend who has a condo here, looking at apartments Brandon and I might share. I was going to surprise him. At the event, we were given these cool square-shaped glasses at the door—a kind of mask. You know, for the masquerade part. We all had our hair done since it was black tie. It was fun. You could observe people without them knowing who you were."

"How do you know Cindi?" I asked.

"I get my hair done at Shear Design. She and I sat next to each other at an appointment and hit it off. Whenever I knew I'd be in town for more than a quick overnight stay, we'd go shopping or have lunch," Heather said.

"Go on."

"That night, we were at the craps table. It was crowded, and I don't make a lot of money, so I was there because Cindi's husband was out of town. She had an extra ticket. I was standing off to the side, and there was this guy shooting craps. He seemed so familiar, with the same blond hair as Brandon. He moved in a way I recognized, although I didn't immediately recognize him at first. I thought Brandon was flying that night. I'll never forget. A leggy platinum blonde with a plunging red minidress was hanging on his arm. Between each roll of the dice, he kissed her hand or neck. Cindi said something about betting, and I turned away."

She sniffed, and I could see she was struggling not to cry.

"While I watched, Cindi put chips on the table, and a brunette went up to Brandon. I looked back in time to see her grab his arm. As he pulled away, his glasses slipped. That was when I knew for sure he was there.

"I thought I was going to throw up. We'd been talking about living together, and here he was with one woman and another arguing with him. The way she grabbed him and her anger, I thought she was accusing him of cheating on her."

"What happened next?"

"Cindi had seen it too. I think she said, 'Don't those women see that guy is a womanizer and they aren't anything special to him? Women like that never learn.' That's when I knew all the rumors were true. I hadn't told her about Brandon. Only that I was dating a man who lived here, and she didn't know she was talking about me." A sob escaped from Heather. "I've never felt more humiliated. Or glad the glasses hid my eyes. I told Cindi I thought a migraine was coming on, and I left. I don't think he even saw me."

"Wow. What a jerk. I can see why you hate him. But I don't understand why you would lie so you could be here to confront him," I said.

"If that had been all it was, I'd have withdrawn my base transfer request and tried to move on," said Heather.

"What else was there? You're not pregnant, are you?"

"No, thank goodness. Worse. I had been feeling sick with a fever that comes and goes. I was exhausted and had been nauseous. My first thought was I was pregnant, so I went to my doctor. She said no, but was concerned so she ran tests."

Heather paused and took a deep breath. "I have hepatitis C."

52

She really was sick. I willed the muscles in my body to hold tight. She was watching me for any reaction, and any change might silence her.

She continued, "My doctor and I tried to figure out where I might have been infected. I haven't received a blood transfusion. I don't work with blood, and I don't take drugs. The only thing I could think of was I used one of Brandon's razors once, and when we went camping we both fell while hiking. I cut my leg. Brandon tried to help me, but he had cut his hand in the fall. I think a bit of his blood might have gotten into my open wound."

My mouth hung open. I didn't know a lot about hepatitis C, but I knew it was a lifelong virus and could cause liver damage. In any scenario, it was treatable.

"I know what you're thinking. It's a virus, but you can live with it. And you'd be right. But my father died of liver disease. He was an alcoholic. I've seen what happens. I've never taken a drink because I never wanted to risk it. It's ironic, don't you think? I did everything to avoid it, and now I'm going to die from it. When I found out, something in me broke."

My heart went out to her. I didn't understand it all, but her pain was real. I could feel it. Her story made my family dramas look like minor issues. She could have used an Aunt Harriett to warn her about Brandon, who appeared to have been a rotting corpse of a man in how he treated women. The solution for that kind of decay was to remove it from your life. Unfortunately, Heather hadn't realized who he was until too late, and she'd suffered horribly.

"I am so sorry," I said. "I had no idea. But aren't there drugs now to treat it?"

Heather didn't seem to hear me. "Even then, I never meant for him to die. I wanted him to take responsibility. And I didn't want anyone else around to know."

"But how did you know where he'd be?" I asked.

"I called in sick and then Lisha and I talked. She's the other flight attendant. She knew I was having a lot of doctor's appointments. She'd checked her schedule and knew Brandon was taking the flight in my place. It made sense. I got a flight on a different airline. You already know I rented the car, don't you? All I had to do was get here and wait in the parking lot of the Pondside Inn."

"Yes, I tracked you through the car. That night you saw the cabs come in from the last flight." It dawned on me that it probably didn't matter I had put Brandon out of the cab.

"Yes. I got out of the car and walked toward the front. I was hoping to catch him before he got to his car but he wasn't in the cab," Heather said.

"You're the woman I saw with the black glasses," I said.

"Yes. I knew you and others saw me, but I hoped, with my hair up and the glasses on, no one would recognize me. Or remember me."

"I didn't. It was much later I realized it must have been you. What happened next?"

"How did you figure that out?" Heather asked.

"I saw the pictures on the website of the party and people in the sunglasses. Then I found a few poker chips in Brandon's apartment. A friend saw your reaction at the Masquerade Casino Night event, and I put it together. It made sense." Telling her who saw her wouldn't help, and I hoped she wouldn't ask.

Heather was silent. "I headed back to my car and was going to leave. Then I saw someone walking toward the motel. I decided to see who it was. I didn't know why he was walking."

"That was my fault. I'd had a horrible day, and he was rude and obnoxious. Ryan, the pilot who had been on the flight, told him to stop, and when he didn't, he asked me to put him out. So I did, about three blocks or so away. If I hadn't, none of this would have happened."

She nodded.

"You saw it was Brandon?"

I watched her thinking back and could see she was reliving the night.

"I approached him. He was coming up beside the pond area, back where they had been trimming the live oak trees. Boy, was he surprised to see me. 'Brandon,' I told him, 'I have hepatitis C, and you've been cheating on me.' You know what he said? 'Yeah, so what?'

"He was irritated and angry. Now I know why. The next thing he said was that I was getting to be a nag. And that no one wanted a girl-friend like me. Especially not him. I couldn't believe how cold he was. I said, 'You knew you had hepatitis C and never told me.' He told me I couldn't get it from casual contact. Then he said he never told me because it wasn't any of my business.

"I wanted to scream. I remember every muscle in my body went tense. 'I told you about my father and his liver disease. That's what hepatitis C does. It causes long-term liver problems. You knew that,' I yelled at him. But he kept on talking. Telling me to calm down. That I could have gotten it anywhere.

"But I didn't. I got it from a man I trusted and cared about. Then he said it was my fault. That I knew what he was and should have known better." Heather paused. "I wanted to hit him. I wanted to make him feel as bad as he had made me. The front of the motel gave off a bit of light, and I saw the tree branch on the ground. I snapped. I grabbed it and swung it at him. I don't think he ever saw it coming. It was like they always describe. Slow motion. I watched it hit him. He fell. I heard him move a bit and I was so disgusted with him and with myself, I started to cry. I couldn't bear to have him see me cry, so I dropped the log, turned around, and walked away. I slept in the car outside the rental place at the airport. I caught an early flight home the next morning."

Heather stopped.

"Didn't you hear him hit the water?" I asked.

"I heard a small splash. I thought the pond was shallow there and maybe his hand had hit it. I thought I heard him move. I didn't think I was strong enough to knock him out. I never even considered he might be face down in the water."

53

I remembered the area in front of Pondside Inn. The moon hadn't been very bright, and there weren't lights by the water, so she could have been telling the truth.

"You know you have to tell the cops all of this," I said.

"I can't. You'll have to tell them. I can't live like my father." Heather ran her hand over the kitchen counter as if steadying herself. "I don't want to live like that. Weekly injections, dialysis. You have no idea what that's like. And I won't make my mother suffer through the same illness all over again. I couldn't."

"But surely there are others who can help you. Friends. And I heard there are new treatments. Wouldn't your mother rather have the time to spend with you than not?"

"It's too hard. My life is over. Brandon took everything away from me. And if I tell the cops, I'll go to jail. I won't subject my mother to that either. There's nothing left for me."

Heather pulled out a package. She unwrapped it, and it glistened in the light. "It's almost poetic, don't you think? I'll use one of Brandon's razors to cut my wrists to end it all."

I froze in horror. "You don't want to do this." I took a step forward.

"Why come back here?" I hoped I could keep her talking long enough to distract her from the razor.

"I don't know. I thought maybe it would help. I felt like I had to somehow, you know? Maybe others should know the truth about him. I'd hoped I'd have a chance to explain. That's so much better than a note, don't you think?"

Before I could ask her why, something grazed my ankle, and I looked down. The same black swirl was back, trying to crawl up my legs. I stamped at it and took a quick step backward. The soot followed. What the ...? "Get off me."

"Who are you talking to?" Heather looked at me like I'd lost my mind.

"There's this stuff on my legs. I don't know what it is. I can't get away from it."

Heather came around the counter to look but kept the razor tightly in her hand as if I might be trying to trick her. I only wished that had been the case.

"That's weird," she said. "I've never seen anything like it."

"Help me, okay?"

Heather took a step back. "No way. I've got enough problems of my own."

I wanted to strangle her. My stomach was clenched tight. The muscles in my neck tightened like I had been on the road for eight hours straight.

"Calm yourself." I heard what I thought was Aunt Harriett's voice.

"Aunt Harriett?" I asked silently.

"Yes, dear. Now stand very still. I've never tried this before, but I have it on very good authority this will help. Close your eyes, imagine white light all around you, protecting you."

Very good authority? What? A bunch of spirits? I was afraid to ask her what it meant. I forced myself to stop moving. The soot continued moving toward my waist.

"Now, dear, the angry one is going to keep climbing. Don't fidget. Let it come. Is she the one?" Aunt Harriett asked.

"I think so."

"Good, then when you can feel it at the corners of your consciousness, turn your attention to creating a thick brick wall in your mind. You want to block it out. Once it figures out you aren't what it wants, it will move on and refocus, maybe on her, if she's the one it wants," Aunt Harriett said.

"But when it focuses on Heather, won't she get hurt?"

"I know it's a bad choice, but it's attached to you. The only way you can get it off you is to let it find what it's after. The girl will have to deal with what she's done to it, and if she does, there's a chance of peace for both of them. Others wait to help her."

I wasn't sure about all this. A coldness reached in to touch my bones, and a darkness snaked closer. Anger rose like a volcano ready to spew hate into the world. I waited and gripped my sanity as an anchor.

54

As the swirl began to take shape in my brain, I heard a shout of "Now" from Aunt Harriett. It took all the willpower and strength I had to hold on to the white light, fight back, and visualize a brick wall.

In my head, I yelled at the sooty mass, "Get off me. Go away. I'm not what you want." Then I strengthened the white light until I couldn't see anything else.

The relief was instant. It fled the light. Whatever *it* had been. There was a small trace of a touch that felt like it might have been Brandon, a slimy bit of swagger reminding me of how he'd talked in the cab.

I looked at Heather. She'd had no warning as I had. Her face distorted as she tried to fight the unseen foe. I took a step forward.

"You can't help her, my dear. As much as you'd like to, she has to do this herself," Aunt Harriett said.

"Heather, fight it. Surround yourself with light," I yelled. "Will the others help her as you helped me? Was it Brandon?"

Heather collapsed onto the ground. She was writhing silently, even while she seemed to have given up on life.

"Only if she lets them. I don't know that she knows how yet. And I don't know that she can hear you. You must leave. Just in case she fights back or the spirit isn't satisfied. I think it's safe to say it was that young man's spirit if he stays with her."

I didn't want to think about what that meant.

I turned and ran to the door as Heather gave out a scream and then went quiet. Smack into Officer John.

"What are you doing here?" he asked.

"It's Heather. She needs help."

As if to back me up, I heard an anguished cry behind me.

John looked past me. He pulled his radio to his mouth. "We're going to need medical help here, stat."

He turned back to me. "Don't you go anywhere. I need to talk to you."

John rushed forward.

55

John gave Heather CPR and tried to help her. He removed the razor from her hand and set them aside. After what felt like an hour but was probably more like fifteen minutes, paramedics arrived. They stabilized her as best they could before Heather was loaded onto a gurney, moaning and incoherent.

"Okay, now it's your turn. What happened here?"

I described how I had gotten here and why. John's frown deepened until I didn't think it could get any darker, then it did.

"How'd you know I was here?"

John explained that Dave, the cute guy I met the first time I came to check out Brandon's apartment, had been keeping an eye on things for the cops. He knew me from my prior visit and once he described me to John, John knew I was on to something but wasn't sure what. He and his partner had rushed over to see what I was after and make sure I was okay.

"I don't understand how she got in the state she did. Why didn't she cut herself?"

I tried to think of an answer that might satisfy him. I decided staying close to the truth would be in order. "I don't know. One minute she was talking and threatening to kill herself. The next minute she was on the ground thrashing around. It was the strangest thing I've ever seen." And that was no lie.

John considered what I had said. I could tell he thought there might be more to the story, but he either couldn't find a question or maybe decided he didn't want to ask. Savannah's long history of strange occurrences gave weight to my answers, although I knew he was more comfortable with cold hard facts.

"You'll need to come down to the station and give a formal statement. And we may have more questions. Can you come now?"

I nodded. Once I agreed, John called his partner and they secured the scene, replacing the bright yellow tape on the patio and front door, locking up. We headed to the station in our separate cars. Better to get the statement over with while I could keep straight which parts I had told him and which parts he'd likely never believe.

56

The day after my long interview at the station, I slept in, even though I had things to wrap up. Bill stopped by and together we drove to Big Louie's restaurant. He'd ordered me not to go without him. "It's not safe," he'd said. For once, I'd agreed and followed what I considered advice rather than a real command. We'd called ahead and met the smiling Big Louie, who thought we were there to pay him off.

His face had turned an angry blotched red as I told him about Heather, even telling him he could confirm it with the cops. That had stopped him cold. In addition to Bill's presence. I thought he might explode when I got to the part of Heather being hospitalized and practically comatose. The last thing he'd wanted to hear was that the person he'd have to collect from was not only outside his reach but might never be conscious.

Then he surprised me. Big Louie said he would make a few calls. If all was true, then I would be off the hook. He'd grinned his broad smile, giving me chills. "If it's not true, you can expect me to follow up."

Ha. I knew that meant one of his henchmen would visit, and likely Geoff.

"That won't be necessary. If there's a problem, you let me know, and we'll straighten it out," Bill said.

I was glad to have him by my side. If it had just been me, I'd have been quivering in my shoes, waiting. And Big Louie's attitude didn't make me feel better as to what that would mean if we ever met again.

LATER IN THE DAY, I called my daughter, Stephanie. I brought her up to date on everything that had transpired. She'd peppered me with questions as to the details. When her dad called her for dinner, we made plans for lunch on the weekend. As much as I didn't want it to be about the investigation, I wasn't going to pass up an opportunity to see my daughter.

Once that was done, Sylvie and I met at her office. Derek was back home and improving again. She had forgiven me for talking to the cops about Geoff. She'd talked to Geoff and the police again. They'd confirmed the fight at the poker game.

"You'll be happy to know I have told Geoff he'll be on dispatch for a day. Same as you were," Sylvie said.

"I'd like to be working that day. Not to gloat or treat him bad. I want him to know I know."

She'd agreed once she was sure I wasn't going to try to take advantage of the situation. We talked about moving forward with the business deal again and I told her I'd be meeting with accountants soon. I left with a copy of the confidentiality agreement to review. Once Bill looked it over with me and I was comfortable signing it, we'd begin reviewing the financial statements.

57

Two days later, I called the hospital to check on Heather. No one would give me any information other than she was under evaluation and couldn't have visitors. I'd suspected I might not have any luck. There was more than one way to skin a cat, as Aunt Harriett always said. Time to try my other sources.

"Aunt Harriett," I called. "Aunt Harriett."

I thought she was near. I wasn't exactly sure how I knew or how I could contact her. I'd heard other people could feel their loved ones who had passed over. This was new to me, but I was learning. I also knew my senses were beginning to heighten.

My mind was another thing, though. My brain was trying to wrap itself around the fact Aunt Harriett was here and probably going to stay awhile. Not a dream. Not a hallucination caused by my mind. I was thrilled I could talk to her. Terrified I could speak to her.

"Hello, dear," Aunt Harriett said, interrupting my thoughts.

"What happened to Heather? Do you know?"

"Oh, my. The poor girl. I checked in on her. The doctors think she's quite mental. Modern medicine has no more ability to deal with something like this than doctors did in my childhood. The darkness has quite overwhelmed her spirit."

Mental? That could be anything. "But what happened?"

"You felt it?"

"Yes."

"That's what she felt, only more so. She had no real way to fight it off, so while you could repel it, she couldn't. It overwhelmed her and fed on her fear and guilt. She will have to find a way to forgive herself and allow the presence to find a way to forgive her. Then they can both be healed."

"I feel awful I couldn't do more. Do you think Heather will ever get better?"

"She has to come to terms with herself and the presence. That's a lot to ask of anyone. It may take something more. I'll see what I can find out in the Gray that might be helpful. Now, I have to run. And no more shouting for me. I have my schedule to keep. I'll know if you need me."

"Wait. Are you gonna be around for a while?"

"Of course. I need to sort out things with Peter. He may not be willing to tell me what's going on in front of Russell. I know he's here because of Russell, but I think he might also have wanted to wait for me. Getting him away from Russell will be a bit more complicated than I thought. You up to the challenge?"

"Always. Anything for you. Just let me know how I can help."

She'd disappeared, so I decided to check back with my secret weapon, Bill.

He thought he knew someone and had promised to check on Heather. Having a paramedic boyfriend had some unexpected perks. I felt horrible for Heather. I hoped I could find a way to help her.

I laughed out loud at the thought of Aunt Harriett on the hunt for her man. It felt good.

58

An hour later, I dropped off barbeque pork sandwiches, coleslaw, and the fixings to the crew at Bill's station. He was a bit surprised until I started asking about Heather.

"Yeah. We dropped off a heart attack victim whose wife was hysterical and had to be sedated. I hung around and talked to the doctor on call, who happens to do psych patient work." He waited for me to plant a kiss as thanks before he continued with a grin. "They're evaluating her, but he said they think the stress of her father's illness and death, as well as her accidental killing of Brandon, finally kicked her over the edge. She couldn't handle all the guilt. For now, they're sedating her until they can figure out a course of treatment to help her."

Which explained Aunt Harriett's vague mental diagnosis. They didn't know what had happened, and I doubted they'd believe my version of her problem. Aunt Harriett had said Heather had the power to heal this. I hoped so.

"Thanks. I had no luck on my end."

"Skill and connections, hon. No luck to it." Bill grinned.

"I'll give you that." I smiled.

"Nice, but I was thinking of a more tangible bit of thanks." His grin turned into his version of a leering smile. "And I think there's more to this story you haven't told me."

I couldn't help myself. He could be so charming when he wanted to be. I laughed. I also knew this was the opening I had been waiting for. If we were going to have a longtime relationship, I needed to be honest with him.

"You're right. You never met Aunt Harriett but she was an important part to this. This isn't the place to talk. She was quite the character and what I need to tell you may sound a bit out of this world, but I'd like to talk. When does your shift end?"

Bill's smile became more serious.

"You want us to talk. That's normally a death knell for a relationship. Although, watching your face, I think this time, it's a good thing."

"Hey, guys. There's food," a male voice yelled as a firefighter walked through a door.

"I'm off tomorrow. How about I bring dinner for a late-night feast once you're off your shift?" Bill asked.

It was my turn to grin. I wanted to spend more time with Bill, get to know him better and let him know more about me. If he could deal with Aunt Harriett being around, we'd get through one of the more complicated parts of my life. Bill knew a bit about my family history, but it was time for him to know who I really was and what he had signed up for in dating me. I had a feeling he might need time to ease it, but I figured he'd manage what I had to say like he did everything else and we'd get through it. I just needed to trust he'd get there.

I sucked in a breath and smiled more broadly with just a trace of the nerves I was feeling. I had hours to prepare and build up my confidence to say what I needed to say.

Bill grinned again.

"I'd better grab one of these before the guys take them all. Don't sweat whatever you need to tell me. Whatever it is, I've probably heard something like it before."

Maybe, although maybe not, but Bill was from Savannah and we had all been raised on the dead haunting the buildings and parks and our own family histories with our unique ancestors. Not to mention that Bill dealt with people who were in trouble and told all kinds of tales in his job on a daily basis. If he could deal with that, what was one more ghost in a city haunted by so many?

ABOUT THE AUTHOR

C.A. Rowland loves traveling and learning about cultures, whether they are exotic ones or small-town life. Ms. Rowland has explored countless places from empty neighborhood houses to Roman ruins that seem to draw her. Those travels inspired many of her stories. Raised in Texas, she now calls Virginia home – a place of history and folklore.

Ms. Rowland writes historical fiction, science fiction, fantasy, and mysteries. She comes by her interest in ghosts, myths, and legends and the paranormal naturally, having spent hours in cemeteries with her grandmother.

You can keep up with her upcoming fiction and travel adventures at www.carowland.com.

Hope to see you there!